NYMPHO

NYMPHO

A *novel by*

ANDREA BLACKSTONE

Q-Boro Books

WWW.QBOROBOOKS.COM
An Urban Entertainment Company

Published by Q-Boro Books

Copyright © 2007 by Andrea Blackstone

ISBN13: 978-1-933967-10-3
ISBN 10: 1-933967-10-2
LCCN: 2006936047

First Printing May 2007
Printed in the United States of America

10 9 8 7 6 5 4 3 2

Cover Copyright © 2006 by Q-BORO BOOKS all rights reserved
Cover Photo by JLove; Model: Shonda
Cover layout/design by Candace K. Cottrell
Editors: Alisha Yvonne, Stacey Seay

Q-BORO BOOKS
Jamaica, Queens NY 11434
WWW.QBOROBOOKS.COM

Acknowledgments

To God:
With you, all things are truly possible.

To my guardian angel:
I miss you. One day, we will meet again. Thanks for keeping me strong, in the midst of it all. You live in me. It's you who helps to keep me going, no matter what people say or do to discourage me.

To my father:
Thanks for everything, including more friendship.

To those who truly supported me:
You know who you are. Thank you for wishing me the best and proving that you are on my side. I won't forget. To those who work with me on my projects, I appreciate your dedication and quality work, too.

To my artistic circle:
You know who you are. I hope each and every one of you blow up! I have such talented friends and family. Just like you tell me, don't give up until you get to where you want to be.

To my readers:
Thank you for giving me an opportunity to take you different places in my twisted mind! Those who like my work should know that it's all done in good fun.☺ I thank each and every one of you who have emailed me, written letters, or spoken to me in person to provide feedback. I am honored to have met so many supportive and positive spirits. Special thanks to my test readers.

To Mark Anthony and Candace:
Thank you for giving me an opportunity to make this happen.
I treasure and value the opportunity more than either of you
will ever know.

Jumbled Thoughts

August 23rd, 2005
Diary Entry #1:

Dear Diary,

   I just want to ask myself one question: How in the hell did
I end up in a position like this? I just finished taking a trip to
the post office box I was smart enough to invest in so my fiancé wouldn't question why my cell phone bill had climbed
to four hundred dollars in one month, and why eighty percent of the calls were from, well, *our best man.* Opening the
thick packet of call records caused my mind to drift back to
all of the pillow and kinky talk with that one man in particular.
Looking at the amount of incoming calls from the same three
numbers—his cell phone, his home phone, and the direct
line from his desk at work, has resurrected the memory of my
infidelity. At first I thought that creeping was cute—the attention I was getting was swelling my ego, right! But since a
whole lot of shit has been hitting the fan that I'll get into a
little later, I decided to take a crucial step in attempting to

break out of my darkness: <u>private admission</u>. I'm the type who would sing *What a Friend We Have in Jesus* in one breath, and tempt the choir director to see what's under my robe in the next. I know that's a pretty scandalous statement, but I'm just keeping it real. I'm the kind of woman who has closet freak cravings. If a leopard can change its spots, maybe there is hope for me to bury my alter ego, Innocence. You know what they say: it's always the quiet ones! It sure is. *Damn—* it sure is. They say it's always the quiet ones or church girls who are the real closet freaks. Even if you're a believer, can you really change who you are? Let me be honest about something up front; I don't like that I appear to be a woman with little or no sexual experience and a low libido. It's all a front and I'm tired of pretending that I'm something I'm not. To put it bluntly—I like sex. Correction, I love sex.

I wished I could've felt good without cheating, but my needs took on a life of their own and I felt trapped—as if there was no other way. Men are always talking about what they want, but what about what women want? It's a terrible thing to be bored, in more ways than one, but not be interested in changing your current situation is even worse. It's a more common problem than most people are willing to admit though. Those with testosterone think they're getting over on stupid people from Venus, and those with estrogen claim to possess superior intellect above those who hail from Mars. What it all comes down to is one big game we play behind each other's backs. Men cheat, but so do women, all because the average person is afraid to tell the truth regarding what they really desire. In fact, some women are worse than the average dog. I venture to guess that there are more cheat-a-holics in this world than those who truly cherish a sacred bond. Marriage has become a business agreement, or a death sentence to those who can't be honest about what it takes to really make it work the way it should. Take half of the credit card bills that have been hanging over someone else's head for years, half of their life's stressors, then take away SEX, add a whole lot of morning halitosis, last minute cheap gifts, walking the dog, changing dirty diapers, forgiving a husband for forgotten birthdays and anniversaries, tossing beer cans, and fussing over the need to wipe pee off the seat because men rarely raise it, and of course, nosey in laws, and see if ten years from now you'll appreciate that shit! Wake up and smell the Folgers—you won't! With that said, who can blame me for taking matters into my own hands by looking for someone else to ring my bell, before I signed up to be Mrs. So and So? Men do it all of the time—they started it! Flip the script and they have the nerve to get an attitude . . . whatever. Why should women be ashamed to admit that we want to have the big "O" and someone to make our toes curl?

I've learned about all these things through struggling to love the man in my life. Trey, I wanted everything with you. I swear I wasn't playing games when I accepted the engagement ring . . . at least not intentionally. You can't imagine what it's like to be a thirty-something woman who wants to be married and have a family in an age where straight, available, commitment-minded, sane acting black men who don't want to date white, Asian, or Spanish sisters are rumored to be an endangered species. I just couldn't stomach throwing myself back to the few wolves in the pack, although there were many issues I was dissatisfied with, including your lack of desire to get your wee wee up enough. When you did bother to give me some affection, you'd watch TV while I was getting it. So what if you're fascinated by sharks—if you're making love to me, Flipper shouldn't come first. When you turned your head to look over your shoulder . . . that was the final clue that our sex life was *finito*, even before we got married. I say don't do it partially, do it all the way, all night long, or at least until my hair is sweated out! After all, I threw no marriage hints your

way. I figured that if I turned it down, I may have been forfeiting my one and only shot to walk down the aisle before my
biological clock stopped ticking. My heart longed to experience solidarity with a brother who was all fucking mine: no
more man sharing, and no more dating disasters. I had the
power to get off the train, and pulling into the station gave
me joy. To me, the thought of all of these things was a much
needed relief. I had a career, my own home, and a set routine
that made sense, but my heart was thirsty, and I needed a tall
glass of water. Never did I realize that I was assigning you to
be my ticket out of being caught up in a stinking mix. In reality, being a savior in my hour of darkness wasn't your responsibility. I never should've submitted to the fantasy by settling
for someone I knew wasn't my cup of tea. That's what you
were Trey, a fantasy that looked attractive. While you were
appearing to become more conservative, I started taking my
engagement ring off, wearing tight booty shorts, and flirting
with men. Your golden lady was hitting her sexual peak, becoming more daring and adventurous, running the streets to
get banged while getting my hair pulled, until the early morning. You were the one who backed me up against the wall by
not letting me be a freak with you and only you. I knew you
wanted a conservative woman, so that's what I tried to be to
fit into your life, but I just couldn't keep up the act. After the
first time I got comfortable fondling a strange dick and swallowing nut, I found out that I preferred being a freak who
stayed on her hands and knees.

Before I write some three-page letter about someone else,
I suppose I should address my individual issues with the person I've never really liked—me. I admit that the struggle is
somehow related to baggage I drag around. I don't know who
is to blame—my parents, my sister, the culture, pressure of
trying to be successful, fate. Maybe if I vent on paper, living
with myself will be a little bit easier. After all, I have to take it

here because I'm tired of playing the role of what I appear to be—a quiet, mannerly, reserved, and high-browed conservative woman who rarely even smiles. I have the game of owning two opposite personalities down pat. In fact, few would ever guess what kind of woman was hidden behind the trips to church, neatly done tight bun, make-up free face, skirts down to my knees, blouses that covered everything, including my collar bone, and school teacher-like glasses. I wasn't that conservative woman who volunteered for a non-profit organization every third weekend in the summer. The real me was a nasty slut with little moral grounding, although I was the one who rolled my eyes, and gave a lingering cough of disgust if a provocatively dressed woman walked by, or if I heard anyone mention they had sex before marriage.

This isn't simple, safe, or easy. This diary is the only one who will ever know the secrets of the real me. Secrets that . . . if they ever got out . . . would complicate an already messy situation. So, even here, I'll leave out some locations and real names. I know who is who and no one needs to use me to understand what's wrong with them while I absorb the brunt of judgment and public persecution. The golden question is: How do I shake off a severe case of nymphomania? I have no idea what the answer is, but the emancipation of me begins right here, right now. *Fact*: Leslie Thompson wasn't ready to be anyone's wife, but she was willing to pretend that she was ready to march down the aisle with a bouquet of flowers in her hand, so long as the dirt that she did didn't come to light and bite her in the ass. The thing is, it did in the craziest way. *Fiction*: I apologize for participating in an affair that never should've been. *Fact:* The bottom line is that it happened and cheating like a heathen was the thrill of a lifetime. If I had it to do all over again, I probably would. *Fiction:* Help wanted. SOS. Save my soul. 911. Attention: Red Alert. I wish something would rise up within this empty vessel and resurrect the good girl that can make me keep my panties up and keep my legs crossed. *Fact:* If I were forced to confess, my biggest secret in life would be that I enjoyed exploring my sexual fantasies with the best man, strangers, and even paying customers. Now that I'm sitting here holding the pieces of a broken marital dream because of it, all I can really say is oops—I fucked up really bad!

1

An Unseen Enemy

The intense summer heat caused my sticky skin to glisten with sweat, despite it being nearly seven o'clock in the evening. As I walked nude around my fiancé's three bedroom brick rancher, I mustered the strength to raise every window, and turned all the fans on high. I began thinking about how my once beautiful life was beginning to tarnish and lose its luster—I wanted a vacation. I crawled back into his bed for a much-needed nap, but feeling restless, I had no choice but to acknowledge that I really had nothing on my mind but fucking. After I did, I ended up lying on my back, closing my eyes, and slowly stroking my clitoris to relieve some pent up frustration and physical tension. I slid my middle finger into my slit as my mind scrolled through the hundreds of photos I'd viewed of fine men on the Internet. Masturbation had become the only way I could escape into my fantasy world—where I felt no rejection, or even a mere inkling of sexual frustration. Although I had a special man in my life, losing control discretely and alone was the only way I could try and stop the throbbing of my tight, hot, and hungry pussy.

Trey and I had been seeing each other less, and I'd been

observing that he was supposedly at work more than he was with me. He stopped telling me that he loved me and would never leave me the way he did when our relationship was new and exciting. We stopped laughing together, slow dancing, flirting, going out on dates—I mean all of the good shit to keep me confident that he was feeling me, just dried up and blew away. I may as well have been invisible as far as he was concerned. In fact, the last time I spoke with him and asked where he'd been all day, he crankily responded that I don't report my whereabouts to him blow by blow, so why should I expect him to do the same.

One Monday night, after arguing on his cell phone for two hours, I stopped craving his touch, stopped thinking about our upcoming seven-day honeymoon in Jamaica, and gradually released the comforting thought of him holding me as we lay under the moonlight. Out of sheer spite, I ate up both pieces of grilled salmon, polished off almost half the bottle of chardonnay, and took care of a healthy bowl of salad while sitting at my circular kitchen table . . . alone. Afterward, I felt sick as a dog.

It was then I realized Leslie Thompson was sick of the rigid computer programmer. Somehow, the love I had for my man was hardly enough to keep me satisfied. Hell, as far as I knew, maybe my man was getting it on with another chick, or these days, even another brother. I wasn't sure if insecurities from childhood were creeping into my psyche, or if I was dealing with cold, hard facts. Either way, whether Trey realized it or not, our bond was blown to a billion smithereens because all traces of trust had vanished. Hell, I didn't know the truth regarding why he wasn't around. This thing between he and I was so twisted, I wasn't sure I had the mental energy to straighten it out, even in light of deposits having been made, and the wedding planner having done her part to make our big day run as smoothly as possible.

Although I was tired of powering my cell phone on and off

late at night, waiting to see if Trey would show up to hold me
in his arms, or come hit it like most normal men, I knew that
he would be an excellent provider, and take good care of the
kids that we discussed having down the road. The thing is, a
new game chose me after someone very close to the situation
reminded me I could make up for the attention I wasn't getting at home by lying and cheating.

In lieu of me not desiring a bridal shower, my best friend
and maid of honor, Tanya opted to take me out for a day at
the spa. The plan was to get manicures, massages, and just
kick it about the old days. After the spa, we ended up eating
at The Stonefish Grill at the Capital Center Boulevard in
Largo. We had a great time eating and discussing the dirt
men do, all on her dime. I opened the present Tanya gave
me—it was a picture of me and her in the second grade, en-
closed in a beautiful gold colored frame. After we shed a few
tears, I opened a card that included a notice for a free sub-
scription to *Essence Magazine*. We devoured our seafood,
settling into the ambiance of the chic, modern place. I found
out she was also having man problems with someone who just
so happened to be my man's best friend, Rico.

"There's something I want to talk to you about, but I don't
want to spoil our day."

"Whatever, Tanya. Lay it on me."

"I answered Rico's phone and a woman seemed rather surprised to hear the sound of my voice," Tanya explained.

"So . . . what's the big deal? It's his phone. Why'd you answer it—you don't pay his telephone bill. A man is going to
talk to whomever he wants."

"A: I'm his woman. B: *this* hussy had that I-thought-he-
was-single kind of tone going on, and C: I thought it was him
calling me since I picked up his keys while he was at work.
He told me to let myself in. I had no idea that I'd find out
Rico was kicking it with his secretary. She and I talked a

while, and she was sure to tell me that they had two tickets to see Raheem DeVaughn. Then, she had the nerve to ask me to hang up so she could call back and leave him a private message. I did and just let the phone ring so that—"

I cut Tanya off. "Don't let me find out that you've got rocks for brains, girl. Come on!" I shook my head with disapproval. "Excuse me, but you can't be nice to the competition. Kicking it was a different story. What's wrong with you? You should've let her have it where it hurts. Everyone knows you and Rico are dating. How in the world did you manage to let her walk over you like that?"

"But it wasn't just her fault. And she said they weren't sleeping together. There's something about Rico that's mesmerizing. He just pulls me in and I can't seem to let go. I can't explain it because I've never experienced this feeling before," Tanya insisted.

"How many ways can I tell you to adopt a zero tolerance cheating policy? You fuck up, you're fired—that's how it should be. If Rico hasn't dipped his wick in her yet, he will. He's no more magnetic than any other sucker out here with cheap lines, a decent job, a few good brains cells, and a mission to weave a tangled web to catch as many women off guard as possible. Don't let that man brainwash you. It's just a matter of time before you find out that he's a pure dud who has no more appeal than the rest of them."

"You think so?"

"I know so. I'm tired of listening to this bullshit, Tanya. This shouldn't be a difficult decision for anyone. This isn't Rico's first time cheating on you. Maybe I should've kept a log and listed all of the times you woke my ass up wondering if he was at home or in someone else's. No, you haven't proven anything yet, but what in the hell are you waiting for—in-person proof that you're nothing more than an onlooker in the hoochie parade? You're celibate, Rico is man who likes to fuck, and you have no ring. Do you really think he's going to be faithful under those circumstances, or do you think he's going to keep playing these games?"

"I don't know what to think anymore—I just don't. I'm just trying to do the right thing."

"Trey's hands stay on me like an octopus, but he knows that I'm not giving him some ass until we get married," I lied. "It's not easy holding out on these Negroes when women are out here shaking their tail feathers in clubs and handing it over on the first night after a man pays for a cheesy fifteen-dollar entree. Somehow, I manage to remind him he's not missing out because I'm worth the wait. I constantly remind him that these trifling hoochies who drop their drawers on demand will only be a convenience to him and those types have nothing lasting to offer."

"What should I do? The last one picked his nose at the dinner table and went on and on about his swollen prostate. The one before that acted as if paying for a lunch date would ruin his savings account. The choice index is very slim out here."

"Stop tripping—forget Rico's peanut head self! Crack down, be tough, and date someone else. Think ahead. He's a waste of your time despite the slim pickings. Rico is what I call a professional bachelor. He's never going to get married, he's set in his ways, and he may not even be trainable to do right by any woman . . . let alone, my girl."

"You're right. I've been acting like he was interested in having a wife and kids. Rico isn't going to rig up a trailer hitch and pull it through weeds just so I can go camping. What was I thinking?" Tanya chuckled and shook her head.

"The blind sees! Thank you Jesus—she's healed! Boo coo improvement! Break up with him so you can find your place in time. After you do, the membership drive of Tanya's fan club will be on! If it's the last thing I do, we're going to find you someone worth keeping. But first I'm going to teach you how to grow a backbone so you can train a man to respect you. You're a beautiful, strong woman, so be encouraged. It's not you, it's him."

"Thanks Leslie. I'm glad I have you. You're my best friend in this world," Tanya told me, smiling.

"Well, prove that you want peace of mind by getting rid of the dead weight in your life. I found a good man and so can you, girl. Keep your standards high. Do what's best for you by hooking up with a man who appreciates you, Miss Tanya. Now get going before you start tripping again," I told her, patting the top of her left hand.

"But what about our girl's day out? This was supposed to be all about you, not me."

"Everything was nice, Tanya. Besides, I can head over to my man's house. I assure you that a sister can take care of herself." Just to pretend that everything was kosher, I dangled Trey's key and grinned. I was showing off like I had Trey on lockdown by having it. My girl knew we didn't live together, yet I had a key.

As Tanya walked away to handle the business in her private life, I began to rewind the situation in my head. Tanya and Rico hooked up after meeting at a cookout Trey threw early in the summer, a few months after her divorce. Like the hypocrite I was, I'd just advised her to cut the cord on Rico while pretending it was all gravy in my world. I wanted to portray the image of a secure woman in love, but in actuality, it was a fifty-fifty shot that Trey would be thrilled when my face met his. Sometimes people give advice they don't follow themselves. You know how that goes.

2

My Best Friend's Man

I made it to Trey's house about six o'clock that evening. He was nowhere to be found, but since traffic had been heavy due to construction work on the highway, I decided to stick around and plug in a good flick. The events that transpired in my own life should've given me pause. Watching porn and giving contraptions like the Rider Rocker Fucking Ball a spin were the only way in which I could become sexually adventurous. As soon as the UPS man dropped the box on my porch, I inflated the ball, attached the six-inch fake penis, and mounted it as if I expected a waterfall of satisfaction. I was ashamed of how far I'd go in pursuit of an orgasm because I claimed to be a born again Christian. Obviously, I hadn't stopped denying my carnal pleasures. The only thing I was good at was leading a double life. In fact, I'd hidden some of the spiciest recorded trysts in the back of a closet that Trey never bothered to clean, in his very own place. Anytime I was tired of hearing my fiancé's explanation that the mother of his children should never behave like a common slut by putting her mouth where he peed, I snuck to watch various women liberate themselves sexually by being very nasty girls and enjoying it. Those men didn't seem to mind; in fact, they simply loved it. I wished I didn't have to learn about the erotic side of life by hunting down someone who made ten-dollar bootleg porn videos and sold them in a pissy smelling cubbyhole near a metro stop. But my profession as a teacher, and Trey's standards that involved placing me on a high pedestal, meant that I could never hold my head up high and openly walk into a sex shop—I had to sneak. And sneak I did, at least twice a week. I became my hook up man's best customer, requesting him to recommend his new favorites and leaving with several flicks at a time.

After I put on my glasses so I could see every detail, I inserted a new freak show into the DVD player in Trey's bedroom. Sex sounds immediately inspired me to stroke my clitoris. Just as my juices began to flow, my phone rang and disturbed my groove. Without realizing how close I was to feeling my first *real* orgasm, I picked up my cell phone, remembering to turn down the volume of the movie first, of course.

"Hello," I said breathlessly.

"Damn, do you answer the phone sounding like that all of the time? I need to call looking for my girl more often," Rico replied.

"Mmm. Mmm. Hold on," I said. The sound of a living man's voice aroused me so much I tried to kill off the naughty feeling, and send it back to its sender.

"I'm looking for Tanya, but from the sound of things, she's not with you."

"She isn't . . . she isn't . . . here. I'm at Trey's place. How'd you get my number?" I replied, watching the TV screen.

"Desperate times call for desperate measures," Rico teased. "Someone was filling my girl's head with a whole lot of garbage. We had some heated words, and I really need to talk to her. In fact, I thought maybe you could help me track her down."

"Whatever went on, I'm not in it. I don't even want to know."

"Fuck it—fuck her! My mind is somewhere else now. You need some company over there, Leslie?"

"Rico, I've really got to go," I said urgently. By this time, I meant to hit the mute button, but instead, I accidentally increased the volume.

"Don't get mad at what I'm about to say, but it doesn't sound like my man Trey is taking care of business in his neck of the woods. Why are you trying to independently inspire yourself, mami? You all acting like married people already, huh? I see you don't knock boots anymore." He chuckled. "That's not right. Isn't it a little early for the big marital drought? You have a whole lifetime to go that route," Rico commented.

I didn't like being busted, but that's what happened. I blocked out Rico's snide remarks and continued struggling to find relief for my body as a woman slurped and sucked on a beautiful looking, stiff penis. When her partner groped at her left breast, I thought of how mine were aching to be fondled, my ass craved a good spanking, and my mouth wanted something long and hard to suck on.

For whatever reason, Trey and I had only been making love about once every two weeks as opposed to our usual three times weekly. Summertime turned me on, and I wanted him to take me to London, Brazil, Paris, and Africa with his good loving, but the only way I'd get a mega-sex-fest was by means of a trip to the bootleg porn spot. Whooptie do. Maybe love and sex don't mix because before Trey and I officially hooked up, he represented like a Mandingo warrior who had been chosen by a master for his baby making talents. I missed those times—they kept my libido fed and interested.

Out of the blue, Rico said, "Stroke it for me, Leslie."

"What? I can't masturbate to the sound of my best friend's man's voice . . . *and* my man's boy," I said innocently. But I was already doing the deed. "Tanya's my girl and your horny ass is the best man in my wedding. Come on, it would be foul to go down this route, especially while I am in Trey's bed," I added.

The thought of Rico's boldness turned me on. In fact, it was causing a steady stream of moistness to run down my brown thighs as I continued watching the TV screen.

Even though sleeping in Trey's old T-shirt reminded me of him, it did nothing for the up close and personal attention I needed. I loved every minute of this smooth-talking brother flirting with me while betraying the one who was neglecting me.

"Everyone likes choices. It's your choice if you want to pretend you don't like this or you can live a little."

"It's not that simple," I said, stroking my kitty kat.

"I know that I'm turning you on, and I can tell your hands are busy, too. Tanya and I broke up, so *technically*, I'm no longer her man. Since I'm putting it out there, just know that I went home and jacked off thinking about you after we were finally introduced. I've always wanted to hit it but the opportunity never presented itself. There's something about you, Leslie—I can't quite explain it. I'd lick you from head to toe."

"You are a trip. Sure, Rico. Tell me anything," I said, half giggling. "For someone who can't explain something, you sure are long-winded," I teased.

"I just think you're sexy as hell, mentally and physically. When I found out your fine ass was a school teacher that just did it. I've always had this fantasy of breaking off a teacher who sports a bun and glasses to work like a sexy librarian, but likes to let loose when she comes home. From what I'm guessing, you have another side to your personality," Rico said, ignoring my comments.

"Ya think?"

"I know what I peeped a while back. The glasses and innocent act didn't fool me one bit."

Rico's choice of words fed my ego and caused me to journey down the slippery slope of betrayal—I proceeded to have
phone sex with him. "Why are you doing this?" I asked. I
began rubbing my clit faster, in circular motions, my eyes
glued to the anonymous woman on the screen who began to
scream as a man with dreadlocks pounded her without mercy.
I lost control and began to heave.

"Are you still playing with yourself?" Rico asked.

I bit my lip and managed to squeeze out a few words. "Yes,
I'm doing it."

"What are you wearing?" Rico said in a voice so sexy it
began to hypnotize me. When I didn't answer, he repeated, "I
asked, what you are wearing?"

"Nothing but my glasses."

"That's what I'm talking about . . . mmm. You're butt
naked? Leave the glasses on. Your girl wouldn't get down like
this. Damn—so are you on your back or on your stomach?"

"I'm on my stomach now."

"I bet you've got that tight and wet freak pussy. Stick your
finger inside. Are you wet? Check for me, Leslie."

"Mm-hmm," I moaned. My answer was obvious without
me articulating the words. I put my body into it, feeling the
electric energy of being hot and bothered.

"Good. I'm coming over," Rico said.

I finally slipped back toward reality and turned my eyes
away from the steamy scene. "No, Rico. Don't. That wouldn't
be a good—"

"Wake up. You're not a married woman on lockdown yet,
and now I'm a free man who is more than willing to demonstrate how Trey should be putting it down. He's lucky to have
a woman who's ten years younger than him. As far as Tanya,
what she doesn't know won't hurt her. She never has to know
a damn thing. As well as you know me, you should know all
I'll do is make love to you like the queen you are. The problem is that you're too much woman for the man you hooked

up with, but you're not too much woman for me. I'm going to beat the pussy up and enjoy every moment of it. Trust me, that nigga you're marrying ain't no saint. I should know. I've known him way longer than you. Stop acting like it's 1920. Just because you and I get our freak on doesn't mean you can't put on your white dress in a few and live happily ever after with my boy. You're not even living together yet, so don't feel bad. Relax and take a chance on Rico…you won't regret it."

The cell phone call ended abruptly, and I heard the signal drop. Apparently, Rico wasn't bluffing and wanted to take our phone fucking to the next level. All that I could manage to do was run to grab the disc from the DVD player and hide it in its proper place. Despite what would or wouldn't happen next, no one needed to know how sexually unsatisfied I really was. I wanted everyone to be completely unaware of my frustration.

What I wanted to do was something many fantasized about but few would admit—fucking their man's boy. Still, there's a distinct difference between fantasy, and making fantasy into reality. Never did I imagine that the thoughts of playing around would fuse with acting them out in real time.

In less than twenty minutes, Rico was knocking at Trey's door. I was stunned beyond belief because he wasn't bluffing about making an appearance for my sake. I knew he was forbidden fruit and I had no right to pluck from the tree. Even so, the rush of adrenaline I felt flowing through me prompted me to slowly ease the screen door open, immediately salivating over the sight of his shirtless deep-brown body. Trey had a horsepower engine, but it was all going to a waste. He wanted to go about five miles per hour on a four lane highway.

Rico, on the other hand, stared me in the eyes, walked through the door without speaking, and headed straight for my lips.

"Where. Where's your shirt?" I stuttered.

"In my hand," Rico explained, revealing a balled up T-shirt. "Do you have a problem with it? Don't you like what you see?" he asked.

I was so nervous, I couldn't even reply. The temptation to reach out and touch him was like battling to stand upright in a 150 mile per hour wind—the temptation was just that strong. Instantly, he became irresistible, and I began to anxiously anticipate him coming toward me. After the screen door slammed, he abruptly pushed me against the kitchen counter and secured both of his hands around my face. His shoulders looked strong, he smelled edible, and his dark, wavy hair was freshly cut. I'd never noticed Rico's looks before because I had no business focusing on them in between marinating lamb chops, him flipping burgers on the grill, or at thecountless number of events where he was in attendance. This day was different. Like a six-foot chiseled, bronzed god, he tilted my head back, pressed his body against mine, and sent shooting tingles through me by doing something Trey hadn't done in months—sticking his tongue into my mouth.

As his tongue danced between my wanting lips, I let my hands wander up and down Rico's back then stopped on his tight ass, drinking in his physical attention like a neglected soul would. I'd set a carton of ice cream on the counter before my surprise guest arrived and had forgotten all about it. Rico opened the Breyers' lid, stuck his finger in the ice cream, and instructed me to suck it off his finger. The next thing I knew, I was tasting the sugary mixture along with his tongue as it darted into my mouth again. I began to enjoy the erotic lesson in Freakology 101, feeling the groove of his seductive moves and his hard dick pressed up against me. Although I didn't want him to stop, after a while I unlocked his tongue from mine.

"Look, Rico, we need to slow down and think about what we're doing. You and I could get busted. Plus, I can't go through with this. It's just not right."

"Shhh. I told you to stop worrying. Plus, it's too late to turn away from what we both really want. It's not like this one little time of being naughty is going to cause the downfall of civilization. After we satisfy our curiosity, we can pretend this never even happened. This can be our secret, Leslie. I can keep a secret, can you?" Rico asked, grinning and slowly tracing my lips with his index finger.

When he dropped his shirt on the floor, I felt my knees getting weak. I noticed his gleaming white teeth, but I tried to deny it to myself. "Are you for real? You expect me to just let you hit it? Trey could walk in any minute," I told him, nearly jumping out of my skin when I heard a random sound. "You're cute, Rico. You should have no trouble finding another woman."

"I did find another woman—*you*. Close the door and lock it, but I know he's out drinking with our crew. After that, they're going to pick up some pussy at H20. I'm just keeping it real with you, mami. Trey isn't in a rush to spend time with you tonight. Don't let no nigga play you like he's got you wrapped around his finger. Wise up, Leslie—a man is going to be a man, with or without a ring and a wife, so get yours. You can play and still stay. In so many words, I'm trying to let you know that's what your man is going to do. Don't feel bad about this. You deserve to feel good—it's just that easy."

"Thanks for being here with me, Rico, and thank you for the wake up call. You can't ever tell anyone about this. It will have to remain our biggest secret . . . for life," I said as the reality of his hypnotizing words sunk into my mind. Rico knew exactly what to say to make me contemplate whether he could really put a big smile on my face by delivering the uncensored, kinky sex I craved.

I shook off my blue state by slowly pressing my lips against his cheek. Just when I was enjoying my lust feast, I pushed his body away from me, trying to decide if I would really accept Rico's invitation to make magic happen. I considered how much money I'd spent on provocative outfits, lingerie, sex toys, love potions, porn sites, tape watching, and chatting on expensive sex talk lines with people I'd never meet in real life. Then I looked over at the two white hangers that lay on the couch reminding me that Trey had been in a hurry to put on his best clothes and disappear somewhere with out me. That's when I walked over to the door and locked it without guilt. As I turned around, I felt Rico's breath on my skin. I grabbed his hand and headed toward Trey's bed. My emotions had swayed in Rico's favor, I was eager to have my world set on fire. I had a feeling that this half Puerto Rican, half black, exotic looking brother was about to set my dull world ablaze.

There was something magnetic about Rico, just as Tanya said. I was wet and wanted to lie down and let him take care of me, instead of returning to the frustration of stroking myself wildly. What was I going to do? I only had one choice: let myself go and get mine. Hey, you only live once. With those thoughts, I was no longer struggling to make up my mind about cheating with Rico.

It was on and popping when Rico whipped out body paint and a little brush from his pocket. I forgot I was living life on the edge. My walls of defense came tumbling down as he appealed to my emotional side, asking me about all the things I didn't like about Trey. For starters, I told him about how Trey didn't touch me, and what it was like feeling as if I would be marrying an invisible husband. He inspired me to open up by dripping chocolate on my body and painting naughty messages on me as if I were an art palate. Without realizing it, I told him vital information I should've kept private. I giggled and giggled as the sticky liquid fell onto my skin in the most ticklish places. After he finished, Rico drew one large heart in a thick layer of chocolate and took his time licking off every drop. As promised, he nearly licked me from head to toe.

His range of foreplay moves ended with properly sucked

toes, licked thighs, a fully explored belly button, and loosened shoulders from an erotic back massage. I was primed to give it up and temporarily forgot that Trey had nearly taken me off the market.

For two hours straight, I had more erotic fun than I'd had the whole time I'd known Trey. Rico knew what to do and exactly how to do it. This fact made me leave my stress behind and scream Rico's name at the top of my lungs like he was the one I cooked and prayed for each and every night. I lost track of time—the sheets were soaked with sweat, and the room smelled like steamy sex. Rico did things to me that Trey wouldn't do in two centuries, and he seemed to focus on my satisfaction before his own. He was serving attention on a platter, and I was enjoying indulging in the sweetness of what he was offering. It was like Rico had the master key to expose what I felt I needed and managed to open my every feeling. I couldn't have asked for a better experience, or a better lover. Unlike Trey, missionary sex was not the primary position, and Rico didn't fear going down to tongue-fuck me.

"Damn, mami. You are so thick. Tell me you'll always be my freak," Rico said, flicking his tongue over my clit.

Trying to keep it together enough to talk, I answered, "I'll always be your freak, Rico, even after I marry Trey."

"Whose pussy is this now?" he said, raising his head from between my legs.

"Yours," I answered breathlessly as he licked my tiny pearl, which was growing with hardness.

"Whose?" he asked, after licking it for the last time. "Say my name for me, mami."

"Trey!" I whined intentionally.

"Trey—oh no you didn't! I'm making you scream and moan like someone's beating on you, and you're thinking about someone who you claim never made you have an orgasm? I'm going to punish your ass for getting mixed up," Rico said. After that I can't recall his exact words, but it

sounded like he was trying to tell me something about wanting me in Spanish. "Mami, yo quiero todo de su curepo. I
want your body all to myself. Do you want mine?"

"Yes."

"You're not lying to me, are you?"

"No."

"Who am I? Who's giving you this good loving?"

"Rico."

"Prove that you want me. Show me, Leslie, and I will give
you something you've never felt. Don't think about it, just
show me like a good freak would," Rico said. I sat upright and
positioned myself on my hands and knees. We were straight
fucking, to say the least. Our session grew sweeter and
sweeter as our bodies dripped with sweat.

I looked back at him. "Hit it from the back and stroke it
good. After that, it's my turn to please you, papi."

When Rico entered me from behind, I held my ass cheeks
open wide and my body began to quiver. My bottom lip
dropped when the smacking noise began and my ass cheeks
began to vibrate. I could feel my eyes roll back in my head
when Rico drove himself deep inside of me, simultaneously
reaching around in front of me to massage my clit. Suddenly,
he scooped me up. The next thing I knew, he was balancing
me in the air as I held him tightly around the neck. My hair
came undone and I had no idea where my barrette had flown.
I hated wild hair and usually confined it to a bun or ponytail.
For once, I didn't mind letting my mane fly free.

"Ah—there it is. That's the spot. Don't stop. Don't stop.
You make me feel so good. Oh Rico. Shit! Oh my God! Fuck
yes! What are you doing to me?" I screamed as his powerful,
muscular legs allowed him to perform some sort of acrobatic
feat.

Rico began pumping me faster; saying all kinds of crazy
madness about him not ever having fucked a pussy as wet, me
remembering not to scream his name on my honeymoon, and

me having an open invitation to get buck wild with him anytime I got sick of pretending Trey was meeting my sexual
needs. My glasses were jumping up and down on my face,
right along with me. I pushed them up on my nose as Rico
laughed. When Rico sat me down on top of Trey's light oak
dresser and gripped my ass while sucking and licking my tits,
I began to tingle all over. He raised his head and slowly kissed
me on the lips.

"You're so beautiful. Damn, Leslie. Does Trey tell you how
fine you are, everyday? Why would he be in the club, when
the finest thing to look at is right here?"

"He stopped telling me that and making me feel special a
long time ago. I guess I don't turn him on anymore, but at
least I know I turn *you* on," I said sadly.

We walked over to Trey's antique wingback reading chair.
As soon as Rico sat down I fell to my knees and began sucking
on his penis. He tilted his head back and gapped his legs
open in front of me as I moved my head back and forth toward his midsection. I imagined he was Trey, as my lips
wrapped around his thick, long cock. After Rico hardened
again and let out a guttural moan, he said, "Oh fuck . . . this
feels good as shit! Now I know what it's like to be Trey. Mami,
he's a very lucky man. In fact, who says he deserves to be this
lucky? Let's make the best of the situation—me and my man
are secretly going to have to share this stuff."

"You want me to get on top of that?" I asked, lifting my
head. "By the looks of your dick, I think you're ready for
some more."

"I'm waiting, mami. I think it's obvious I didn't come here
for a quickie. I knew you were a closet freak. So what's up
now—que' pasa?" He flipped the script and added, "What do
you want? This is your fantasy—I'm just here to fulfill it."

I tugged at Rico's hand, grinning. He followed me to Trey's
bed. Rico lay down and left the next move up to me. He
began to moan as I lowered my vagina on his penis. When I

did, my wetness began to gush all over again. This was the first time I had ever dominated a man, and I loved it. Finally, my body relented and I experienced my first orgasm with a man.

"I think I'm cumming. I'm cumming! Yeeeeessss! I'm reaaaaaally cumming!" I screamed with delight as I bounced wildly on top of him like a three-time-winning rodeo champion. As I creamed, I heard one of the slats break under the bed, but I continued responding as if I was oblivious to what had occurred.

I felt years younger as my sexual frustration evolved into toe-curling satisfaction. After I climaxed, I attempted to climb down from my brown horse and catch my breath but Rico bit his lip with excitement as his penis began to swell. Like a tidal wave, he began to cum then pulled out of me to let semen trickle on my face and glasses. I licked Rico's happy ending from my glasses. Although they were cloudy, I put them back on just to be funny. All of the sudden, I heard glass shatter in another room. Like a bolt of lightening, I jumped up off the bed, pushing Rico away from me. Without thinking, I ran toward the noise, removing my glasses to wipe them between my thumbs for a quick cleaning. Of course my visibility was still compromised when I put them back on, but what I couldn't see clearly, I could surely hear.

3

The Backstabber

"Oh my God!" Tanya said, shaking her head and taking breaths in between each word. "I can't believe this. Bitch, how could you? See how you do me! You're the godmother of my two children. I'm the maid of honor in your wedding! You're like a blood sister. You told me to break up with Rico and come to find out ya'll are fucking each other! I thought you were celibate too. Ain't this some shit!" Tanya mumbled teary-eyed as the volume of her voice escalated.

"What do you want me to do? I'm sorry! Now just calm down, Tanya," I said, pleading with my best friend. I was shocked to see her but tried to play off the awkward moment.

"Calm down my ass! And what a weak apology! I came over here to vent after I broke up with Rico, but I see whose side you're really on, you back biting, bitch-ass ho," she said, jerking her head all around her neck like a girl from the hood.

My usually mild-mannered friend, who swayed next to me while singing in the church choir, picked up the same brick from Trey's flowerbed she'd apparently used to break the picture window. Tanya knocked the window out completely, then walked through it to gain entry into the house. In a fit of rage, she threw the brick across the room, knocking over an imported Asian vase I'd given Trey on the anniversary of our one year commitment. I looked at Tanya in awe as she stormed past me, heading toward the bedroom.

Upon her heated arrival, Rico said, "Ladies, ladies. There's enough to go around for the both of you, so don't fight. All three of us can have some fun. Leslie can suck my shit, and Tanya can open wide and swallow. Now are both of you down for the next round?" He continued stroking himself. I couldn't believe what a perverted ass he was!

"You're not funny, Rico. And the big beef I have is with you, Leslie. I was outside listening near the bedroom window for a while," Tanya said, wildly waving her finger in my face. She moved closer then continued, poking me in the middle of my chest. "I had my suspicions that he was no good, but you, you take the motherfucking cake! You're supposed to be a Christian!" she screamed.

"Look, Tanya, slow your roll. I'm saved, not dead. Oh, so now I'm supposed to take the blame for everything? I didn't twist his arm to come here. Apparently, I'm a member of the cleanup committee because you don't know what to do or how to do it. You were too busy pretending God said sex was nasty. Furthermore, I never made a promise to love, honor, and cherish you. In case your high and mighty uptight ass has forgotten, I'm marrying my man, not you, and I'm strictly dickly. If you didn't know what to do with that fine pretty boy over there, you left the door open for anyone to satisfy him. In this case, he felt I was fit to do the job. Call next time. No one told you to show up without announcing your visit. Don't trip—since you were eavesdropping on how I get down, I hope you took some damn good notes!" I said, erasing every-thing I'd told her during our bonding time earlier the same day.

I have no idea where my arrogance came from, but my lips were moving, saying all sorts of nasty things, regardless of how I betrayed my girl. The more I said, the better it felt to lash out at Tanya, although I didn't know why I wanted to be so mean. Apparently, my last audible jabs were fighting words, and the camel's back was officially broken.

"Good things come in small packages, bubble ass!" Tanya screamed. She intentionally broke my four hundred dollar glasses, and then pushed me down on the bed, grabbing handfuls of my hair and punching me all over my body. We rolled around, and I managed to slap her in the face and poke at her eyes. Rico should have been trying to pry us apart but he seemed to become more aroused by the girl fight. I heard him moaning when I managed to peel Tanya off of me. She fell to the floor. I kicked her in the ribs and held my size nine on top of her petite frame.

"From the bottom of my heart, I'm sorry you had a shitty day, but take a deep breath and move on my sista. See, something good did come from this. At least you know the Rico Suave knock off is not the one for you. Pick up your pride and move the hell on. Begging isn't cute my friend. Didn't you learn that from your failed marriage? Touch me again and I'm going to knock your ass out and hang you on a telephone pole. You know I train in the gym and can drop you like a dude. I'm warning you, Tanya. Make it a priority to calm your five-foot-two ass down in three seconds or less, and stop acting like I offended all of mankind. Why are you fighting over leftovers, sweetie? Were you looking for a daddy to be a father figure for your rug rats?"

Tanya began to cry like I'd dealt her the lowest possible blow. I knew my words cut her deeply but I didn't care. Making her miserable made me feel powerful. "Get out, bitch," I continued. "No one wants to hear all of this drama. Why'd you break my glasses? These are the pair with the scratch-proof lenses. They cost me four hundred dollars!"

"So what? Wait until I tell Trey about this. *And*, I'm going to tell pastor what you pulled when I get to church on Sunday. Let's see what he thinks of Ms. Leslie then," she threatened.

"If you do go there, I'll have to call the police and report you for breaking and entering and assault. And for the grand finale, I'll see to it that your ex takes your kids away when he hears about you being an unstable, violent mother who tried to wreck your best friend's wedding after trying to fuck her man. Try me and I'll turn it all around in my favor. That's the part I'm telling you about, but there could be more where that came from. If you want to open your big mouth, bring it on."

"You wouldn't! *You* were wrong, not me."

"Welcome to the real world, Miss Hooked on Stupid! Don't threaten me with wrecking my wedding. I'm good for it. Try me. By the way, try ordering some ProActiv for your adult case of acne, and tone up that accordion looking belly if you want to wear shirts that show your midriff. Flabby, bumpy, blubber is not a good look. None of that is cute. Now I can finally tell you the truth since you wanted to start the Battle of Little Big Mouth!"

"I never want to see you again, you closet freak! I had no idea you were like this! You're disgusting! You need prayer!"

"Get the fuck out. Should I call 911 or what? I have a witness and I'm not thrilled about having to repair the shit you damaged. What's it going to be?"

Tanya spit on me and stormed out of Trey's place. The only reason I didn't chase her down was because I was naked and didn't want to attract any more attention to Trey's house. After the tires of her four-door Toyota Camry squealed, and she took off, I dressed so I could see if she tried any funny stuff before stepping off. Sure enough she plastered the word NYMPHO on the door and underlined it twice in bright red lipstick. When I thought of the lie I was going to have to tell to explain this mess to Trey, I stormed back to the bedroom to throw out Rico's horny ass. I knew I had to get rid of the evidence quickly because the house next door was up for sale and people had been trailing in and out of it on several occasions. I didn't need the realtor knocking on Trey's door asking questions about anything.

"Ding, ding, ding. Your time's up. Game over, baby boy." I began picking up slithers of glass from off of the floor, carefully placing them in the palm of my right hand.

"Already?" Rico said, grinning. "You church girls are wild as hell. Let me find out I need to hunt for sisters in the house of the Lord."

After I dropped the glass in the trash, I turned around and rolled my eyes at him.

Without saying another word, I shooed him out after making him dress quickly. I made it clear that he better not breathe a word to his boy, and he should forget what happened between us like he'd suffered the worse case of amnesia. Suddenly, my spirit turned icy, and I couldn't tolerate the sight of Rico. I cussed him out and explained that he'd worn out his welcome. He thought I was joking, but I wasn't. I stuffed his black Calvin Klein drawers in his hand, found his balled up t-shirt, and commanded him to clean the lipstick off of Trey's door on his way out. After he left, I returned to the bedroom to start cleaning up whatever I could in a hurry.

My gaze fell on something green. Apparently, Rico had paid me three hundred dollars cash money for fulfilling his fantasy. There was a note sitting underneath which read: I WANT YOU TO KEEP YOUR MOUTH SHUT TOO. TAKE THIS AND GET SOME KINKY SHIT FROM FREDERICKS OF HOLLYWOOD FOR YOUR HONEYMOON. I KNOW YOU'LL WEAR IT WELL, MI AMOR.

I smiled as I ripped up Rico's note and flushed it down the toilet. He had no idea, but he'd just given me the idea to get paid to get my rocks off. After all, how I rolled officially made me a freak and maybe I liked the idea of men screaming *my* name. At that moment, I decided my pet name when I was acting devilish would be Innocence. Round one of my official secret life was about to begin. Fortunately, I made a habit of keeping a spare set of glasses in my glove compartment for *freak* accidents. By my standards, I think this scenario qualified, but it was worth it because I enjoyed learning that tasting forbidden fruit could taste so very good. On top of it all, I became hooked on having orgasms—amen, amen, and AMEN!

Although I had already opened up Pandora's Box, I was in search of the next opportunity to work my hips.

4

Playing With Fire

Trey came home smelling like liquor and smoke around five in the morning. No doubt, he must've been bar and club hopping with his other gray-haired player friends, just as Rico had explained. When I felt him crawl into bed next to me, I pretended I was asleep, but I wasn't. With the exception of the broken window, there were no signs remaining of the shake up . . . or shake down, depending on how you'd like to describe it. Even so, I had trumped up a lie and it was ready for delivery. I planned to tell Trey some bad, unsupervised kids hit a softball through the window, but I couldn't tell who did it since they all ran in various directions. No real worries with his ass though. As luck would have it, he decided he wanted to make love, instead of spoon. I guess the liquor got his typically limp dick hard, or maybe some well-prepared bitch made him take Viagra when he was out on the town doing whatever it was men do.

Trey's fingers wandered toward my vagina. After he asked for it, I let him hit the skins just to shut his half-inebriated ass up. I didn't mind obliging since it gave me an opportunity to give him his fifteen minutes of fame on the same bed where his boy had his way with me. I behaved as if I craved Trey's touch, but I was really thinking about the naughty things I'd done on the same bed with Rico. Trey's ego was eating up the sex talk as I put it on him like never before, but when I looked at the clock, I was surprised because the ordeal of lying on my back lasted an entire twenty minutes as opposed to his usual fifteen. *Whooptie do, Trey*, I thought. *You're a little too late.* Damn shame. Trey was as fine as Rico, but couldn't put it down under the sheets like he did before he was banging me and all the other chicks on his tap the punani list. God should've given his big, fat tool to someone who would've appreciated it enough to use it properly. Oh well. Even drunk, my man looked hot. The one thing I couldn't take away from the Negro was his looks. The older he got, the finer he became and the more I wanted to prove I was approaching my sexual peak.

The next morning, I offered to cook Trey bacon and eggs—his favorite morning indulgence when he wasn't wolfing down cereal or coffee.

"What happened to my window?" he asked after finally observing the plastic tacked over the area where the glass was housed.

I tried to act cool.

"It's getting fixed today, don't worry about it," I said.

"Leslie, what happened to it?"

"You were a kid once. Let it go. Some kids in the neighborhood were playing football and accidentally hit your window yesterday. I cleaned up the glass, put some plastic over it, and called for someone to come out and put a new one in. They're coming tomorrow. I plan to wait for them to get here because I know you won't be home."

"Let it go, nothing! Why should I? I'm going to find out who did this. I shouldn't have to pay for the repair. Where's the football?" Trey asked, looking around the room.

"I said I've got it. You don't have to pay for anything."

"You shouldn't pay for this either."

"Why are you sweating the small stuff? I said I took care of it. I know kids. I'm a teacher, remember? If you go around banging on doors, no one's gong to own up to it. What would it do besides run up your blood pressure? They will be more careful because they know you'll be on the look out now. Give them this one free pass. We've got enough going on in our world."

"I guess you're right. Thank you for keeping me calm, Leslie," Trey said.

"That's what I'm here for. So, can we spend some time together now?"

"I'm meeting my boys to play ball, then I'm running errands all day. Keep your phone on in case we can hook up later though."

"Playing ball? How ironic. What about me?" I mumbled.

I rolled my eyes, and then rolled out. Of course it never occurred to him that I may want to have some quality time with my man on a sunny summer day, but what's new? Nothing.

When I made it home, I peeled off my clothes, cooked myself bacon and eggs, straightened up a bit, then checked my email. I also decided to also search for another vase on the Internet to replace the one I had given Trey before it slipped my mind. He was so pissed about his window, he put on his shoes and was about to start knocking on doors to question every brat in the neighborhood who could've broken his window. The last thing I needed was for Trey to fly off the handle again after noticing the vase was missing, because that would definitely put holes in my story regarding how the window was broken. I figured I might be able to replace it before he noticed it was missing in action. That's when I stumbled onto a website called craigslist.org. I clicked on the for sale section of the Washington D.C. link. Although I didn't see a description that matched what I was looking for, there were so many interesting goodies, I promised myself that I would revisit the website.

Before leaving the website, my eye zoomed in on something strange. Toward the bottom section of the many links, the word *erotic* was listed under the service section. My curiosity swelled and I clicked on that link too. A disclaimer popped up stating that unless certain conditions were met, the user should hit the back button and exit this part of the site. The individual who entered that portion of the site had to be at least eighteen years old, understand that explicit sexual content may be included, couldn't bothered by explicit sexual content, and agree that when proceeding to click on the link, they released creators, owners and providers of craiglist from any and all liability which may arise from its use.

After I got past all of the legal jargon, I entered a world I never imagined I'd find on the Internet. My eyes fell upon strings of countless ads where people posted sexual services and each post was dated to separate the new from the old. Captions such as: DO YOU WANT ME TO BE YOUR SEX SLAVE, LUNCH SPECIALS UNTIL 2:00 A.M., REVIEW OF KOREAN CUTIE, AND LADIES UP FOR SOME FUN AT FOUR STAR HOTEL IN AR-LINGTON, were just a few of the headings. Obviously, the world's oldest profession had gone high tech. The illegal offerings far outnumbered the web cam and sex line "call me now" ads, legitimate massage descriptions, stripper solicitations, and photography service announcements for females in need of erotic photos. The funny thing was that a few girls even posted fabricated stories about their panties being for sale because they were short on their rent at some college campus. Try again hoes in training—sure you're right.

I was so intrigued by what I'd stumbled upon, I spent the entire day clicking on ads, studying terminology, service offerings, body shapes, ages, and reviews of women who were apparently formally having sex for money. The prostitutes described themselves as providers and those who were providing erotic services ranged the full gamut: people in debt, single mothers in need of extra cash, male and female college students strapped for cash, preachers' wives, pregnant women, big beautiful women, porn stars, wanna be models or dominatrixes, gay men, and regular hookers who discovered they could get paid more to arrange lunch break quickies or business traveler delights. Some providers showed their faces while posing in the buff, while others hid their identities within silhouettes or picture free ads.

The beauty of the set up was that no real email addresses were shown. A provider could remain anonymous until they chose to respond to a curious person. No doubt, all of this fostered the ability for married men, singles, executives, and whoever was looking for sex to hook up. In addition to that, some providers traveled from state to state and posted under other cities to let "fans" know when they could get the hook up. All of this should've raised a twenty-four foot red flag for me, but instead, the idea of getting paid to lust became my objective. I suddenly felt walking through this door was an option for. In some twisted way, I felt playing with fire would help me get the thrills I deserved. Every time I'd open my legs, it would be for a stranger. And each and every stranger understood the one, simple, three syllable word that was the code terminology for getting paid to give up the booty—*donation.*

After I moved to the front of the class in understanding how to dodge law enforcement and give customers what they wanted in exchange for the moolah, it was time to get ready to give a GFE, a.k.a. girlfriend experience, where I'd perform as the trick's woman in the bedroom, complete with kissing, cuddling, caressing, and sappy shit like that. It was funny how many married or committed men believed that living in a fantasy world with a woman who *pretended* to be into him would

do the trick. Speaking of tricks, it was time to begin my legitimate secret life turning tricks. Before signing up to be a
housewife, I figured I may as well try something freaky and
new by giving professional whoring a shot. Maybe if I had
more penises at my disposal, I could quiet the throbbing between my legs before it was time to live my boring life with
Trey.

The ad that read: EARN AS MUCH AS YOU WANT in the cap-
tion caught my attention. I ended up calling a number and
setting up an interview to become a working girl for a man
who claimed to collect a finder's fee after hooking up busi-
nessmen and high rollers. He told me if I passed his test, and
honored his rules, I could make as much as $1200 a day—
fulltime. That was all I needed to hear to give up my conservative looking bun, shave my legs and bikini area, flat iron my
hair, and prepare to show him what sweet Innocence was really
made of. Although I'd only had three lovers in my entire life,
all of them were conservative between the sheets, but watching my fair share of porn had me well prepared to release the
freak within.

Later that day, I was off to the address I'd been given over
the phone. I left my glasses and confined hairstyle at home. I
wanted to feel like someone else, the same someone who
made Rico forget his girl and hit his boy's piece in the same
day. My car wheels halted in front of a tall, black, wrought iron
gate. A mansion sat behind it, and I was stunned. I gulped when
two burly looking guards asked me for some sort of code word.
I could tell they were guards based on their demeanor, and
the fact that they were both dressed in all black.

"Code word?" I replied looking bewildered.

"Yeah, what's the code word?"

"I wasn't given a code word. I'm just here to see—"

"He's joking, sweetheart. May we please see your invitation?"

"I don't have one of those either. Invitation for what?"

"There's a special event going on today. You don't know? This is the biggest private party of the year."

"Well I wasn't told about any of that. I'm just here to see some guy name Brian Delgado."

The guard with cornrows looked at me and spoke into a radio. "And your name is?"

"Innocence."

"She says her name is Innocence," he said.

After he put down the walkie talkie device, he tapped the other guard on the shoulder and whispered something in his ear. Afterward, he turned back to me and pulled out a clipboard and piece of paper. He shoved it through the window with his right arm. "You'll have to sign a waiver to come in. If you choose to sign, we'll need your real name," he explained.

I read it over as I wondered what the waiver of liability was all about. My mind flashed back to craigslist. *What could be inside of those gates that would require my full birth name and a few other details?* Although I hesitated for a moment, I scribbled my John Hancock and then was directed to park on a sprawling lawn. All sorts of vehicles were lined up side by side—Hummers, luxury trucks, and a few exotic cars. As I walked up to the front door, I was greeted by two very attractive females.

"Are you a model?" one asked.

"Me?" I asked, half laughing. "No, I'm not."

"Well welcome," the black one said. The other woman placed a lei around my neck and opened the door for me to walk through. When I prepared to shut the door, I suddenly realized I was not alone. I looked back and noticed one of the guards towering over me. Apparently, he was escorting me to my final destination.

"Turn right," he commanded.

When I did, I passed two more guards standing in front of a set of steps. I pretended not to notice them nodding, and continued walking down a long hallway with fluorescent blue lighting. After the guard commanded me to turn left, I stood in front of a large office with about twenty security cameras and a short Italian looking man with gray chest hair poking out of a black shirt.

"You must be Innocence. I'm Brian," the man told me.

"Yes I am. Nice to meet you, Brian," I replied. Before I knew it, the guard closed the door, but I had a distinct feeling that he was standing on the other side of it.

"We're having a special party today. I thought you should come at a time like this so you can get a flavor of how things can be."

I looked around and my eyes fell upon a large window that revealed a small pool—the kind that was perfect for skinny dipping. Women of all races were walking around in bikinis and heels, sipping on drinks, and chatting with all sorts of men who ranged from corporate looking types to celebrities I could easily recognize. A few were sun bathing in solitude but I noticed that everyone had access to a cell phone.

"So tell me about yourself, Innocence," Brian said, interrupting my daze.

"There really isn't much to tell. I'm just your average girl, living an average life," I answered, my eyes focusing on his Movado desk clock.

"You don't look average to me. In fact, average is not what I'm looking for. I don't like average women with average personalities or average bodies. I like the best because my clients pay to enjoy the best. The L.A. types with big implants who can't explain how a bill becomes a law, or who aren't aware of foreign policy and current events are not what I'm after. An airhead who looks good on the outside but whose brain is empty on the inside is a dime a dozen. Now let's try this conversation again. Tell me about yourself, Innocence."

I suddenly felt like I was being interviewed to win the Miss America crown. Apparently, Brian wanted more than a whore.

He wanted the appearance of a cultured lady—at least on some level.

"Hello, Brian. It's a pleasure to meet you. My given name is Leslie, but I prefer to call myself Innocence. I'm thirty years of age, teach for a living, and am on my summer break. My favorite hobbies include studying history, fitness, traveling, and meeting new people. I prefer to regard myself as a new millennium woman with discerning taste. Don't let me fool you—I'm not all Innocent though. I'm capable of going toe-to-toe with a man in a boardroom or the bedroom. In fact, there's nothing ordinary about me so if I were you, I wouldn't expect it."

"Name the seven continents."

"Europe, Asia, Africa, Australia, South America, North America, and of course, Antarctica," I replied, smiling victoriously. "Do you have any real questions, Brian? If you do, fire away. I'm waiting."

"Take off your skirt and top. Let's see what you have underneath. That's not exactly a question but—"

"I know what it is—it's a command. I'm a teacher, remember? And I have nothing to hide or be ashamed of. My body is tight and it's a ten. No, I'm being far too modest. It's a twelve, at least in my opinion. It's only fair if you draw your own conclusion though," I said, shedding my military inspired outfit. My pink and green mini skirt fell down my knees and I pulled my army green tube top over my head. "What if I'm not wearing a bra . . . or panties? I hope that's okay with you."

I stood tall in nothing but my gold heels that just so happened to be Trey's favorite pair. He did manage to tell me my feet and calves looked sexy in them each time I wore them. I could tell by the manner in which Brain glanced over me that he was impressed by my physique. Although I wasn't some L.A. skinny bitch, I knew I was a head turner.

"All right—you passed those tests with flying colors. Before you take the last step in the interview process let me ex-

plain something to you. I take good care of my girls, Innocence—an expense account, shopping sprees, a nice place to
say—no fear of being arrested. I'm not a pimp and never force
a client on anyone. My girls come and go when they please.
Drug use and alcoholism is prohibited, but I ensure that
everyone goes home happy and comes to work happy. There is
nothing to do until a call comes in for you. You can sit by the
pool, talk on the cell phone, which I provide, watch TV, or just
relax. You don't have to worry about being marketed because I
make sure that is taken care of. If you accept a client, you deliver my finder's fee after you are paid. I have no fear of not
getting my share because you'll definitely want another pre-
screened client with the same qualities as the last guy. I am a
businessman and a damn good one. I work long hours and expect complete cooperation with all of the talent, so everyone
can benefit from this. Dress and let's take a walk."

After I dressed quickly, Brian allowed me to walk out of his
office first. Next, he told the guard to take me to get a swim-
suit, and then to escort me outside to the pool area. I slipped
on a red string bikini with moveable letters that spelled
BLING. They were strung on the side and midsection of two
strings. When I finished changing, I followed the guard down
winding steps that led to our final destination. My eyes
scanned the open bar, lavish outdoor buffet, and umbrellas-
topped circular tables. I heard girls suck their teeth and hiss
at me as I walked past them to find a seat near the pool.
Heads turned as I whipped out my sunglasses and lay back on
a lounge chair in my heels.

By the time I strutted over to the bartender to request a
mixed drink, I could feel eyes burning a hole in my back.
Clients who were supposedly occupied were already lusting
after me. I knew I was the center of attention and loved every
second of it.

About forty minutes later, a guard I hadn't seen before
pointed at me while a young man wearing diamonds in both

ears and a huge dollar sign emblem necklace around his neck
headed toward me. Despite him wearing a plain, large white
t-shirt, I recognized the well-known rapper. In fact, I couldn't
believe he was looking at me as if I was some sort of scrump-
tious entrée he'd picked out. *Doesn't his fame get him enough
ass?* I was confused as to why a famous man would pay for
sex—especially one who could pop bottles with super models.

"Hi, Ma," he said. "How come I never seen you here before or at the VIP lap dance parties Brian hosts?"

"What parties?" I asked. The rapper grinned.

"Never mind. You'll find out if you're good with your hands
and can work them hips right. So . . . wassup witcha?"

At that moment, all of Brian's I better be an intelligent
woman talk went flying out of the window. Before I could
greet him properly, he said, "Get up and turn around." I did.
"Yeah—you straight. Let's go. Come take a little walk wit
me."

Apparently, the rapper's definition of "me" was more like
"us," and included his personal bodyguard. I questioned this
at first, but then decided that despite his limited vocabulary,
he must've had at least half a brain cell to want an extra pair
of eyes along for the protection of his money. Smart thug.
Correction: smart businessman. Obviously, he'd cracked the
millionaire's code and wanted to keep his money under his
thumb.

Once again, the girls sucked their teeth with envy when I
followed the men. Since the competition tried to give me so
much bad attitude, I added to the hate index by switching
past them like a confident piece of ebony eye candy.

When the three of us walked down a long hallway inside of
the mansion, we passed between the same set of bodyguards
I spotted upon my initial arrival. We then proceeded up a
flight of steps that I logically concluded led to the VIP area.
When we reached the top and turned left, another set of

bodyguards were blocking the hallway. Upon spotting the rapper, their eyes shifted slightly, giving the approval for him and his small entourage to enter the door at the end of the hall. As we passed several doors I could hear sex sounds with a twist—several staggered moans and groans of various pitches escaping through the air at once.

We moved a little further and then his personal bodyguard frisked me down, feeling me between my legs, then holding his finger to the rapper's nose to sniff it. He inhaled my scent and I knew he obviously approved because he ordered the bodyguard to "get the merchandise ready for purchase." The bodyguard began to slowly undress me, rubbing all over my body, then smacking my ass. As he did this, the vain rapper showed off his lyrical skills by singing about ghetto love. The little tune went something like this:

> Money is power—
> All those paid for hoes
> Wit da pedicured toes
> Jump on my dick
> And show me mo' love
> 'Cause they know my paper thick
> Don't need no credit cards on the bar
> My ice, my cars
> Hanging out wit movie stars
> I told ya I'm living da life
> Hell yeah, that's right.
> Hell yeah, that's right.
> East, South, North, West;
> they want me
> 'cause my shit tight
> and I rock the mike the best

When he stopped, so did the bodyguard. Standing nude in my heels, we locked eyes. I was dripping wet because the star who was lusting over me was the same one I fussed at my students over for trying to mimic his disjointed hip hop dance, and singing his lyrics everywhere in school, even during class. If I had a quarter for every time I reminded the young people that men like him don't know how to treat a lady, I'd be the only rich teacher in the world. And there I was the role model, mentor, and child advocate, watching him lick his lips over my ass, and listening to him refer to me as the best of the best eye candy. Suddenly, I was just as impressed by his cockiness, fame, tattoos, and the long platinum necklace that looked like Jacob The Jeweler had custom made it for him,. I was being a hypocrite, but the bad girl in me loved the fact that I'd been led to have the opportunity to be in this position. I felt like a star in my own right because I was getting ready to have sex with one.

"Stop acting like a virgin. Fuck the bed—up against the wall. Show me all dat ass," he said, correcting me when I got ready to assume the position.

I turned around, pressing my breasts against the wall. I wasn't sure what to do with my hands until he said, "Play wit' yourself a while." He palmed both ass cheeks and then pressed his lips press against each one. He stopped touching me. "Make it dance," he commanded.

Instantly, I recalled some of the music videos I'd seen with women clapping their asses, particularly those with that popular video honey Buffie the Body. Since we were about the same size, her tricks became my tricks.

"Shit, you're a pretty little thing—that's what Blaze is talking about. I bet that apple looks good in jeans," he mumbled. "Come on sexy. Enough bullshitting wit dat foreplay. Let's see if you got whip appeal." He turned me around and looked me up and down. "What's your name?"

"Innocence."

"I likes that. So take me to heaven, Innocence. Do whatever ya do that will blow my mind. Prove that you ain't got nothing but love for me."

Knowing that all men love oral sex, I sucked on his dollar sign necklace to give him a hint that I was good at licking and sucking it like a lollipop, then I yanked at his belt buckle. Blaze's bodyguard walked over to pull down the star's pants. When the bodyguard moved out of the way Blaze's jeans fell to his ankles. I dropped to my knees in the middle of the room and stared up into his eyes while running my tongue around the rim of his swollen knob. Then I wrapped my lips around the largest, thickest penis I'd ever encountered. When he began to moan, I wrapped both hands around his tool, bobbing my head faster, and mesmerizing him as Innocence began to defy logic. Blaze grabbed my head by my hair and pushed it toward his dick until I could barely manage to breathe. My lips felt as if they were stretched as far as they would go as I sucked what I hoped would soon be inside my pussy. Although I was thinking he was nearly too big for my mouth, I wasn't about to complain. The harder and larger he grew, the more I felt as if I was nearly gagging . . . but I loved being his cock sucker.

"Damn! That's one bad ass, freaky bitch right der! She sucks a mean dick!" his guard said.

The sound of the bodyguard's voice reminded me of his presence, and the thought of being watched turned me on. I'd always wanted to give Trey head while someone watched, but I knew I could never recommend such a thing. My fantasies were off limits although he'd probably lived each and every one of his.

Blaze let go of my hair and without speaking, I rose from my knees with saliva and pre cum swimming in my mouth. I began to moan and pinch my breasts while walking back toward the wall. I stood about two inches from the wall and bent straight over, preparing to show off my flexibility from when I was active in creative dance and gymnastics back in my college days. When I made my breasts touch my chin, the rapper snapped his fingers and his bodyguard presented a condom, tore it open, and handed it to him. He rolled it down on himself.

"Gimme dat. This bad boy's gonna tear your ass up," he stated. The next thing I knew, my back was completely touching the wall and I could feel the vibration from Blaze's intense pounding. I screamed as the pictures on the wall rattled and my legs began to spread wider apart like an upside down V. After a few minutes passed, I stood up and pulled off the condom. Like a professional head doctor who sucked dick for a living, I dropped to my knees again. This time I moved my head around wildly, sucking on him until my own saliva streamed down my chest. I opened wide and deep throated his juicy penis once more, and then we made our way to the bed. He clicked his fingers once and before I knew it a fresh condom was covering his penis.

"Let me stick this up that big phat ass," he said, holding himself.

"Oh no, honey. The back door is closed. Translation: my booty hole is off limits. You'll have to stick to the front opening," I told him, switching gears.

Instantly it was as if a needle on a record had slid off and ruined the flow, mid-groove.

"Now ma, stop trying to hassle me and rip me off! I thought you knew—I'm paying $5,000 to tap this. Not five grand per hole; just five grand—*period.* Show some respect. You know what I'm sayin'? I got da hottest single out here. If a superstar like Blaze wants to open the back door, you're supposed to turn that ass up with a smile. Some women would pay to fuck me, not the other way around, so get your head right," he said, sounding frustrated.

"Brian said everything I do is my choice, and I'm choosing

to reserve my asshole for my husband, so enough of the yang popping," I insisted.

"No one wants to hear all dat shit. Show me some love before I lose my hard on. C'mon, bitch, back that thang up and cooperate like you know your place," he growled.

"Well this *bitch* is engaged, and I meant what I said."

"No one gives a fuck about whatever nigga you got at home," Blaze said, grabbing his balls, shaking his penis in my direction.

"You can shake that thing until 2007 but it's not going to make one iota of a difference. I know you think you've got all the power in the world, but I'm not letting you drive *this* Benz down the Hershey highway. Five grand or not, it's not going to happen. In fact, I'm as kinky as the next bitch, but that's not enough to even get me to start up the car," I said, jumping up from the bed.

"What seems to be the problem?" Brian asked, suddenly appearing. I guess he got a glimpse of things not going so well on the monitor and decided to come survey the situation.

"Anal sex—that's the problem," I complained.

"Well, give the man what he wants."

"That's not how you explained it," I shot back.

"I thought you would fill in the blanks, you learn fast—never argue with a client. You're always to deliver an unforgettable experience."

"I tell you what. Why don't you take the five grand and let him stick *you* up the ass with that tree trunk looking thing he's slinging? After you do, I guarantee you won't be able to shit for an entire week—let's see how you like delivering an unforgettable experience then. Why don't you drop your pants and your drawers and put your hands on your knees? Go on . . . ass up, Brian," I said.

"Do you know how many black girls are selling themselves for fifty bucks a pop? Asian girls, easy sell. All American blondes, easy sell. You're lucky you can get top dollar. My clients pay for discretion and cooperation, and here you come treating one like a crack head with no money. You're far more stupid than I thought. Get out!" Brian screamed, pointing at the door.

I left my clothes behind and even the bikini that I borrowed when I first changed. Feeling angry and insulted, I began storming out butt naked in my heels.

On my way out of the room, I heard Blaze cuss and request two white girls and one Asian one, I said, "As the kids would say...get on your A game. Your rapping sucks. You probably can't even get your music played on the air. Hottest single out here my ass! By the way, you look like something crawled out of the swamp and bit you in the face. The only reason paid for hoes with the pedicured toes jump on your dick is because money is power, just like you said. *I* don't do it for the *money*, I do it for the *excitement*, so you can keep your five grand, Blaze."

I don't know what came over to me, but exerting my power made me hornier than ever. When I reached the bottom of the steps, I exited by the pool area longing to pull every man in sight by the arm and take them all to bed at the same time. Their eyes glazed over as I proceeded to sashay to my car like a confident exhibitionist. When I reached my vehicle, I unlocked it and masturbated until I began screaming and shaking, my legs waving back and forth. I knew I ran the risk of being watched publicly, but I didn't care. My body found relief. Holding my head upright, I saw two of the guards pointing at me, confirming that I'd just put on a show for them. I pulled a blanket that I'd washed at the Laundromat around myself, started the car, and squealed tires as I left the premises.

This was the first time I realized I was officially out of control. Although I knew I was playing with fire by ignoring logical personal boundaries, I just couldn't stop living out my sexual fantasies. I promised myself I would try my hardest to simmer down before the consequences crept up on me and ruined my life. Whether my effort would work was wholly a question of a different nature.

5

Guess Who's Coming To Dinner?

Sunday morning rolled around and it was time to switch gears and revert back to my original persona, even if I felt like dragging my feet to get it done. While I sat in the house of the Lord, I kept nodding off, tired from my adventure with Blaze in my new secret life. Despite the fact that I could barely focus or stay awake, when Trey nudged me, I sprang to my feet and managed to sing *This Little Light of Mine* on key as if I'd been awake the entire time.

Needless to say, my mind wasn't on the sermon. Instead, I was reminiscing over me having the guts to sex a man who couldn't have been shaving long and who still dressed the part of a free, young spirit. I kept thinking about being banged by the young buck with the exceptionally large tool. Just thinking about what I'd done made me reach over and grab Trey's hand for a moment—not because of guilt, but because opening my legs for someone so different than him turned me on and allowed me to pretend I was content.

Luckily, I didn't attend my church, so Tanya couldn't start any static regarding what had transpired earlier in the week—a cooling off period was a good thing. After I finished sitting in a church pew in Leslie mode, I was stuck having to spend time with Trey's family for the second time since we've been engaged. I made sure to slick my hair back in a neatly done bun and wear a skirt that touched my knees this morning. Boring Leslie had returned to the building. I was most comfortable looking *boring* when I sought to make a good impression on others—especially those over fifty years of age.

Although I didn't know his family well, I got my daily scoop on the conservative Southern Christians through updates from my beau. Every day there was new piece of something that made me despise those strangers for almost everything, beginning with how Trey was reared. It was insane for a young person to be prohibited from dancing, watching movies, television, and doing the normal things any teenager would want to enjoy. I guess all of this explained why Trey wasn't wrapped up into dishing up ghetto fabulous loving. After we got engaged, he always held back and even appeared to feel guilty when we made love.

Since Trey believed we should be serving the Lord *together*, I joined his church and occasionally went there with him. In Trey's eyes, I was a Christian girl with old-school beliefs. But in actuality, I was a Christian with worldly habits, hence my desire to get my freak on. In my mind's eye, there were worse sins I could be committing than lusting over the man I planned to marry.

What I perceived as ambivalence frustrated me and quelled my desire to experience my first orgasm with Trey. It was screwed up that thanks to his family's puritanical outlook the first man I experienced an orgasm with was our best man. Thanks to Trey's cock blocking family, smiles on my face caused by hot, passionate lovemaking were few and far in between. This was new for me because I was used to fighting men off, not begging them to jump on the bandwagon.

Speaking of puritanical outlooks, all Trey's immediate fam-

ily seemed to do was judge people, and I was not looking forward to a second inspection. I'd have to tolerate seeing them
at wedding rehearsal soon enough anyway. Trey's mother had
her dress altered four times. Maybe if she would've stopped
sampling different types of menus for the wedding plate, she
would've kept a stable size. I sensed that before long, the
total amount paid for her alterations would surpass the cost of
my wedding dress. It seemed as though she was the one walking down the aisle instead of me. She and her mother seemed
rather comfortable planning how many friends and family
would be attending, and how the seating for parents and relatives would be arranged. She was also intent on dictating
that grape juice toasts be made since champagne was off limits, and explained that the vows would be read right out of the
Bible, even though I made it clear that Trey and I had agreed
to compose our own commitment of marriage. Arrangements
for the honeymoon and moving in together also came up, but
I tuned the suckers out hours prior, reminding myself that
the person footing the bill should have the final say so—me.

Since I was estranged from my family and they wouldn't be
involved, I was responsible for coughing up the money by the
contract due date. Our modest wedding would cost around
fifteen thousand dollars. I planned to use my savings to pay
for most of it. The remaining tab was small stuff, which I
wasn't going to sweat, although it did cut into my reserve
stash. My reasoning was that Trey was worth it, and he meant
enough for me to part with my rainy day fund.

Hopefully, Trey would take time off from his job and walk
down the aisle with me. It sounded like a basic premise,
being available for your wedding and honeymoon, but who
could tell, especially since he still gave his mother and grandmother spending money every week. Perhaps he wouldn't
have had to be a workaholic if he took them off of his payroll
account.

"There's my son," Trey's mother said, hugging him tightly. "Leslie," she grunted as I walked through the door behind him.

Mabel inspected me from head to toe. I could tell she didn't approve of my outfit although it was conservative. Even so, I didn't give a damn.

"Mrs. Williams, it's always a pleasure," I lied in the same unpleasant tone.

Her ass was looking more and more like a train caboose every day. I'm not sure if she ever thought about gastric bypass surgery, but the option should've been considered. Tyler Perry's get ups had nothing on hers except that hers wasn't a get up—it was something she wore in real life.

As we passed through the living room, I felt an overwhelming sense of fear that I was being suffocated by plastic. I noticed that *everything* was coated in plastic—transparent plastic on the furniture, yellow plastic runners covering the carpet, fake plastic fruit on the dining room table, plastic figurines tucked inside of nooks . . . plastic, plastic, plastic! When I noticed a painting depicting a cowboy scene and cellophane on a lampshade below it, I stopped myself from laughing at the thought that she and Fred Sanford would have been great friends.

I had an inkling of an idea that something was amiss when I spotted an unused, yellow legal notepad and a Parker pen sitting on the table. Before long, Trey's mother was writing down everything I said. I couldn't believe she was actually taking notes on what I was saying to her son. When I turned around and addressed her rude intrusion, she said something outlandish that made me feel as if I were on the second round of a job interview. I was amazed that she was serious, but when her shriveled up mother sat alongside of her like the member of a panel, I knew she wasn't bluffing.

"Okay, Leslie, you will be read a series of questions. Since you will soon be a part of our lovely family, we'd like to get to know *the real you*. The only way we can do so is if we have a heart-to-heart talk and ask you everything that we've collectively discussed in a family meeting, and would like to know. I would greatly appreciate your cooperation. Now please pay attention and keep up. Do you owe any money for student loans? Is that your hair? Are you still employed as a teacher? Are you a faithful servant of the Lord? Have you ever smoked, puffed, or inhaled a marijuana cigarette, blunt, or any variation thereof? Are you a virgin? Can you cook, bake, and sew?"

While Trey's mother paused awaiting my thoughtful replies, his nutty grandmother added something way over the top. "Would you submit to a polygraph exam? I see them things used on lawyer shows on TV—maybe that would be more accurate."

"Ma—Grandma—easy on my wife-to-be. Stop it. You're insulting her," Trey said. "This is ridiculous," he added.

"Something is wrong with someone who says they have no family. You ought to do a background check. She knows everything about your people, but what do you know about hers? We've met not one of her folks—that's what's ridiculous!" his mother added.

"No disrespect intended, but I'm a grown man with my own home," Trey shot back. "I think I can pick a wife, and you must respect my choice. Please don't do this. You can't protect a forty plus year old man from life—it's just not your place to try and control who I fall in love with."

"I pushed you out and your grandmother did the same for me. I own you 'til death because I brought you into this world. If I need to, I can take you right on out. You're not equally yoked. This woman isn't a true woman of God—I know these things. Don't be stupid. I have a right to express myself, and its no secret that I don't like this little fast, hot in the tail girl you picked out. Her drawers aren't golden. What is it you see in her that's got your nose wide open like a hypnotized fool?

If you marry her instead of a nice church girl, your life won't end happily ever after," Mabel said, ignoring my presence.

She had definitely said too much in my face, and I wasn't going to hold Innocence back much longer.

"I'm not a child. Stop it, Momma."

I put my hand up and interjected. "No, it's fine. I'll answer. Look you two—you're messing with the wrong girl. I've tried to be respectful, but you've pushed me beyond my limit. My social security number is 212 . . ." I said, rambling off the numbers. "As you know, I'm a teacher. I earn $40,000 a year, before taxes, that is. I'm not a virgin. By no means am I rich, but I can more than cover the mortgage and light bill. The next matter I'd like to address is that I do like dick, and I'm not going to apologize for my appreciation of God's precious art, otherwise known as the penis. To you, it may seem that I'm all worn out and used up for admitting that I'm not a prude, but rest assured, you can still put Leslie in a room of high-classed people or church folk. Furthermore, I attended church today, although I may miss a Sunday here and there.

"I do owe a few more payments on my student loan but Uncle Sam is well aware of my payment schedule. He and I get along well and are on speaking terms. I know what you may be thinking—I'm thirty and Trey is forty. In case you have it twisted, I'm not looking for a man to take care of me. I am an independent, educated woman, and there's no reason that I can't take care of myself. I don't want to marry your precious Trey for his money or whatever you may feel would cause a younger woman to accept a ring from an older gentleman. If I wanted a sugar daddy to take care of me financially, I could've had one a long time ago.

"Next up, the hair issue—unlike the wigs you two are wearing, if and when I choose to style my hair with extensions, no one will know. As far as the pot smoking, I've considered taking a few tokes when I've been highly stressed, but I never have. Try it, you may like it. Then again, Momma

Mabel, you can't afford the munchies. With whatever sort of genes you have, you'd blow up just *looking* at a cupcake.

"I'm not trying to be rude here, but neither of you will be sticking your nose in my business, commenting on how I scrub my kitchen floor, my douching regimen, or how often I change my bed sheets. I will be marrying Trey, so wake up and accept that he picked me, and I said yes. I'm madly in love with him and his opinion is the only one that counts in my eyes.

"Now all of this is out of the way, we can talk about more important things. I'm starving. Is dinner almost ready? What's on the menu, family?"

"Leslie, may I have a word with you outside?" Trey said, once I finished my tirade. He had the nerve to look upset.

I pushed the chair back, rose to my feet, and walked out behind him with my head held high. When we reached the comfort of the outdoors, all of his tension was released.

"What did you just do? What got into you?"

"What did *I* just do? Are you kidding, Trey? Those two bats started it. I could've said far worse things than what I did say."

"They're elders. I could've handled it. You were out of line to speak to my mother and grandmother that way."

"I'm about to become your wife, and I'm telling you that if you don't grow a dick and act like you know how to use it, we will have big problems. God should come first, and I should always come second," I blurted out in one explosive breath.

I opened the door, walked back into the house, then sat at the table and pulled out my cell phone to play games on it while dinner was cooking. I did lose my temper but like I told Trey, I didn't start it—they did.

While playing games on my phone, I heard the ring tone signaling a text message had been received. When I checked to see who'd sent something my way, I found out it was that damned Rico.

U SEEM SHY BUT 1 ON 1 U R DA BOMB! BTW, U GOT DA MOST SQUEEZABLE BOOTY! JUST WANTED 2 SEND YOU A TEXT 2 BRIGHTEN UR DAY.

Trey and his fan club were in the kitchen. His mother was letting him sample some homemade tomato-basil bisque off of a tablespoon, petting him up, and treating him like a punk in a dress as he raved over her cooking talents. Mabel continued to try to put a wedge between her son and I by letting him know she would keep plenty of home cooked food around, and that he had an open invitation for breakfast, lunch, and dinner. I rolled my eyes wondering what he'd need me for. Trey was already too self-sufficient—almost to the point it made me feel ostracized—he didn't need any help treating me as if he really didn't need me. Since he didn't seem to need me emotionally, physically, or mentally, I no longer craved the fullness of an ideal relationship.

Although I fought the feeling for a while, I had to admit to myself that his boy, Rico, turned me on about as much as Trey turned me off. Since no one was paying me any mind, my fingers began traveling to the middle of my skirt. I found myself reading text messages without feeling guilty, holding the phone with one hand, while rubbing myself through the fabric with the other.

IT'S ME AGAIN. GOT 2 HAVE YOU. I WANT 2 ROCK YOUR WORLD ALL DAY LONG. MAKE SOME TIME 4 ME. GET AT ME WHEN YOU READ THIS.

The more messages Rico sent my way, the dirtier they got, and the more I touched myself, fighting off the desire to hunt for an orgasm. He was bold, decisive and daring—Rico was my kind of player.

I looked to the left and the right, closed my phone, and then took it with me to the bathroom. After I shut and locked the door, I feverishly stripped down to my panties. I sat down on top of the toilet, squeezing my thighs together, continuing to allow him to turn me on. I stuck one of my fingers in my mouth, imagining that I was sucking cock, as I continued to read several more messages from Rico. When the moistness between my legs began flowing faster, I deleted the messages, shut my phone, and began to dress. Then, I made a fatal mistake and opened it once more. I found an erotic picture of Rico's beautiful erect penis staring at me.

U NEED INCENTIVE. PERHAPS FOREPLAY WILL DO. WHAT HE DOES, U KNOW I'LL DO 5X'S BETTER. LET'S B FRIENDS WITH BENEFITS. U'LL HAVE THE BEST OF BOTH WORLDS.

His words were enticing. I found myself responding by licking my breasts, walking over to the mirror to play with myself while typing a reply in between. Watching my body in the mirror heightened my arousal so much that I removed the bobby pins from my bun, shook my hair loose, and let if fall on my shoulders. I felt free, adventurous and sexy.

Rico kept sending texts, telling me what to do, and I'd send replies back. I liked what he brought out in me. I set my phone down then palmed my ass with one hand while fingering myself with the other. When I heard footsteps approach the door, I quickly picked up my cell phone and hid it behind the shower curtain.

"Leslie, are you okay?" Trey asked. I didn't answer. "Just because I'm mad at you doesn't mean that I don't love you," he said softly.

"I'm fine," I answered through the door in a snappy tone.

"Are you sick? Open the door. I want to make sure you're all right." I drank exotic fantasies from a fountain of lust that Rico created. As they danced through my head, I quickly opened the door. Although Trey often told me he thought oral sex was nasty thing for me to do after our engagement, I was determined to prove that he'd enjoy it once again. I dropped to my knees, pulled Trey in by his hand, unbuckled his pants, and licked him from him from his asshole to his balls. At first, he tried to push my head away. His body twitched a little as his tool grew; reminding me that he was a pretty big dicked brutha, he put up far less resistance. Leaning forward I prompted Trey to slide his thick, long meat into my mouth. A warm feeling covered my body as I moved my head back and forth, enjoying the taste of him. Trey was on the cusp of erupting and I wanted to make him cum until he felt too weak to walk. Seeing him turned on gave me pleasure, and I yearned to remind him all about the joys of having spontaneous sex with me.

Suddenly his mood shifted back to a distant, frigid place. "This is my parent's house. I can't do this. No way."

"That's just some weak excuse. You liked it, I could tell. I need you. Please, Trey, let me. I really need to do this to you," I begged, nearly in tears from feeling sheer agony.

Trey pushed me away from him, muttering something about this house was sacred ground. So much for the thrill of getting off in a taboo place—homeboy wasn't having it.

"Get dressed, Leslie. We really shouldn't be having sex before we get married. In fact, as of this second, we're not going to any longer. Now I've got to get back to the kitchen before someone comes looking for us," he said, stuffing his privates back in his slacks.

"You mean looking for you, not *us*," I shot back angrily.

I knew this wasn't how love was supposed to be. I was sexually frustrated and felt emotionally distanced from someone I wanted to give myself to in every way. After Trey left, I rinsed out my mouth, put on my clothes, fixed my hair back into a tight bun, and returned to the table. When I did, there was a totally different vibe. To my surprise, Rico was seated on one of those plastic lined dining room chairs holding a square piece of cornbread in his right hand. I gulped and tried not to panic.

"We said grace without you because you took so long," Mabel said in a hostile tone.

I ignored her gastric bypass needing ass because I was caught off guard by Rico's stunt. I sat nestled in between my man and my piece of forbidden fruit. From the moment I took my seat,, things got a whole lot hotter. I trembled inside and knew I wouldn't be able to eat with Rico in my personal space.

After I made my plate, Rico began copping a feel on my legs with his left hand while he ate with his right. Quick brushes turned into him lifting my skirt and rubbing steadily between my thighs until I grew sticky. I wanted to moan, grab him, and beg him to take me higher, but my hands were tied. When he began kicking my chair I came up with a plan.

"Trey, I feel ill."

"If you need a ride, I'll take you home Leslie. It's not everyday that Trey gets to eat his momma's good cooking," Rico responded quickly.

"You okay, Les?" Trey asked with concern.

"I'll be okay, baby. I just need to lay down in the comfort of my own place. If it's okay with you, I'll take Rico up on his offer so you can spend time with your family."

"Thanks, man. Call me when you get home, Les," Trey said.

I couldn't believe he would allow another man to take me home. Suddenly, I felt justified for wanting Rico to change my oil, since my own man could let me slip way so easily, especially knowing I was feeling horny and insulted. No one else said goodbye, and I was headed out the door with Rico, who was as smooth as butter.

6

Mr. Right Now

As soon as we drove away, I began unleashing my frustration on Rico. I was angry that Trey announced we'd be going from sparse sex to none at all . . . at least until our big day.

"Are you crazy, showing up like that and doing that shit under the table!" I screamed in Rico's ear with hostility. When he smirked I truly felt like slapping him silly.

"You ran across my mind, and I care about your needs. I wanted to see you . . . you know you want some more of this." He smelled good, and I hated him for it. My anger was beginning to transform into lust. "How could you stay away so long, when I was the one who set your body free? I thought you were in need of sexual healing . . . how amazing," Rico said. He was oozing with cockiness and sex appeal and made my defenses melt.

"It's only been a few days. I let you hit it one time, and you think you've got it like that? I slept with you because you're close to Trey, and I was angry at him for neglecting me, not because of anything else. So stop smothering a sister 'cause she gave you a little bit," I said, playing it off. Rico was a tough act to follow but he didn't need to know how my thankful body was already craving another orgasm, another session of slam, bam, thank Rico the fuck buddy man.

"I do have it like that. You're full of shit—you know you'd rather be with me. I'm taking you for a nice, long ride so you can relax and fix that bad attitude of yours," he said, pressing the button to put the top down on his sea green convertible BMW.

Rico used a remote control to crank a rap tune, and I crossed my arms. As the wind gently caressed my face, Rico kept looking over in my direction. He took a back way toward my house and the car hugged each curve as he shifted gears. I drank the sunshine, closing my eyes on and off. That's when I realized I recognized the familiar rap tune that was playing. Apparently it was Blaze's new single—the one that he performed before attacking my booty hole at the mansion. According to the radio disc jockey, it was a hot new single that was climbing the charts. *How's that for irony?*

"Get your damn hand off my leg, Rico," I snapped. Inside, I loved how his hand felt there. It got me hot and bothered.

"You know you like it. You can lie to yourself, but what you really want is a man like me who can keep it up all night. As you know, I'm man enough to tame that freak pussy. Now take that off," he said, tugging at my skirt.

"What?"

"You heard me. Like the Nike slogan says, *'Just do it,'*" he said as his right hand traveled up my leg.

The wetness began to flow, and I fell back into the place he took me when I masturbated in the bathroom at Trey's mother's house. I unbuttoned my skirt, wiggled out of it, and then pulled it toward the floor. Rico unfastened his pants and freed his penis. I was blown away by the fact that unlike Trey, he was so open with his body. They seemed like opposites in almost every way. Trey still covered himself up with a towel around his waist after showering, hiding himself from my eyes. Rico, on the other hand, was a free spirit and I loved that. I felt like I'd jump over mountaintops to get my hands on Rico. I buried my face in his lap and gave him pleasure as he reached an open highway. He kicked up his speed to about eighty miles per hour, and the danger of the sex game we were playing ignited the risk-taker in me.

"Keep your eyes on the road," I said, coming up for air. "Drive steady."

"Mmm. Oh Leslie, yo me gusto," he whined.

When we approached a light, a nosey truck driver kept looking down into the car, staring at the game we were playing in our own private world. I casually glanced upward in his direction, then kept my head low while licking Rico's shaft up and down, putting on a free show for the trucker. All I can manage to say is that Rico was giving me the ride of my life, but the fun wasn't over—not even a little bit. I didn't realize that I'd have to finish what I started, until right then.

"Take off your top, let your hair loose, and get ready to get *fucked*," Rico said, emphasizing the last word.

"Oh, hell yeah. I like the sound of that," I said as we pulled into an isolated park.

By the time I loosened up, it was nearly pitch black outside. The stars were twinkling, and Rico's spontaneous idea of having hot public sex awakened the freakiest part of me. I found myself craving his touch all over again, as I watched him tune in to a jazz station and turn off the head lights. Next, he walked around to open my car door and I got out of his ride butt naked. Rico lightly manhandled me, pushing me onto the hood of the car before thrusting himself in me just as his pants dropped to his ankles. I continued looking at the luminous stars and drinking the mellow tones of soft jazz. Rico pumped me and made me moan over and over again. I felt my nipples harden and my mind wandered. At that moment, I felt Rico had to be the most passionate brother on the face of this great big and wide earth. Although I wanted to immediately smother him with affection, I remembered that I was supposed to call Trey.

"Trey . . . I need to call Trey," I said, struggling to make sense as I spoke.

"No," he said, completely unaffected.

"What if he's looking for me, Rico!" I complained. He pulled his penis from my vagina and began licking me with a skilled and willing tongue. Time and time again, Rico proved that he was a highly educated freak who didn't mind getting his face wet in some suckable pussy. In fact, he ate my dripping wet kitty kat like it had never been eaten before.

"Oh fuck! Rico. Rico. Oh fuck!" I yelled like a broken record. "I need to call Trey. I need to, I need to—"

"Five more minutes," he said between licks, as he traced the contour of my half naked body with his fingertips.

"No. Now," I whined.

"Rico!" I complained. He pulled his penis from my vagina and began licking me with a skilled and willing tongue. "Oh fuck! Rico . . . Rico . . . oh fuck!" I yelled like a broken record. "I need to call Trey. I need to . . . I need to—"

"I think you're kind of busy right now. I told you, five minutes," he said between licks.

"No. Now," I whined.

"Okay, have it your way then." He stood erect, snatched my cell phone from my purse, and then handed it to me. "So dial your keeper, Leslie," he told me, placing my legs over his head and driving his penis into me again.

"I can't," I said, gasping for air.

"Do it. Call your man while the best man is pounding you like nobody's business. If he cared about what might happen, we wouldn't have had the opportunity to do what we're doing. Relax and enjoy all of this. Stop being overly analytical, mujer. I'm trying to give you a way out."

The more Rico talked, fucked me, and talked dirty, the hornier I got. So much so that I followed his insane suggestion to lie and say that I made it home, and got comfortable after Rico left, all while having him inside of me. Thankfully, Trey didn't keep me on the phone long, so I didn't have to hold in the near explosion of guilty sounds for too long. I told Rico to call him five minutes later and give him the same version of events, and he did, while still enjoying our romp. As soon as he hung up his cell phone, I pushed him away and managed to rise from the hood.

My mouth wandered straight toward his middle as I crouched down in front of the headlights. Rico began moaning as I gave him oral joy, seemingly to the point in which he lost control of his thoughts and reached his orgasm.

"I'm not trying to smother you, Leslie. I just don't want you to marry Trey because I know that I'm crazy about you. I'm falling in love with you. If I had one wish, it would be for you to really be mine without having to sneak. I've waited all my life to feel this way about someone," he blurted out as he released a load of semen into my mouth.

"Damn, I'm a freak. I can't believe what just jumped off," I mumbled, standing up and spitting out the fluid on the black top.

We both got into the car. I wiped my mouth, and lay nude in his lap, looking up at the stars. Part of me didn't want to address what he'd slipped and said, while the other half wanted to enjoy his warmth on such a romantic night. After a while, I lifted my head and looked into his eyes. I began to dress fearing a policeman or voyeur would soon find us.

"I don't want to throw my relationship away, Rico. Let's go," I said firmly.

When he tried to stick his tongue into my mouth, I turned my head, snubbing him. A spurt of guilt fell upon me, and I knew that what Rico and I had been doing was cold-blooded. The loud stillness of silence consumed the rest of car ride. I was only interested in getting off; I wasn't trying to fall in love again. Didn't Rico understand where I was coming from? He was just my temporary boy toy—something for my enjoyment. I didn't give a shit about anything prolific and earth shattering.

The full moon tinted by a subtle yellow hue, lit up the night as Rico pulled into my driveway. The turn of events had given me a reason not to invite him in for another rendezvous. While proceeding to my front door, I had a bigger annoyance than Rico following me. The closer I got to my steps, an eerie feeling swirled around me as my eyes were drawn to a foot tall picture that was affixed to the front door. My head was cut out of the enlarged photograph. I got her message, loud and clear. It was my favorite picture; one we took together while we were in Cozumel, Mexico. Crossing this emotional line stung a little bit, but it didn't hurt me as much as Tanya probably thought it would.

When I reached the door and turned the key, I found trails of pink fabric lining the floor—pieces of what had once been Tanya's maid of honor dress. Each trail led to a mirror. NYMPHO was written on each large mirror in the same shade of red lipstick as before. I looked at Rico. I assumed Tanya wouldn't be creating the welcome baskets for the out-of-town guests as promised, since she was forfeiting her maid of honor title. *Shit!* How was I going to explain that? I wasn't surprised she'd pulled out of participating in my wedding—it was more that I hadn't thought about how and when she'd actually do it. I suppose I was more focused on other matters.

When Rico still tried to pull me into my bedroom and suggested that we undress and crawl into bed and make love to me despite all of this, I realized he truly was getting too attached. Without a doubt, I'd have to find a way to cut our affair off. Now I had two problems: him *and* Tanya.

As I walked around in back of him and physically pushed him out of the door, I truly began to feel ill. A migraine began to fester, and it grew to astronomical levels of pain when Rico opened his mouth again.

"I know you feel this thing between us, too. You may choose to look the other way, but I know the truth about your feelings, and so do you." He shook his head, then chuckled. "If I were your man, I'd come home to you every night. If you were sick, I'd never let someone else look after you. In time, you will see you're making a mistake marrying Trey. This is all such a shame. I almost reached Heaven and now it's about to slip away, mami. We've got good chemistry—much better than the sham with the person whose ring you're wearing. I see who you really are, and it's not who Trey would like for you to be. He may be older and established, but that doesn't mean he's the one. Dame su corazon. You know I'm a good man. You know. Give me your love, Leslie."

"Out!" I commanded. "You said what we did the first time would be a one time thing!"

"How was I to know I was going to feel this way about you? I've got nothing but time, Leslie. I'm going to get to know you. You'll see."

"Like hell you will. Don't call, write, send Indian smoke signals, or fax me in this lifetime. You're tripping, Rico. You're really, really tripping like you're on something. Shake it off . . . I'm not the only woman in the world. We're through, end of subject."

"Whether you like it or not, this *isn't* over, Leslie. I won't let us go our separate ways. Rico always gets what he wants. I've got my eye on you. I don't want to just be your lover, and I don't just want to be your friend. As far as I'm concerned, you are the only woman in the world," he said, walking out of the door.

In my book, the subject of our short affair was over. Unfortunately, in Rico's mind, it wasn't hardly that simple. It didn't seem to matter that Trey regarded him as a brother and trusted him with his back turned. What I didn't know was that I'd live to regret the stupid decision of stirring up drama too close to home with a half Puerto Rican lover boy who had nice abs and the ability to speak broken Spanish. Even when he spoke the Spanish, I had no idea what it all meant, but I could identify words here and there. I hate to admit it, but hearing the whispers of a part-time Latin lover was a turn on. That is, until Rico began dropping major indicators that he was overly possessive of me. In his mind, he and I were just getting our private party started, while I was fighting to say one of the two Spanish words I knew the best—adios.

7

Ménage Trois

"Leslie, I'm just calling to check in with you. Momma has some tickets to see the Washington Nationals play. Take it easy and be sure to put some food in that stomach. Take care and have a good day."

"Trey, I got your message. You were supposed to take me dancing tonight, remember? Did you forget about our date?" I asked, feeling frustrated. "It's Friday night," I added.

"Oh hi, Leslie. I guess you got my message. I have some tickets that may never come my way again. I'm not sure what time I'll be back home. You should stay home and rest, since you haven't been feeling well anyway. We'll go another time. I promise, baby. You understand, don't you?"

I rolled my eyes. Not feeling well, hell! When did he become my father?

"Sure, Trey."

"By the way, do you know what happened to that vase you bought me? I can't find it anywhere."

"It got broken when those kids broke the window," I lied.

"I knew I should've said something!"

"Forget it—it was just a cheap ole thing anyway," I commented.

"You gave it to me and I liked it."

"Enjoy the game, Trey. Obviously, *that's* what is most important," I said, then hung up the phone.

"Hey, that was a cheap shot and it wasn't fair," Trey remarked after calling me back.

"Not fair? I'm beginning to think that you take me for granted. Perhaps you don't think that men perceive me as a hottie given the fact that I have a conservative image. Perhaps you don't take me seriously because I'm a younger woman. I just don't know what to think, Trey."

"I make good money in my field, and this hectic schedule is the trade off. In case you've forgotten, I work hard. It isn't just to my benefit. It will be to our benefit. Right now, I need a break, and you can't seem to understand that I have needs, too. At first, you liked that I gave you freedom to live your life with lots of choices, but now you're sounding like you feel attention deprived."

"Well maybe I feel attention deprived because I am."

"Why are you being such a drama queen? All I want to do is go to a stinking game with my parents! Nothing has changed between us, sheesh."

"Like I said the first time, enjoy the game. Never mind, Trey. You're right, I'm wrong," I answered in a sarcastic tone. I hung up the phone with small tears forming in my eyes.

Football, basketball, baseball—it never mattered. If a game was going on, Trey wanted to sit his ass in a seat with someone other than Leslie. I came second, once again. I tried to occupy my mind with something productive, but I was too upset. I did love Trey, I just didn't feel totally fulfilled. A week of taking a breather from Rico gave me time to think about my feelings, including why I'd been so wishy-washy. I didn't want to get caught cheating because Trey did mean something to me. On the other hand, the void in our relationship reignited my "ho tendencies."

Obviously, being engaged to an almost forty-one-year-old man wasn't a foolproof situation. Trey was too calm around me, and part of me longed to get with a man in his thirties, but the other part knew their typical lack of maturity would drive me crazy. Knuckleheads were a turn off, and someone in my age range would probably fit the bill. No thanks. I had a ring on my finger, so why would I return to the dating jungle? Most women would kill for a proposal, given the ratio of women to men, even from a man who behaved like a cold fish.

Sometimes I just felt like giving up on Trey, but I truly wanted a family of my own with him. My biological clock was ticking, and I wanted everything a normal woman should want at my age. I wish he could've understood how ostracized I felt, but he didn't seem to hear the desperation in my voice when the subject came up.

In his defense, I wasn't perfect and shouldn't have expected my other half to be. The concept of marriage has changed in modern society, but it is what it is. For starters, I began buying into the notion that how I was living wasn't all that bad. I even started taking off my ring before heading out to certain places—clubs for one, yet I still felt as if the reward of a devoted husband was in order.

My wedding was now less than twenty-six days away, and from morning 'til night I fought with feelings that my marriage would be more like a business agreement than the happily ever after I wanted.

I was thirsty to the point I felt I would lose my mind if I didn't get a cool drink of pleasure—one, two, or even three sips wouldn't do. There was no passion in my life, at least not from the correct person. I no longer wanted the pleasure I was being offered, courtesy of the new thorn in my side. Rico texted me all night long, professing his love for me and explaining that he'd turn in his player's card if I promptly broke off my engagement. Hurricane Tanya was pushing her luck by calling my home line and hanging up over and over again. She finally shot her last marble my way when she bothered to leave an unsettling message.

"Look, I don't want to talk to you, but I do want to give you a reality check," Tanya stated. "I hired a private investigator to get the goods on you and Rico. How was your walk in the park, Leslie? You looked like you were enjoying the stars. Maybe Trey would like to see how you've been spending your time. I'll keep it simple—if you try to make good on any of the threats you made, I'll see to it that the pastor, the entire congregation, and Trey get to see how orally talented you are. Your keys are on your lawn. I expect you to mail mine within the next business day. I deserve a man like Trey, you don't! There you have it, folks. Tanya the quiet church mouse officially flipped the script on Ms. Bitch; located at 666 Whore's Lane—home of the devil's daughter."

After hearing Tanya plunk down her two cents, I peered out of my window. As promised, emergency keys to my car and home were sprawled out on the lawn, held together by a large Atlanta key ring. I ran downstairs to collect them. As I opened the door, eggs pelted my body from head to toe, and then I heard tires squeal. I sighed while the slimy texture of the yolks slid down to my feet. I wasn't sure how I was going to handle Tanya's streak of revenge, but I knew I'd think of something after I took a mental break from the entire ugly scenario.

With not much else to do, I managed to survey my messy place and decided to clean what appeared to be the site of World War II. I began picking up things, including leaves from dead plants, and the empty cartons that were flowing out of the trashcan. I also decided to tackle the dishes that had been sitting in stale dish water for at least a week. I had been in such an ugly funk that week I hadn't lifted a finger to clean a thing. When I first turned on the radio, Yolanda Adams was singing something inspirational, in her silky, smooth voice. I turned the dial of the radio, searching for something else, although I wasn't sure what. As a song I never caught the title of played, the lyrics about a woman not taking shit flowed from the radio. The beat and message of the catchy tune fueled me to clean my dirty place. As I listened intently to every word, I reminded myself that a workaholic prude was what I felt Trey had become. When the reality of my unhappiness resurfaced, I decided to compensate by putting on my come hither attitude and indulging in a makeover.

I took a trip to the M·A·C counter at Nordstrom's, purchasing lipsticks in several colors, and eye shadows to accentuate my sultry eyes. While I was out, I splurged on sexy clothes, and even took a plunge and got a tattoo and wig. I finished my attitude with a Brazilian wax job for my bikini line, and a deep tissue massage from an upscale day spa. I could always pretend to be conservative whenever Trey decided to give me some time. The thought of having two personalities was exciting. I was backsliding as a Christian, but didn't feel regretful about it—I'd repent with Jesus later. I'd lost interest in church, but that wouldn't affect my wedding plans. I had time to find a preacher to preside over the ceremony if I was kicked out of the congregation for not bothering to show up faithfully. Besides, I'd already decided we would have everything in a hotel as opposed to a house of worship. That settled, I was done beating myself up and putting myself down. I decided to get my ass up in the club to get some stress off my chest.

Once I got to the club, I intended to put my skills to use. If I could pull a rapper, I could surely get my boogie on solo, especially looking as fly as I was. At first I was going to head to a typical club, but then I made a U turn so I could go to a spot in D.C. I'd heard about. It was rumored to be wild as hell. I didn't know if the stories I'd heard were true, but I was about to find out, since I was looking for some erotic fun above and beyond the average experience.

I parked the car about two streets over from my destination, according to map quest. I was decked out in a hot pink spandex dress that stopped about four inches below my kitty kat and hugged my ass firmly in the back before sloping down a bit longer. I was bra-less and loving how my breasts felt full in the V shaped front that scooped low enough to reveal my belly button. As I walked along the dark street, I heard a voice.

"You left your car lights on," a male said.

"I did?" I replied. I walked back to check the front of my car but the only lights I saw on were on someone else's car.

"You didn't leave your lights on. I just wanted to see you up close. Where's your man?" he asked.

"At home," I lied, turning around.

"You better be careful walking around like that. There are some perverts out here like me."

I smiled without uttering a word. In that brief moment I'd already assessed him. The man was not on my level. His caliber was too low to turn my head. He had too much gut for his height, which was a tell tale sign of eating too many fried foods, and all of nine and a half teeth in his head. Additionally, he was busy drawing up on a marijuana cigarette, looking as dirty as a soap-deprived refugee. As far as I was concerned, he could take his compliment and shove it up his ass.

When I reached the entrance of a place that will remain nameless, a few people were standing outside. I pushed my way through the crowd and opened the door. After showing my ID, I paid the cover charge, and then walked down three small steps. I could hear remnants of the conversation behind me floating in my ears. Apparently, all men needed a date to get into the club, and one man had to hit the road because of the rule.

I stopped near the bar where a small crowd of people were assembled around a young black woman who was topless. She waved her arms around in the middle of the circle, bragging about her assets and about how they should want to see much more. She was a trip. I couldn't believe the maniac was imitating a wobbly bobble head, allowing her audience to inspect her cow udders which each had nipple ring. The funny thing was that no one outside of the circle gawked at her. Acting sexually liberated and free appeared to be the norm.

I walked into the next room and entered a whole new world of freakiness; the aura reminded me of an old-fashioned house party. People were grooving and grinding to Little Kim's "Lighters Up." It was so dark, all I could make out were shadows of faces and bodies. Women were dancing with women. Couples were dancing with couples. One man was indulging by getting his penis sucked as he stood against a wall. Next to him sat a brother who was enjoying a lap dance. The room was definitely hot, and not in a way that the fan in the corner could cool it off. As rumored, this place was off the hook, and I enjoyed being a voyeur. People stared at me a lot, but for the most part, I was left alone.

Next, I took a walk upstairs to find out what that scene was like. As soon as my foot hit the top step, I observed a crowd watching three women dance in a large cage. One was topless, bent over, and gripping the bars while another simulated screwing her doggy style. They appeared to be college students, no doubt on the rolls of a university less than fifteen minutes away. As they laughed and enjoyed giving a freak show, I wondered how their parents would feel if they knew what was going down. I would sure they were clueless, believing their kids were studying hard in summer school. Yeah, right—studying. They were studying Freakology 101, just like me.

Long, loose curtains flowed, brushing the floor almost in

)

time with the strange music that was playing. There were benches built into the sides of both walls, and I assumed they were for the convenience of other voyeurs, or those who needed the leverage. The atmosphere and the music conjured a strange vibe that proved to be too eerie for my taste. I carefully pushed my way through the crowd and walked back downstairs.

Suddenly, I felt as if I needed a cool, stiff glass of liquor, although I'd never had anything stronger than organic cran-apple juice in my life. One drink led to two, and two led to three. Before I knew it, I had exceeded my alcohol tolerance, which was, apparently, extremely low. I quickly learned I was the type who could nearly get drunk just smelling communion wine, let alone consuming it.

I pulled the cherry from my last drink, and tilted back my head to bite it from the stem, just as I'd seen sex sirens do in old, low budget movies. I swallowed it and noticed that my nipples were peeking out of my dress. When I looked up, a handsome-looking man was staring at me.

"Hi, I'm Rich." A tall brown-skinned man with smooth skin stuck out his hand to shake mine. "This is my girl, Deja."

"Hello." I looked at the both of them, wondering why they had me hemmed up.

"Are you seeing anyone?" he asked bluntly. That's when I noticed his mustache and goatee.

I smiled. "No ring . . . no man. I do have a friend with benefits, but I don't think that's quite what you were asking about."

They both laughed as I held my hand up and wiggled it.

"So, you're seeing Deja?" I asked, confused.

"Deja is my wife, not my girlfriend."

"Your wife?"

"We can both do what we want as long as we discuss it," Rich explained.

Then it hit me—they were swingers, and this club was swinger, bisexual, and gay friendly. Being open-minded was a requirement. It wasn't like anyone was here just to listen to the music, drink brews, and have a good time. They were here to hook up.

All of those apple martinis I drank started to cloud my judgment. Rich and Deja began drinking a concoction I'd never heard of called Sex on the Beach, of all things. The next thing I felt was a pat on my ass, and then I was on the dance floor nestled between the two of them. Deja was bordering on the full-figured side, but still what I considered drop-dead gorgeous. She definitely changed my mind about what society may classify as an ideal size. She stood about 5'2 and began sliding her hand up my dress, feeling on my legs.

"You have the most firm legs," she told me.

I knew I'd exceeded my alcohol limit when I said, "If you like my legs, you'd *love* what's in between them."

Rich winked at me, rubbing up against my kitty kat, causing my thoughts to become thoroughly soaked in lust. Just when I thought that I'd heard it all, he whispered in my ear after the song ended.

"I bet we would. You're really impressive. So what are you doing tonight?"

"Nothing in particular," I answered.

"Come home and party with us, Leslie," he offered. I felt my nipples harden as I listened to those taboo words that added up to one freaky invitation.

"I don't know if I should," I said, half giggling. "I don't know you and you all don't know me," I flirted. My head felt light and my coordination took on a life of its own.

Deja pressed her two mountain peaks against my back, reached around toward mine, and gently touched my nipples with her fingertips.

"I think you just may have the biggest nipples I've ever touched. They're as big as Lemon Heads."

"Lemon what?" I asked, smiling.

"The candy. I bet they taste sweeter than sugar, too," she

said. I was too inebriated to freak out. Instead, I felt relaxed enough to take the naughty trip with her.

"I really like you, Leslie," Deja continued.

"I really think your man is hot and you're cute for a girl. I never said anything like this to a woman before, but you're really pretty. I think you've got the perfect shape. And your titties are so huge. How big are they?"

"I'm an E cup—all natural. So you are attracted to us. Since that's the case, I'm rather certain there's something we can do for you in private. In fact, it would be our privilege to do some things to you that you've probably never experienced. You'll never know what that entails unless you accept our invitation to come home with us," she explained softly, with a hint of seductiveness in her voice. "You only live once. If you're even a little bit curious about our proposal just say yes to doing something spontaneous. No worries, just kinky fun and pleasure—I promise," Deja added while still massaging my nipples.

That's all it took to cause my wheels to turn. Her erotic stunt led to the three of us leaving in search of something I had no business finding—a ménage a trios. Although I should've run like the wind, this experience spelled instant gratification, and I was game to be instantly gratified by two hedonistic and horny strangers. Although I wasn't willing to admit it to myself, part of the reason I decided to experience a threesome was to get back at Trey for ditching me to go to that stinking game. In case it's not obvious, I hate getting stood up. Two wrongs don't make a right, but I felt getting a little bit of pleasure could make me feel better than a mad, sexually-frustrated bitch.

8

The Freaks Do Come Out At Night

As we walked down the hall leading to their apartment, our equilibrium proved to be slightly off kilter. Rich and Deja pressed every button that I had at the same time. Rich began handling his business before the three of us even made it inside of their apartment, signaling Deja to flirt with me by verbalizing what she planned to do to my body. I giggled and felt a rush of excitement. I could hear the desire in his voice. I wished Trey would play with me emotionally and physically the way they were doing, but that was unlikely so I allowed these two strangers to get off on the thought of seducing a single, lonely woman.

The venue where we got our party started was beautiful, to say the least. It was equipped with several fireplaces, parquet floors, and antique furniture. I guess Deja was the one with the eclectic decorating style. Antiques and modern furniture coexisted in the same rooms. I spotted a baby grand piano, a chaise lounge, brass candle sticks, various limited edition prints, and authentic looking Tiffany lamps on our way to their bedroom. When we reached a king-sized bed topped with a lightweight gold colored silk comforter, I fell backward.

"I'll do anything for you and to you," Deja said, leaning on her elbows and kissing me all over my face. Her large breasts brushed my chest.

"We're pretty open-minded and fun. Tell us what you like, and we'll make your erotic dreams come true," Rich added, removing my high heels and panties. When I looked at his body, I noticed he was all muscle.

The pair made me feel like a goddess, so I just giggled without answering. My mind was relaxed and a smile covered my face as I anticipated how Rich and Deja would tease me. I dropped my purse on the side of the bed. Deja took the opportunity to help me undress while I sat up slightly.

"Your shit is right. I knew it. You're the one with the most incredible body," she said. "Look, Rich—she has an outtie. Look at her big clit."

Deja affectionately began kneading my breasts and sucking on my nipples like I had her undivided attention.

"You're right, Deja. It looks delicious. My wife doesn't mind sharing, so may I kiss your clitoris?" Rick asked in the cutest way.

All I could do was nod my head yes. "Relax and enjoy having a handsome black man eat you, nice and slow. You don't even have to return the favor . . . unless you want to," he added. I felt Rich licking between my thighs, so I went with the flow and locked my legs around his head as his wet and welcoming tongue moved steady and slow.

"Oh. Oh. Shit!" I screamed. My legs flew open, quivering, and my face felt flushed. The next thing I heard was the buzzing of a vibrator. Rich held it on my clitoris while Deja watched and began kissing me on the lips. I thoroughly enjoyed their hands, fingers, mouths, and tongues exploring my body. Every sensation was soothing and intense. I became completely engrossed in what we were doing, and for the first time, my mouth experienced what it was like to suck another woman's nipples. I nestled my face in between Deja's plump breasts and let my mouth explore her peaks, one at a time. Before I knew it, I shut my eyes and I did my best to gently suck them the same way Rico had done mine. The vibrator continued to hum steadily, teasing my clitoris, and I enjoyed giving and receiving a whole lot of pleasure.

In the midst of having my world rocked sideways like I was participating in my first live porn flick experience, I thought I heard a knock at the door. Deja grabbed the vibrator and continued to pleasure me with it while Rich left our presence. As my moans escaped into the air, I heard him speaking in soft, low tones.

"What in the hell do you think you're doing? We have company," he said.

"And? I am *not* scared of you," a bold, feminine voice replied.

"You know you shouldn't be here."

"Says *who*?" she asked. "So now you want to play favorites? Oh no. I don't think so. I'm your girlfriend, remember?"

"You know the rules. It's not your place to just show up anytime you feel like it. You're my girlfriend, *not* my wife," Rich told her.

"I'm trying to get some, and you're not trying to give me any. That wasn't the agreement either."

The conversation ceased, and by this time, Deja was licking me in between my legs the way a thirsty dog laps up water from a bowl. When Rich returned, he picked up where Deja left off with my breasts. In the background, I heard the shower running. The mystery woman entered the room, dropped her towel, and then joined us up on the bed. The threesome turned into a foursome. Hands were groping all over my body. As thirty fingertips touched and stimulated me, I suddenly felt the need to reciprocate. I thought of Trey while I sucked on Rich with Deja and the newest stranger pleasuring me below.

Rich put on a condom, and then he screwed all of us, one by one. He was a beast. When my turn came, I craved the pounding sensation that I'd watched him give Deja. All kinds of swapping went on all night long, until the sun came up. I didn't have an orgasm, but having all of that adventurous sex was a welcomed distraction.

A ringing sound awakened me. I lifted my head from under the covers and saw people all over the room. At first, I couldn't recall what had occurred the night before, or whose bed I was in, but I did I realize my cell phone was going off in my purse. I reached for it and took my phone out.

"Where are you? I was worried about you. I called you after I went

out with my boys and didn't get an answer on either phone. I've left six messages," Trey rambled.

I smirked. Since I hadn't been available to take his calls he was suddenly able to see how facing the unknown felt.

"I was hanging out with Tanya and fell asleep at her place," I lied, looking around at the snoring people. "I was up all night playing with the kids. We were watching Barney, and I helped her wash six loads of clothes. You'd be tired too, Trey."

"Hurry up. I want to see you. I fly out for a week on Monday."

My head was pounding because the after effects of the liquor began to kick in. I struggled to hold my lies together. The manner in which I ended up in the strange bed flooded my memory bank, and I realized my drinking binge had led me there. As I bungled through holding a conversation with Trey, an angry-looking man blew into the room talking loudly.

"What did I tell you about this shit?" he exclaimed.

"What's that noise?" Trey asked.

"Cable, I gotta go. I told Tanya about watching adult movies around the kids." I abruptly ended the call. Everyone began to stir, jumping up like they were waking up from a bad dream.

"Get your hot ass in the car. Hurry up! I swear you can't make a ho into a housewife," he spat, cursing at the strange woman. "You're not moving fast enough, Linda." He shook her foot, then she scrambled to comply. The couple moved against the headboard and leaned on each other. "You have nothing to say to me? *And* you want to take your time? Oh, hell naw!" He dragged the naked woman out of the bed by her hair. "You're not leaving those squealing kids on me. Get up! I give you affection. I've been a good husband to you. I give you love. I put you through school. I keep a roof over your head, and I am the one who keeps you fed. Still, you fuck around and sleep with these freaks. Ever since they moved in the neighborhood you've gotten out of hand. This is the last time I'm going to have to show up and snatch you up because the house is going on the market today, and we're moving to Kansas, Mobile, Alabama, or somewhere far away from Chocolate City or anywhere like it!"

The woman scurried to her feet. With his left hand, the man pulled a nine from out of his pants and began waving it around the room like a lunatic. He walked over and stuck his gun between Rich's legs. "Unless you're willing to share your woman with me every night, leave mine alone." He hit his wife upside the head with the gun once and then stared at Deja. "I hate you, you snatch-licking, dyke bitch—stay away from my pussy! This is your last warning! Next time, I'll pop a cap in your freak ass."

Deja looked terrified, but not half as much as the man's wife whose ponytail attachment was getting a helluva work-out as he pulled at it like a caveman. It finally gave up and fell off. He glared at me and blurted out, "And you . . . go home to your man. I'm sure you've got one you're cheating on—out here being a ho."

As soon as they left, I didn't contemplate getting out of

dodge. I hopped over the ponytail piece, grabbed my shit and moved as fast as I could to 'go home to my man.' All I knew was that I better get out of there and pull myself together before Tanya blew my cover. I was scared straight, at least temporarily. I had no idea whether she'd played along and be an alibi if Trey called or if the heffa would play more hardball.

9

The Medicine Man

I pulled into the driveway like a rabid bat out of hell. I made a mad dash for the door, jumped in the shower to wash away the scents of my sin, then got my nerves together in a New York minute. Something told me that Trey was going to show up and use his spare key to my place, and I was right. I made it home with only five minutes to spare. When he stared me in the face my skin was still wet. In fact, I was wrapped in a towel and hadn't dried off yet. I knew he was searching for a host of explanations by the look he was wearing on his face.

"First of all, you left your keys in the door," he said.

"I did?"

"Yes, you did. You've got to be more careful, Leslie," Trey warned, placing them on the counter. He turned around and faced me. "You don't look like you were dressed like you were at Tanya's house, and according to your girl, she hasn't seen you in quite some time. She also said that she won't be participating in the wedding. What's that all about? What's *this* all about," he asked, holding out the pink dress he picked up on his way into my house. I left it in the living room where I stepped out of it. I prayed that Trey wouldn't hold it close to his nose to inhale the smoke scent of the club. As I struggled to look expressionless, he added, "In fact, what's up with the hair, new dress, and attitude?"

"Hold on a second. You are not in charge of my life just because we're getting married. As you know, although my heart is yours, I no longer think its right to track your every move. I backed off after you went to that baseball game with your folks, but now you want to question me down. Look Trey, I don't want to argue. Let's move forward with this conversation." I was feeling overwhelmed but refused to be a slave to guilt. "All right, fine. I really wasn't at Tanya's, if you really must know every nook and cranny regarding when I come and go. I have a right to wear what I want, and I've been working on spicing things up between us. I bought that dress for you. I was out shopping last night, getting a bit of a makeover, and taking care of some things for the wedding. *Is that a crime?* As far as Tanya, I didn't want to say anything, but she's bitter because I mentioned we applied for our marriage license the other day when she and I went for my final gown fitting. In fact, Ms. Maid of Honor didn't even want to learn how to bustle my train or fasten the buttons for her girl. I could just feel the tension mounting up even after I changed out of my dress.

"Can't you see what's happening here? I'm getting married and she's weary from dating knuckleheads. It's pure hateration—nothing more. I was going to replace her and not make an issue out of it. The green-eyed monster will change people—even those you've known a long time. Think about it, Trey. She has no man—all she's got is a baby's daddy. Please don't give me drama because I've had enough from my *former* sister friend. Enough about that scenario. We don't get to see each other that much. I miss you, and that's where my focus should be. Let me make you breakfast."

To my surprise, instead of snapping at me, Trey tongue

kissed me and let me taste his sweet lips. "Hey, I can't wait to marry you. I'm on your side. Just believe what I'm telling you. We're going to make it. I can't wait to build a family with you—you're a good woman. I know I don't tell you this very often, but just because I don't come out and say those words doesn't mean I don't know I'm a lucky man. We need to stand together, Leslie. We're blessed with real love, and I'll never leave you."

As I pressed his body against mine, everything felt perfect. I found myself slipping into shadows of the old Trey. Romantic and reassuring Trey felt as if he could chase my storms away, ending my personal suffering and doubt. In his arms, I felt the compassion of a bright sunny day and the peace of its presence. He began caressing my breasts, holding me tightly. I reached for his shorts and felt his penis stiffen. I wanted him, all of him—mind, body, and soul—today, tomorrow, and forever. At that moment, he was all I needed and the intensity of my love for the attentive Trey returned, gripping me without warning. When he released me, I walked to the bathroom, grabbed a robe, and put it on.

After cooking breakfast for him, we sat down and ate together the way I'd longed to for some time. I couldn't wait to get my arms around him. Trey must've felt a mirrored reflection of my feelings. Usually I would clear the table and wash the dishest, but this time, after we both finished eating, he grabbed my hand and initiated walking to my bedroom. When we arrived, I heard a strong voice despite the silence. As I watched my love undress, the voice was telling me Trey was sorry for not spending as much time with me lately, and reminding me I was truly the woman he wanted to spend the rest of his life with. I smiled, dropped my robe, then I crawled on top of him. We kissed and caressed each other, and talked about our future. It was intimate and nice.

With a smile on my face, I slipped under crisp, clean sheets and basked in the glory of Trey the romantic, Trey the future father of my children, and Trey the sacred protector. As we held on to each other, I felt guided to make changes in my behavior. The only reason I didn't want to give my body to Trey was because I was tired from giving it to others. Instead, I slept a delicious sleep with the man of my dreams—one who had decided fornication was a sin.

Two hours later, my love was still knocked out. I carefully lifted his arm from around my waist and tipped out of bed to get a glass of water. After I drank it down, I suddenly felt losing what I had was not an option, even more so than before. Placing a call to protect my relationship became a must do after Trey showed so much emotion. He gave me a reason to want to fight back. Without thinking, I grabbed my purse from the table and eased out onto the back porch so I could have some privacy while I used my cell phone. I pressed speed dial and called Tanya. Even if I threw the first blow, I would prove that she didn't want none of this.

"How dare you, bitch! I warned you," I said, snapping as soon as Tanya answered. "So you tried to make trouble with me and Trey? You stabbing me in the back isn't going to stop me from getting my man so don't think you've tied my hands down. I guess you forgot you told me your ex used to beat you and you had to find a shelter and start life over to get away from him. I tell you what I'm going to do for you since I'm getting tired of giving your hardheaded, two-foot-one ass so many chances. Get ready to reconcile, because when I get through, he'll have the kiddies."

"No, don't. No, Les. He's a crazy man. I love you. Just understand that you hurt me. Let's sit down and discuss things today. Don't let a man come in between our friendship," Tanya rambled.

I knew she had done the nasty with Rico, and I wanted to rub it in her face.

"Oh, now I'm Les? Now you love me, miss our friendship, and want to act like you have some sense—talking about not letting a man mess up how close we were? You act like you slept with Rico or something. If you're the big Christian you act like you are in church, surely you haven't been physical with Rico. You go around judging me, and look at how you're living." Tanya didn't comment.

"I never said I did," she replied faintly.

"And you never said you *didn't*. You think you're bad, trying to ruin my engagement? You knew what you were doing. You tried to play me like a fiddle. Kiss your job, peaceful life, and rug rats adios. It's hypocrite bitches like you that make it hard to . . ."

"Listen, please have a heart. I thought you cared about the children. Don't take our problems out on them. Give them a chance to grow up and be happy. We've known each other since the first grade. You're like family to me."

"If you have the resources to obtain positive results, you'll be straight my sister. The case would have to be investigated before the children are taken away. It's not like you'll have recent charges against you for breaking and entering and assault. It's not like you leave them unsupervised sometimes when you have to work overtime, and the neighbors know about it. And it's not like more than one person will be saying you drink, smoke, and get high."

I began rummaging through my purse while I talked and realized that Deja had slipped her cell phone number in it with a request to call for a hook up behind her husband's back. Without realizing it, I slipped and called Tanya the wrong name. "Deja, I'll tell you what I'd tell my blood sister. Take my advice and wiggle your way out of this one because you set yourself up." When I decided I'd made my point enough and grew tired of Tanya's whining, I hung up, letting her panic over what I'd said. My phone rang immediately, but the word *private* displayed on my screen. I thought she'd called back, blocking her number so I'd listen to more of her moaning. Before I could cuss her out I heard my least favorite male voice.

"What you been up to, mami? Where've you been hiding, Les?" It was Rico. He was the last Negro I wanted to have a conversation with. I found myself wishing Tanya was still trying to chase him down and kept that dog on a leash.

"It's 8:00 A.M., what in the hell do you want? Wake the bitch up next to you and chat with her. I'm not the one. Your presence in my life has truly become annoying. Get a grip!"

"I bet you smell good," he said, ignoring my comment. "You have that sweet smelling thing down pat. Leslie, I want to take you motorcycle riding then out for a romantic dinner."

"Now is not a good time. I'm tied up. In fact, I'm tied up for a damn lifetime. I told you we're through. Can't you get that through your thick head?" I snapped.

"Find a way to spend some time with me. Look, I want to do something freaky to you, just the way you like it. I want you here. No exceptions, no excuses," Rico explained, flipping the script.

"Or else what?"

"Who was there for you when you were lonely? Trey wasn't. I was taking care of your emotional and physical needs while he was out running the street."

"Look, do what you want—I'm not coming."

"Okay, you'll be sorry."

"What are you implying?"

"I'm just making a simple request. I have a fantasy of having a woman dress sexy, me picking her up on my bike, then having a romantic evening. Don't question me, Leslie. It's much wiser to play along," he said, sounding on top of his game.

At that moment, I remembered Rico was a lawyer. A bolt of fear rushed through me, and I felt threatened by his vague words and his profession. As a preventative move, I decided to entertain his invitation to feel him out.

"Fine. I'm coming, but only to talk. This has to stop. This is the last time I'll see you under these circumstances," I told him, feeling forced into some sort of reconciliation.

"Fine. Just get rid of the dead weight and be ready by five. I know an under cover freaky bitch like you is standing naked while you're on the phone with me." He laughed. "Dress to impress and I will pick you up on my bike. Make sure you do Trey good before he leaves, and call him daddy when you do it."

My head began to throb as I ended the cell phone call. Rico had given me the chills. I crawled back into bed. I wanted to be warmed by Trey again but his eyelids opened.

"Did you rest well, baby?" I asked, kissing him on the lips. I pretended as if I'd never left the bed. Trey turned toward me then yawned and stretched. "I have some errands to run, baby. Maybe we can hook up later."

"What's on your agenda today?" he asked.

"I hope to catch the eleven o'clock service at church then I may hit the gym, chill out and play the rest by ear."

"Good, baby. I need to be going to church myself but maybe next Sunday. When you get in the gym, make sure you work on those thunder thighs. I wouldn't want to see you catch on fire from all of the rubbing and friction on a hot day," Trey joked.

"What did you say?"

"Nothing," he said, grinning.

"I heard that," I answered, sitting on top of him, swinging my pillow in his direction. Trey began tickling me, and I laughed as I struggled to catch my breath.

"Remember, you're mine and you're all I need. Now do you still love your daddy?" he asked after we stopped our horse playing.

"Of course I love my daddy," I answered. "Can't nobody do it like he does, and that's a fact. I know we're doing the right thing and I can't wait to make love to you, Trey." Half smiling, I was thinking that even when he did do it, he still wasn't doing much!

I was off the hook since he'd be leaving shortly. Things

were getting ugly and absolutely out of hand. Either way, I was off to see Rico after kissing my fiancé's lips with tenderness sweeter than anything I've ever known. After Trey left, I programmed Deja's number in my phone under florist and dropped her note in the shredder.

10

An Indecent Proposal

Since I still wasn't confident Tanya had gotten my message, I took step one of fucking up big-mouth's life by calling and reporting her for child abuse. After I hung up the phone, Rico pulled up on a nifty-looking crotch rocket, hog, or whatever the hip name for bikes was these days. I was impressed to find out it was a Harley, but I didn't let on. I stood in the doorway of my house and watched Rico's eyes glaze over me like he was in some sort of trance. I was wearing heels, extra tiny booty shorts exposing my tattoo of angel wings just above the crack of my ass, and my hair was out, swinging freely. I had applied a light layer of MAC makeup to accentuate my lips and eyes. My bedroom look had quickly become my every day look.

I'd be lying if I said I didn't enjoy the way his eyes traced every curve of my body. Trey often mumbled compliments while watching women on TV, but rarely complimented my figure. Negroes out in the street hooted, hollered, and even cursed while running out of barbershops to shake my hand and get up close to me when I walked by, but my own man acted as if I were invisible to him.

"Que pasa? Mami, you look fantastic. What video shoot did you just step off of? Go get your tennis shoes and a bathing suit. I'll put them in my bag."

When I returned, Rico's sticky compliments made me temporarily forget our previous heated conversation. He always seemed to know what to say, and how to say it. I warned him that he'd better not pop wheelies or mimic Evel Knievel, after which he wasted no time letting me know he belonged to a motorcycle club and drove with the utmost care. Once that was settled, I popped a helmet on my head and experienced my first motorcycle ride, holding tightly onto Rico's trim waist.

We arrived at a restaurant on Wisconsin Avenue, in North West, D.C. Rico's manners were as impeccable as his looks. He opened each door until we reached a hostess who looked up Rico's reservation. To my surprise, Rico knew more than a few things about Japanese culture. As we followed the Japanese woman, I noticed bonsai plants, paper lanterns, bamboo-and-wood trim, and Japanese prints. The schoolteacher in me enjoyed walking into another culture, if even for a short time.

I was quite puzzled as to why we walked past the main seating areas, but I continued following Rico and the hostess. Rico took off his shoes, and I followed suit. I did know that in the Japanese custom, shoes are taken off upon entering certain spaces to preserve the sacredness and cleanliness of the room.

"Do you know what this is?" Rico asked as we stood in front of a room with a sturdy fabric sliding door. I didn't answer. "A zashiki. It's perfect for a romantic evening or business meetings." Rico pointed to the floor. "*Tatami* mats are used for the flooring; this is the traditional floor covering in Japan."

"I had no idea you'd eat at a place like this or knew anything about Japanese culture," I said, sounding a bit impressed.

"If you want to be successful in life, you've got to network and rub elbows with the right people. I'm sure Trey means well when and if he takes you out to eat, but he's a buffet and butter roll kind of guy. I prefer to balance out my life with exotic experiences, and this is only the beginning of the things I could show you. A man owes it to his lady to help her to grow culturally, among other things, mami. Kneel on the cushions. In casual situations, men usually sit cross-legged, while women sit on their knees laying both legs to one side."

Rico and I sat across from each other at a rosewood table in the appropriate positions on cushions that were placed on the floor. A server delivered a little basket with hot, moist, almond-scented terry-cloth towels, and the hostess delivered fresh, warm tea. Rico ordered for us and they both left us alone in the room, closing the sliding door behind them. I didn't have a problem with his desire to choose what I would eat since I obviously didn't know much about Japanese cuisine.

"I'm not here to listen to you bash Trey, and I won't tolerate it, Rico. So what was so important that you wanted to see me?" I asked, pouring a cup of tea.

"Don't play with me. Isn't it obvious? I told you what I want, and now I'm showing you the whole package you could have with me."

"All that's obvious to me is that you like stabbing your boy in the back." I took a sip of what I discovered was green tea and put it down.

"And you don't? And you didn't? The way you made love to me spoke volumes, Leslie."

"Everyone makes mistakes."

"That wasn't a mistake, and you know it. You wanted it. You enjoyed it, and you've thought about me every day since then. What happened between us was something we both needed."

"It's nice to know you think you have ESP, but I beg to differ."

"Why are you fighting this, mami? Why are you being so tough on a man who adores you?"

"What do you mean by that?" I asked, playing dumb.

"I wish you'd get past your hang ups. Why are you fighting me by closing your heart? I know you feel what I do. This isn't my imagination playing tricks on me—you're feeling Rico. Admit it."

I raised my right index finger and pointed at him. I knew it surely violated some Japanese custom, but I felt like being rude. "Rico, don't trip over your ego. Not this again. Remember, you forced me into submission today. I was not a fully willing participant, if the truth be told. You know what you did and what you said to get me here." I let my arm fall.

"I didn't force you to come. I just made a simple request. Many business deals in D.C. are done over a meal and a cocktail."

"Don't play with my head, Rico. You know the truth of the matter."

"I just want you to know you can always count on me. Think about what I said every time Trey treats you like dirt. When you find something you like, the smart thing is to stick to it and make it stick with you. So, I'll pay your bills and give you whatever you want. Money is no object. I'll take good care of you—much better than you think. I choose you, and I want to bless you with some of the good fortune I've got."

"I don't need a man to throw money at me to be impressed. That's not my m.o. at all."

"Maybe not, but don't lie. You are impressed by exotic experiences such as this one, and this is only the beginning. All I need is someone to manage my money and take care of me. I'm used to dating white woman because they give me what I want."

"Well go back to dating them then," I snapped.

"I know you feel proud to be engaged, and I know you feel secure with Trey. Mami, I want you—you may not see it yet, but you're my soul mate."

"Right. I bet you said the same thing to my girl, Tanya," I told him delivering a verbal jab.

"Quite frankly, Tanya didn't have what it takes to keep me interested."

"Why, because she's not white?" I teased.

"It's more like this: if a woman wants a faithful man she has to be worth it. That part has nothing to do with race or color. I know you're a sex on the washing machine, hang from the chandelier type of girl. Boring and conservative just won't do. Rico can show you a finer side to life. One that's far better than what Trey can deliver. You have what it takes to settle my heart. What are you waiting for?"

I was considering whether that was a rhetorical question but was let off the hook when a waitress brought in our food. After she left, Rico began educating me, once again.

"You are supposed to eat a sushi piece in one bite, mami. Never try to separate a piece into two. You don't want to destroy beautifully prepared sushi. I'm teaching you all of this because one day, you'll need to know this and more. Here, let me show you. Open your mouth for me." Rico poured some soy sauce on the small plate that was provided, and then dipped the sushi in it. Morsel by morsel, he fed me. It was a sensual experience and I hated him for it.

"I can feed myself. All I need is a knife and fork."

"Knives and forks are only used for Western food. Spoons are sometimes used to eat Japanese dishes that are difficult to eat with chopsticks, but this is not the case. Now eat for me. It's not everyday that a successful businessman wants to feed a beautiful woman Japanese food using chopsticks. I'm a man of many talents."

"I know what you're thinking, but Trey is doing just fine," I lied, swallowing the sushi.

I thought of how many times I'd tried switching up our usual lovemaking spot, lighting some aromatherapy candles, and even drawing him a bath. Nothing. No response. Rico was correct; boring and conservative wasn't my idea of compatibility with a mate either.

"Bullshit. When's the last time he got inside of your head and had a heart to heart with you? When's the last time he talked to you about investments, asked you if you're making the money you'd like to make, or took the time to rub your feet? Don't get me wrong—I know that there's more than sex to a relationship. I have a checklist of requirements, and watching you has shown me you meet almost all of them. To put it bluntly, I want to be your man, Leslie. I think we could have a lot of fun together, and I want to be more than a shoulder to cry on. Get with Rico for real and *all* of your needs will be met. In my eyes, you're my ideal woman." Rico's cell phone rang. He decided to answer it. "What is it? Cool. I'll call you back later. I'm in the middle of an interview."

"In the middle of an interview," I repeated, confused.

"Excuse the interruption. That was one of my good friends who's a district attorney here," Rico said, bragging about his contact. "If you want another job, you've got it. I'm looking to hire a few new people for some projects, and I brought you here because I wanted to interview you."

"And what kind of interview is *this*?"

"My fantasy, that's what. I've always wanted to interview a woman dressed in sexy clothes. You're doing a good job. How does $80,000 a year sound to you?"

"I'm doing all right for myself, Rico. I'm not some hoochie with claws for nails who wants to work in an office but can't spell and answer the phone properly, or thinks knowing the booty call steps is a sign of sophistication."

"I know that, mi amor. What I'm saying is you're a school teacher. I already know you're not earning what you're truly worth. Play along with my fantasy, Leslie. All you have to do is enjoy yourself and keep me happy. If you can do that the rest of the evening, I'll offer you a once in a lifetime opportunity. I want to introduce you to some new things Trey can't. We can work and play hard together, Leslie."

"How do I even know I can trust you?"

"I've got too much to lose, that's how. I'm not desperate, Leslie." He grinned. "I'm just behaving as any sensitive ladies man would," Rico added.

"I don't understand something here. You don't even seem to care about your friendship with Trey? How would you feel about losing that?"

"May the best man win. Enough talk about this subject. Calletee y cierra la boca, mami. Comer conmigo. Yo soy su nuevo novio. Cada dia de su vida, yo quiero su amor."

"What did you say, Rico?" I asked, half frowning, but somewhat smiling.

"You love it when I talk dirty to you, don't you? I know it gets you all hot and primed to give Rico what he likes. It doesn't matter what I said. You're having the time of your life. Now shut up and eat. You know you don't know how to use chopsticks, mami."

When I felt inspired to laugh, all signs of tension broke. Rico fed me sushi, morsel by morsel, and all I could think of was how Trey was indeed a buffet and butter roll kind of guy, and how he'd never arrange something as romantic as what Rico had done. The truth was the wrong man managed to soothe my soul and give me the attention I craved. I never admitted it, but it felt good to have someone like Rico hanging on to my every word like it was air required to breathe and live. While kneeling on the floor being fed by an obsessed lover, I realized that Rico's growing obsession was making me feel alive again.

✿   ✿   ✿

After Rico and I chowed down, he paid the bill and explained that the evening was still young. When I asked him what was next on our agenda, he told me I should wait and see—all I had to do was hold on tightly to him and enjoy the scenery. As the wind hit my back, I discovered I liked riding with Rico. We jumped on Route 50 toward Annapolis. I'd never been there before although it was only an hour away from the DC area. Rico took me on a mini tour of the small town which was packed with local history. We crossed a bridge and traveled a short distance more where the streets were lined with bricks and opened into a dock area. We saw a statue of the famous writer, Alex Haley, The United States Naval Academy, the state house, the governor's mansion, and a historic Ivy League school called St. John's. Rico stopped at each location to tell me the history of each landmark. The teacher in me couldn't help but be impressed. I began to question if Rico really was the total package he claimed to be on numerous occasions. The brother actually had a brain to go with his body, sex appeal, and beautiful face.

By the time Rico and I covered most of *Naptown,* as the locals call it, he took me to an isolated section of the city near a waterfront area. Frederick Douglass' house was located in a neighborhood that was the first black township called Highland Beach. Just when I thought my history lesson had ended, it had just begun.

"Now that I've filled up your mind with many wonders, it's time to relax your soul. Doesn't that sound good right about now?" Rico asked.

Darkness covered the sky and Rico found a quiet spot on a beach that poured into the mouth of the Chesapeake Bay. At first we sat at a weather beaten picnic table, enjoying the cool breeze and splashing of the gentle waves. As I inhaled the fresh air, I closed my eyes and longed for my heart to feel the way it did at that moment, every day. Forgetting that Rico wasn't Trey, I put my head in his lap and looked up at the stars while lying on my back. Rico brushed my hair away from my face then told me to get up.

He led me to a corner of the beach that was populated with more trees and felt a bit more intimate. I felt Rico's hard dick as I sat in between his legs on the wet sand. After whispering a lot of sensual things in my ear, Rico suddenly switched positions. He pushed me back and leaned over top of me as he began delivering light kisses to my skin under the moonlight. I felt cool and hot at the same time. Rico unfastened my shorts and gently pressed his lips on my stomach. He lay on top of me, kissing me, and holding my arms back in the sand.

"Oh, Leslie. Baby, you're turning me on. Oh, mami," he mumbled between kisses.

Rico was turning me on too. The wetness began to flow between my legs and I found myself wanting to do something about it. The next thing I knew, I was kneeling in the sand, removing my breasts from my bra, and fondling them with my eyes closed. Rico kissed my back, making my nipples hard and causing dampness to drip between my thighs. At that moment, I could've sworn time stood still and the world stopped turning. The passion that I longed to possess pulled me in, and I didn't want it to let me go. Once again, Innocence had conquered Leslie and every inhibition the conservative part of me would've had for living out an erotic scene in public vanished. Innocence was proud of her body, her sexuality, and her ability to let go and enjoy the sensual side of nature.

A quiet storm began. The rain felt soft and warm. Rico and I were intertwined in a passionate embrace when a light drizzle turned into a steady flow of a summer rain. The sand was our mattress as the waves continued to crash. Although my hair was wet and we were a soggy mess, I didn't want the romantic scene to end.

"Venga," Rico said. "Come—follow me." Rico led me to a

pier. A man and a woman were sitting on a large boat. "Watch your step," he told me as I stepped on the boat. "This is my boy, Melvin, and this is his lady friend, Camille," he said.

Without thinking twice about what I was doing, I shook their hands and sat down. The men disappeared into the belly of the boat and left Camille and I no choice but to find something to talk about. About ten minutes later, music started playing, and the boat began to move. Rico returned with a drink and kissed me on the forehead.

"You're safe with me. Don't worry. You'll have fun," he said. "Why don't you let me show you where you can change your clothes—you're soaked. Put on your bathing suit and enjoy the ride."

Rico directed me to a small bathroom, and I took his advice. When I returned, he was shirtless and dressed in a fresh pair of shorts. Camille was swaying from side to side, singing to the old reggae standard, *Telephone Love*. I believe the drink she slurped and joint she was puffing on had something to do with her limber shoulders and waist grinding. After the song ended, she disappeared, heading toward her man, no doubt. Rico disappeared and returned with a joint and a drink, too.

"Which one do you want? Rules of the boat are everyone gets crunk."

I was surprised a lawyer indulged in the sorts of habits that could lead to being disbarred, but I didn't care. "I'll take the drink," I said, grinning.

"That's the spirit, mami," Rico replied, taking a drag of the cigarette.

I noticed the boat stopped moving. I guess the liquor and smoke went to my head because I suddenly began to fantasize about putting my heels back on and deep throating Rico as we rode on the Chesapeake Bay.

"You scratch my back and I'll scratch yours," he whispered in my ear. He threw the cigarette in the water. "I guess now is a good time to tell you that we're stuck. I can't ride my bike in the rain anyway. My boy is too fucked up to drive this thing. If you don't believe me, go check. He and Camille are loaded. Plus, it's still drizzling. Now what?"

I knew Rico set the whole thing up but I was having too good of a time to care about his manipulative streak.

"You scratch my back and I'll scratch yours, Leslie," he repeated, leading me to a small area in the bottom of the boat.

To my surprise, Rico pulled out something that looked like a string of pearls. I don't know why, but I allowed him to push my face down into the bed and lube up my ass. Then he began inserting the long string of silicone beads. I contracted my sphincter muscles as he pushed in each bead.

"Black ass—no more white women for me. How does it feel to know Trey is cheating on you? This is my pussy and ass. Fuck Trey! Rico is in the house and now Trey's woman is mine," Rico said as Camille and Melvin reappeared from somewhere.

I found Rico's words odd, but curiosity got the best of me as I complied. After the beads were completely inside of me, Rico began to screw me like he was getting paid to pound me passionately.

"Scream for me. It's ok, mami. Let it go. We're in the middle of the Bay. Scream like you like it, damnit! Let me know you feel what I'm doing to you."

Camille rose to her feet, walked over, and quickly pulled the beads out of my ass. I screamed freely as an unexpected orgasm caused me to explode. Rico was right. It did feel good. I don't know if Melvin sitting on the small bench observing me getting turned out in a new way had something to do with it . . . but it could've.

The liquor had me feeling loose enough to behave like an exhibitionist who was well acquainted with these sex games. I got down on my knees and gave Rico head and then let him bang me some more, all in front of Mel, who was stroking his dick, and Camille, who was pushing her right breast up to her mouth to lick her own nipples. Rico and I screwed each other like dogs in heat as it rained. The four of us moaned as the sexual escapade of a different flavor unfolded.

When I awakened in Rico's arms, I sighed. I didn't mean to get busy with him again, but I had crossed the line like I couldn't manage to use my common sense. When we made it back to the dock area, and Rico collected his wheels, I felt the strain of realizing I was sleeping with my future husband's best man. I wanted to cry. As I held onto him while we rode his motorcycle to my home, I became more and more disgusted with myself. Like it or not, I'd slipped and dug my hole a whole lot deeper.

Rico attempted to deliver a long goodbye when we reached my house. Instead, I turned my head and showed him no affection.

"If it matters to you, you got the job," he told me.

"I don't want it, and I don't want you." I blurted out. I swung my head around, stormed off, and slammed the front door after I stepped through it.

While looking out of the window, I watched as Rico fastened his helmet to his head. He jumped on his bike, and sped off without saying a word more. Five minutes after I got into the house, my cell phone was ringing.

"Why didn't you call me back, Les? Where have you been? I gave you a ring after I took care of my errands," Trey told me.

"Where have I been? I'm home, of course. I'm sorry I was a bit forgetful. I didn't charge my cell phone, so I didn't know you called."

I knew my signal was bouncing when I was on the water in Annapolis—the real reason I didn't receive Trey's message. I heard a pesky beep interrupt my lie. Rico's number was flashing.

"I'll call you back in a few minutes from the landline, baby. I have something on the stove that smells like it's about to burn up," I lied. I mentioned calling Trey from the landline to reinforce the fact that I was home.

"At six thirty in the morning?" Trey questioned.

"Yes, at six thirty in the morning. I eat breakfast too you know," I answered. In reality, I was brewing a pot of strong coffee to help me wake up.

I clicked over and heard Rico's voice. "Leslie, I realize you weren't in a talkative mood this morning so I thought I'd give you something to think about. I'll mail your clothes to Trey's job. I have pictures of you in my phone. Pictures my boy took of you in the boat. Pictures of my earring in Trey's bed. Text messages. I'll ruin you. If you really love him and want to protect your relationship, get rid of him. If this is what I have to do to keep you, I'm willing. If I have to, I'll make you love me."

"You don't have shit on me. Stop bluffing, Rico. I'm not going to fuck around with you anymore. You can't make me do a thing except stay black and die since that's already a done deal," I said firmly.

The next thing I knew, picture after picture popped up on my cell phone. The dirty dog had actually snapped nude pictures of me, and his boy Mel must've been helping him make a Kodak moment out of the time we all spent on the boat. I saw snapshots of me holding a drink in my hand, snuggling up to Rico, others with my legs open as I looked like I was enjoying his pounding, and finally a picture of his earring in Trey's bed. I was fucked. I couldn't believe Rico actually strong-armed me into spend time with him and then got the goods on me when I showed up. *Damn, he ran game on me.* At that moment I realized how ruthless some men could be. After seeing what I saw, I was speechless. I sat down on the couch and held my aching head in my hands.

My trance was broken an hour later. A large truck pulled up into my driveway. Someone had furniture delivered: a full-sized bed, two night stands and a wardrobe, and a three piece living room modular. I knew who did it. Rico had flipped his lid.

"I don't want this shit. Take it all back!" I protested as the driver and his helper began unloading it.

"Ma'am, this delivery is paid for. If you don't want it you'll have to take that up with the sender. I'm just doing my job."

After a while I gave in, but I was hot as a July day. I directed them to leave the bedroom items in the guest room until I figured out what I would do with them. I was forced to allow them to set up the modular in my basement since that was the only remaining place I had room to store anything. As if I needed any more surprises, I heard a knock at the door. This time, it was a flower delivery for me.

I signed for them and snatched the box without thanking the delivery man. I opened it and found a dozen long stemmed red roses with a card:

To my future wife—

I'll be over later to break in the new bed and watch TV, sitting on the couch snuggled up with you. What man wants to sleep on a mattress where you once did intimate things with someone else? What man wants to enjoy quiet time where another man chilled? You're mine now and I hope you know how much I enjoyed our time together. I'll always remember our first date and everything that brought us to this moment. I love you more than you could ever know. Don't ever say goodbye because it's you that I'm living for every day. My fantasy is your destiny. Eliminate the middleman and submit to your Medicine Man. Count on more surprises to come, mi amor. It's time to play.

This time Rico had outdone himself for sure. He was charging ahead like a burly bull running through a china shop. He wasn't concerned about whom he may hurt or the end result of his sick behavior. All Rico wanted was his way, when all I initially desired was to remember what it was like to have a fling before I couldn't have one anymore. Obviously, Rico was on some different shit. His obsession to prove things were more than just straight fucking was beginning to give me the creeps. I wanted to undo every tie that I knotted with him, but he was fighting to maintain every one of them, moving fast and carelessly. That's when I realized I was dealing with a psycho who happened to hold a Juris Doctor degree. I stripped the sheets on my bed and hoped that the new Simmons Beautyrest mattress would be built to last. Either way, at least it came with a twenty-five year warranty. I wished I'd followed my intuition and left him alone on the day he made my toes curl like never before, but it was much, much too late.

11

Computer Love

Monday morning sneaked up on me like a skilled thief. It was a beautiful clear day, but who would've known it? Trey, now back in town from his short business trip, came home from playing basketball and showered, and dragged his tired, famished ass, along with a load of laundry, over for dinner. Hugs and smiles of bliss warmed my spirit, but things headed toward rock bottom, in a mere five minutes—the time it took for Trey to discover the new items that were sitting in my place.

"I can't wait for us to be together every day," Trey said, wrapping his arms around my waist. "I'm the luckiest man in the world. I'm so happy to have a woman like you to marry. Leslie, you accept me faults and all. I just want to say thank you for really wanting to be with me for the rest of our lives."

"You just said all of that because you know I cooked for you," I teased.

"No, that's not it. I'm just excited that in a few weeks, this whole wedding thing will be behind us. The stress and pressures that have been tugging at us will be all gone."

"I'm excited about our big day too, Trey."

Before I could stop him, Trey let go of my waist and disappeared into the basement to throw his clothes in and returned with a disgusted look on his face.

"Wait a minute, Les. Why all the new furniture. It's nice, but why?" Trey said, letting go of my waist.

"How could you go out and spend money on furniture when you're supposed to be on a budget? How much did all of this cost you?"

"Trey, I've got it all under control. It's not like I'm paying on it until 2007. Stop being a professional skeptic. How about a little patience here? It's not like you haven't ever splurged on something. Relax. Come sit down with me, eat, and tell me all about your day," I said, trying to change the subject. Apparently, Trey didn't want to let it go.

"You seem to lack direction, and we need financial security, Leslie. You've always been frugal from what I've seen. I just don't understand why you would go out and buy expensive things you don't need at a time like this. There are bills still owed for our wedding. We need to be moving forward, not backward. Why didn't you consult with me first?"

"Why should I consult with you over how I spend my own money? I have my own checkbook, and what I do with my piggy bank is my business. As I *said*, I've got it under control. Can't you hear? I'm well aware of our bills and my responsibilities. Maybe your family is putting shit in your ear about me—poisoning your mind against me. I am not marrying them, I'm marrying you. And if Leslie wanted a new mattress so Leslie could get a good night's sleep, then she should have it!"

"Maybe my mother and grandmother have some good points I've never thought about," Trey defended with frustration.

"And maybe I haven't thought about the fact that you're a momma's boy who can't navigate your way out of a wet paper bag without her approval. It's either them or your damn friends. I never come first. I'm tired of being an afterthought."

Trey banged his fist on the counter. I watched his brows

form a line. I knew I'd hit the wrong button. I'd never seen him act so emotional.

"I have a right to go out. I bust my balls every day at work, and playing ball or hanging with my boys is something I deserve. Unlike some people, I'm not on summer vacation. I work all year long in corporate America. You have no idea what it's like in a competitive market like D.C. You talk about the things I do and have no idea why I need what I need. Hey, someone has to have a real job."

"And you have no idea what it's like working as a teacher in this school system. I take less money in my check during the year so I can get a summer break. Don't act like I'm a shiftless bum who is looking to you for a handout. I'm bringing something to the table as an asset, not a liability. I've got my own place, my own car, my bills stay paid, and I'm an independent woman. I'm not one of those D.C. or East Coast gold diggers you're used to. You don't even appreciate that about me," I said with my hand on my hip, yelling in his face.

"You have no idea what kind of day I've had at work. I don't need to come and listen to this foolish talk. Maybe coming here tonight was a big mistake. I've got a great family. Where's yours? Are they really all dead like you said? How could all of them be wiped out without a trace? Maybe I don't really know you at all."

"I am tired of bickering with you. Get out!" I pointed toward the door. All I could do was watch him leave as tears streamed down my face.

"You're overreacting, Leslie! I need to be in a relationship with an adult. You're just so emotional, and all you do is complain. Can't we talk about something different for a change?" Trey mumbled.

"Overreacting? If you want to see overreacting, then I'll show you overreacting!"

I threw a lamp across the room at him. He ducked then slammed the door.

"Go get fucked up in a bar with your boys. The way things stand right now, I don't give a shit," I screamed long after he'd gone.

Instead of communicating with Trey, I began lashing out at him because my patience threshold and the love I felt for him was fading quickly. I lied about paying for the furniture because I couldn't tell the truth about it coming from Rico. There was so much I needed to say to him, but I couldn't put the truth out there for his inspection. All I felt was an empty space, despite my wedding being only four weeks away.

Although I started the fiasco, I was so angry at the things Trey said and I wanted to get back at him. He knew any talk about my family was a sensitive issue, and he'd twisted the knife in my back by throwing the issue up in my face. As I wiped the tears from my eyes, I felt the need to resurrect Innocence.

I was feeling the stress of being stretched to the limit and decided to do something about it. If I couldn't have the life I really wanted, at least I could make another one up in private. My double life fed my libido and gave me a break from life's day-to-day troubles.

Hours later, I couldn't resist the temptation of taking the edge off; I had plenty of nervous energy to burn. I didn't want to jump in with both feet by purchasing a prepaid phone and setting up a website. Instead, I logged onto craigslist.org, read over many of the provider ads to learn something more about how to set up shop, and then posted an anonymous ad under the erotic services section of Washington, D.C.:

Dipping a few toes into the waters—30
Let me first explain that I've never done this before and never considered it until recently. I'm going through some tough times and am wondering if I could give

someone out there a girlfriend experience. I'm eager to learn how to give the best experience to men and couples, but I'd like to let you know I won't be giving full service. If you need someone to strip, massage, or date you, I may be your girl. I'm an articulate, degreed professional who is smart, has a sense of humor, and is very attentive. I have amazing hands and was also blessed with luscious lips and a curvy body. If you like chocolate girls, I'm confident you won't regret meeting me! If you're willing to sneak a peek at a new girl who is considering getting into the field, please contact me for details by responding to this ad. Don't forget to include your phone number, but keep in mind that I won't accept blocked calls. Upscale, clientele preferred. Discretion is a must.
Hugs and Kisses,
Innocence

I went to the basement to finish some laundry and was shocked to find about fifty responses by the time I returned. I cut and pasted a reply with rules to each ad:

1.) *Please arrive clean.*
2.) *I will not deal with pushy or rude people.*
3.) *My donations are non-negotiable. $150 per half hour and $200 for a full hour. My rate increases by $50 if I have to travel to you within the local DC area.*
4.) *When you arrive, please place your donation in an envelope and place it on the table. I will not discuss money or explicit requests over the phone or in person.*
5.) *I repeat; I will not accept blocked calls.*
6.) *I will entertain most fantasies and fetishes although my rates may increase.*
7.) *I do not speak all languages; I do not provide Greek services and will not perform any sexual acts. I seek to deliver the highest quality erotic experiences!*

After I took a nap, there were twice as many responses as before. I had no idea so many people would want to meet me, even without viewing a glimpse of a picture. Then again, I'd read so many posts about dissatisfied customers. Explaining that I was new meat may have been the draw card. I closed my eyes, pointed to my flat screen and picked out a random email. I read the winning entry and decided to read about my first customer—a man whose best friend was getting hitched. *How ironic!* It seemed harmless enough, so I decided to go for it and called the number provided. We agreed on the terms and set a time. Part of the terms specified that if he saw me and didn't like me, all bets were off. I knew that wasn't going to happen though. My confidence was growing, and thanks to Rico I'd gotten a very swollen ego.

Late that evening, I arrived at the address I had scribbled down on a notepad. A man answered the door, but the funny thing was he wasn't the type who seemed like he'd be trolling a message board full of prostitution ads. I'd been paying so much attention to Trey I didn't realize how many good-looking men there were in the area. Although I'd traveled about thirty minutes from D.C. to the 'burbs, I still considered it in *the area.*

The gentleman standing before me was the young, executive buppie type. With the exception of his neat shoulder length dreads, he reminded me of a polished stockbroker. The man dressed in the well-made suit made me want to jump his bones. When he opened his mouth and spoke, I wanted to melt.

"Innocence?" he asked with a slightly crooked smile.

"Yes, that's me."

"Please come in," he said, extending an arm of welcome.

"Only if I meet your approval," I teased. "Do you like what you see?"

"Do I? You're a chocolate Barbie doll, just as you said. Perfect." He formed the okay sign with his fingers. I quietly sighed in relief, glad that he was pleased. "Here, let me take that for you," he said, reaching for my things.

"Oh, thank you." I walked in first. He followed. I stood in the foyer with a small bag on my shoulder.

"There's someone I'd like you to meet. Dougie, where are you?" he called.

"In here, Maxwell." The voice sounded like whoever it was possessed a chronically stuffed nose. When he appeared, I was stunned—he was the opposite of his friend. What I saw was some real freaked out shit. A short, pudgy man appeared wearing a Breathe Right Nasal Strip on the bridge of his nose and linty, blue polyester high water pants. He walked slightly bent over, and even had masking tape holding the middle of his glasses together. To say the least, the guy was a social loser. Nevertheless, it wasn't my job to judge him by his looks or the smell of all the Old Spice he was wearing, which, by the way, could've easily opened his nasal passages. I was there to provide a service, and I was determined to do so.

The three of us talked awhile to add to the comfort of my visit. It turned out Dougie was a loaded, eccentric nerd—an investment guru who still lived in his mother's basement despite his worth of over five million dollars. He recently became engaged. I guessed some woman decided to love him after finding out he'd saved the first paycheck he ever earned and continued saving and investing, rather than because of his charm, or the sparkle in his eyes. After Maxwell demanded that he remove his breathing strip, Dougie even snorted in between laughs as he explained he was never a ladies man, but looked forward to moving into a small cottage with his new bride. You didn't have to tell me she had other plans for an abode, but I didn't say a word—I just listened. Maxwell, my bronzed hunk, was divorced with one child. He worked with Dougie at an investment firm, and seemed to have to fight women off with a stick. Quite frankly, I saw why. The man's game was tight, *plus* it was quite apparent he had a brain. After we chatted for a few moments it was time to get down to business. After all, these two were on my time clock, no matter how interesting they appeared to be.

"Shall we get started, gentlemen?"

"Wait just one minute. I have to take my Alka Seltzer," Dougie said. "When I get nervous my stomach burns. When my stomach burns, I sit up all night with gas." He got up.

"Stop stalling, Dougie. Hurry," Maxwell told him.

Dougie drank down the fizzing solution. He finally returned then sat back down on the couch. "Okay. Oh boy. Oh boy, I'm ready. Now what?" He began to snort as he laughed.

Maxwell and I ignored him, and I noticed that Dougie didn't move. "Oh, you'll be staying? I though this was for just one person," I asked.

Maxwell explained, "I'm sorry for the mix up, but I'll be staying too. My friend here is so shy that if I don't stay he wouldn't even look at you. I'll pay for the inconvenience."

I didn't believe his explanation. By the way he was eying me, I knew he wanted to see if I could work what I had and also discover what I had under my denim skirt and tank top.

"Very well then . . . I'll accommodate you. I'm sure you recall my list of rules." I said with a smile. "So, what's your desire?"

Dougie whispered in Maxwell's ear. "A strip tease," Maxwell responded.

"Let him tell me in my ear. Come," I said, motioning my finger in the direction of the shy man. He trembled as he walked toward me. He even tripped over his own feet. Surprisingly I didn't laugh. I gave him time to get up. Then I repeated my words. "I'm still waiting," I said, flirting.

By the time he stood in front of me, he was trembling and sweating. It was hard to imagine he was really getting married to anyone. I felt his breath on my skin as he stuttered into my ear.

"La-la. La-la. Lap dance. Please." He quickly ran over toward his friend, standing next to him and pushing his glasses up on his nose.

"Very good. All you had to do was ask. Your wish is Innocence's command," I cooed.

"He's a virgin. Need I say anymore?" Maxwell stated.

"No worries. I'll be as gentle as sunshine," I said.

Maxwell poured liquor into one shot glass and the remaining dribbles of Alka Seltzer in the other. I didn't feel as if I had a right to laugh so I didn't. In fact, I felt like some sort of sex therapist who was hard at work with a troubled patient.

"All right, Dougie. Today you will no longer be a solitary man," Maxwell shouted, handing him the shot glass filled with fizzing antacid. "To my business partner," he said, raising his shot glass. "Here's to feeling ten feet tall and changing your life around!"

"Here's to ten feet tall and me," Dougie said clanking shot glasses and smiling like Steve Urkel.

"Where may I change my clothes?" I asked as they drank the liquids down.

"Right this way," Maxwell told me, getting up.

"Is she stripping in the bathroom?" Dougie asked with a white mustache above his lip.

"No. She's coming back. She's putting something else on to strip in," Maxwell explained half annoyed. "Wipe that junk from around your mouth, geez!"

"Ooooooh," Dougie said, cleaning it with the back of his arm.

When I returned, I oozed with confidence. I was now wearing five and a half inch, platform stilettos with a row of rhinestones across each strap, and a black, embroidered mesh shelf bra and panty set under a tight red mini dress. I painted my lips with bright red lip gloss, but left my sassiest wig at home. Instead, I freed my hair from a small ponytail and let it brush my shoulders.

"Music please," I requested.

"Wow, she looks great! Is she going to dance to The Spinners? That's my favorite group," Dougie said.

"The Spinners? She most certainly isn't! Why don't you shut up and enjoy the show—damn! This is why I couldn't take you to a strip club," Maxwell snapped.

"Okay, okay. Take it easy," Dougie answered.

After the two men sat on the leather couch I turned around with my back toward them, holding one hand up in the air like a spotlight shone one me. The first number I danced to was an old standard by Terrance Trent Darby. When the beat started, I transformed myself from Leslie, into the vixen, Innocence, gracefully lowering my arm behind my back. I turned around seductively, just as I'd practiced many times in front of the mirror in the privacy of my own home. One of my fantasies to fulfill was to strip for men at least once in my life. The most I could do about it was order an exotic dance DVD from the Internet to teach me how to strip. Visiting a strip club to watch another girl grind under low lighting had been out of the question. Thanks to Maxwell and Dougie, a closet desire became a reality. Now I was that naughty girl who was about to prove her erotic potential.

My hips swayed slowly as I shifted my weight from one leg to the other. I pointed my toe, threw my right leg out straight, and then did the same with my left, keeping my palms next to my sides. When I stopped I felt the groove of the music, lowering myself to the ground. I leaned on my left elbow and slowly extended my right leg in the air while using my right arm to lift it. I seductively looked both men straight in the eye as I gave them a peak at my pussy. After I lowered my leg, I got up from the floor, sticking my ass out to accentuate my healthy rear as I proceeded to stand. When I rose, I lowered the zipper of my dress with the artful precision of an experienced stripper. Once my breasts were exposed, I began running my hands over them. Dougie's eyes bulged and Maxwell crossed his legs, looking as if he'd like to eat me up.

I took my arms out and let my dress drop to my feet. I stepped out of it and walked around in a circle to the beat of the music. When I faced them again, I had also let my black shelf bra fall to the floor. Standing in nothing but my stripper heels and crotchless panties, I spun around, groped my ass cheeks then bent over with my eyes closed and smacked myself on the ass three times. When I opened my eyes again, I moved in for the kill.

Dougie was my first victim. Sitting in his lap, I straddled him, letting my knees rest on the couch. I bounced up and down on top of his middle, pushing my breasts in his face. I swung around and put my hands on my knees, slowly rubbing my ass against his crotch in a repetitive motion while looking over my shoulder at him. His lip dropped open and his face became flushed. I stood upright, faced him, and extended my leg on top of his shoulder, showing off my acrobatic skills while simultaneously squeezing my breasts.

As soon as my leg hit the carpet, Dougie jumped up. "Gotta go. Bathroom. Oh God. Ooooh God!" He took off running, covering the middle of his pants. I knew he came and wanted to clean up the mess.

Without missing a beat, I turned to Maxwell who seemed more than happy to cop a feel as Prince's *International Lover* began to play. For him, my attention was more sensual and genuine. I pretended he was Trey as I buried his head into my full breasts, sensually moving my hips, imagining he was stroking me. After a minute or so passed, I turned around and placed his large, strong looking hands on my thighs and pushed my ass cheeks against his rock hard stomach. Next, I arched my back and wiggled my ass over his crotch as I rocked and rocked to the beat of the music. We both started breathing heavily as his hard-on grew.

Without speaking, his eyes told me he wanted me to get up. I did. He grabbed my hand and led me into a room that housed a Jacuzzi. I dropped my panties and unbuckled my shoes, then he showed me everything God blessed him with. All I can say is boy did God bless him! We stepped in and began making out like high school kids taking a skinny dip. His hands were everywhere as the bubbles jumped in the water. I moaned slow and long when he stuck his tongue in my ear. My lips begged him to kiss me all over. I was in heaven. In fact, I forgot this was not supposed to be for pleasure.

Just as things began to really heat up, Dougie appeared. Instead of his usual chatter, he was silent, apparently catching the vibe. He shed his clothes with the exception of his smiley face boxer shorts. As Maxwell enjoyed exploring my body, Dougie slowly began to join in. His inhibitions seemed to have faded. He removed his glasses and gingerly set them on the side of the hot tub. Without them he didn't look half bad, although he and Maxwell could never be mistaken for twins.

By this time, both men were kissing the sides of my neck and rubbing me softly.

"Go stand over there," Maxwell suggested.

"But why?" I asked.

"I think you'll enjoy something if you do," he added. My adventurous side led me to follow his suggestion. When I did, I felt a strong stream of water shoot onto the back of my knees. I crouched down slightly, realizing the jets could give me more pleasure that I'd ever imagined.

"Oh shit! What in the hell? MMMmmm," I moaned.

"It never fails. I told you," Maxwell said with a slight trace of victory in the pitch of his voice. I bit my upper lip and gripped the sides of the hot tub as I let my head fall back. By that time, I managed to lift my head and open my eyes. Both men had changed positions.

Just as I began to take note that four hands felt much better than two, my erotic massage turned into something more. Out of the blue, Maxwell began sucking my nipples while his friend moved away and watched the expression of ecstasy cover my face. I felt as if I was standing in fields of gold and I know it showed. Dougie must've enjoyed being a voyeur because I began to hear him moan lustfully.

"Up to my bedroom," Maxwell softly whispered in my ear.

"No sex. We've done more than planned already," I answered.

He twisted my nipples and made me gasp. "Eight hundred. How does eight hundred sound just to let me eat you out?" he asked.

"Eight hundred. How does eight hundred sound just to let me eat you out, too?" Dougie asked, mimicking Maxwell.

"Fine, sixteen hundred for the both of you. That's it though."

"Deal," Maxwell said.

"Dripping wet, the three of us exited the hot tub and walked up two flights of stairs.

When we reached Maxwell's room, he said, "Shower with him first."

I motioned for Dougie to come behind the glass partition with me and gave him the soap to let him enjoy lathering me up. His eyes widened again as he did the job. I tilted my head back and wet my hair, rinsing myself clean. I lathered him up although my mind was on Maxwell. I was dripping wet thinking of him repeating the same events with me. Dougie exited, drying himself off with a towel.

"Go sit on the bed and wait for me. Tell Maxwell I want to see him," I explained. Dougie walked away, nodding his head.

"You called?" Maxwell asked in a deep voice. He towered over me, running his hands through my hair, then stroking my left cheek. He stepped into the shower and I closed my eyes. I initiated touching him by pressing my cheek into his chest and hugging him tenderly. I opened my eyes and his mouth was waiting to kiss me. Steam began to fill the shower, and we both began to moan as his hands rested on my waist.

"Now. I want you now. You're sexy as hell, Innocence," Maxwell uttered. He turned off the shower, and we took turns drying each other off. The time had finally come for my tongue massage, and I couldn't wait for my pussy to get sucked and licked like I was a queen.

When we made it to the bed, Maxwell gently pushed me backward and spread my legs apart. My next sensation was a kind tongue on a neglected clit. Rico didn't count. I'm speaking of Trey's ability to ignore the fact that I may enjoy oral sex being performed on me as much as I did giving it. As the three of us moaned, I heard my cell phone ringing in my clutch purse. I'd forgotten to turn it off as usual. I'd become accustomed to leaving it on in case Trey wanted to talk to me at any time of the day or night.

"We're important clients. Two thousand dollars if you stay put. I'm feeling you, girl," Maxwell told me, once again breaking all the rules by discussing sex for money.

This time I didn't respond because it wasn't really about payment. I told myself to fuck those rules. I moaned and groaned more than I think I ever had. My eyes rolled back in my head, and I was reminded what it felt like to cum. I did, all over Maxwell's tongue. After that, Dougie expected the very same performance. Once I lived up to what was expected of me both of them begged me to come back. The business partners and best friends threw all sorts of dollar amounts in my ear.

As I prepared to leave the house, they each stuffed a thousand dollars into envelopes. I felt as powerful as any stockbroker, CEO, or man's man. This made me confident that being a freak of the week had its benefits. Dougie drew several large hearts on his envelope, but so what if he wasn't playing with a full deck? Obviously, I got *my* rocks off and planned to think of that damn sexy Maxwell again the next time I pleasured myself—in between fighting with my ball and chain to be.

12

The Train Ride

I left my first true independent provider gig depleted and damn near dehydrated. All I wanted to do was sleep, but I checked my messages as I rolled down the highway. After I discovered I had zero messages, my cell phone rang. Although the caller's number was blocked, I answered it anyway. Unfortunately, it was Rico's way of catching me off guard so I'd accept his call.

"It's going to be a beautiful day today with a high of eighty degrees," he told me.

"A: Don't call me from a blocked number. B: What does that mean to me?"

"Stop being so cold. I know you've missed me, so I'm getting out of the office at a reasonable time today, letting the paralegal finish up some tasks."

"Miss you? In your wet dreams when you're whacking off, Rico."

"I just love your sense of humor. Now look, Leslie. This is my third call. Respond promptly next time or Trey will hear about your interesting extra curricular activities. Where were you?"

"What? None of your damned beeswax, Rico psycho. I'm not a dog on a leash. I know you're sprung, but ease up with the choke collar because I didn't sign up to be your obedient pet."

"Why are you being so selfish? I want to see you now! I said, where were you?"

"None of your business. I told you that the first time you asked."

"You *are* my business. So, did you like the furniture or not?"

"You're over stepping your bounds, and this is all very annoying."

"And you're not cooperating by giving me what I want."

"I don't want the damn job, so pack and stuff it where the sun don't shine. Game over. I keep telling you to let go and let me have my peace. You are not relationship material!"

"You've got to keep me happy no matter what you say. I'm not letting you off the hook until I'm ready to. We made a pact. You can't just abandon our agreement like that."

"We did no such thing. I wish you'd quit blowing up my phone. What does your psycho ass want now?"

"I want to fuck you today, that's what. And we did make a pact. I'm your lover. I've got a thing for you, baby. I'm not in your life to hit it and forget it. Maybe that's how it was with those other fools, but Rico has a different agenda for Leslie, mi estrella muy brillante."

Huh. My lover, my stalker, has a different agenda, I thought. Instead, I said, "Don't you ever get enough?"

"Not of your sweet, wet pussy. Before this affair is over everyone's going to know that Rico is the one for you. Get ready to open your legs or cancel your wedding plans. Those are the rules—Rico's rules."

"I'm not doing either. Our connection was built on a damn lie."

"Look, I'm the one who's in control, and for the record, I'm in a bit of a selfish mood today. I really don't have any patience for your back talk, so I suggest you follow my directions. For the last time, correct your attitude, and do whatever you have to do to inspire yourself to get in a giving mood. You have until five o'clock to arrange your plans to meet with me . . . unless you'd like for me to prove the things I've said can come true. As soon as I'm finished working, I want to hit it. I already checked Trey's schedule, and he's keeping his nose to the grind late for a project deadline, so that means the one who holds my heart is free and available for private time with me." Click.

Despite Rico's pushy demands, I wasn't planning on opening my legs or canceling my wedding plans, even though Trey and I were skating on thin ice. I orchestrated a little scam to teach Rico a lesson that required me to book a cheap hotel room and invest some of the money I made in provider fees. I knew his stalker ass would meet me anywhere I instructed, as long as I made it clear I'd be present. Unfortunately for him, he'd walk straight into a trap that he'd remember until his last day on earth.

"It's open," I shouted.

He opened the door. "Where are you, Les? Are you in here?"

"Of course I am, Rico. I changed my mind. I'm ready for my papi" I said in a seductive manner.

"That's more like it," he said happily.

"I'm on the bed. Come get it. What's taking you so long to wrap those beautiful, muscular arms around me? Or would you prefer for me to lick on that ass?" I asked. Maybe you need to loosen up first. Here," I said, getting up to pour him a glass of champagne. I poured myself a glass as well.

"It doesn't get much better than this. I love it when you talk dirty—that's my mami" Rico said, sipping bubbly. I sipped mine as slowly as possible, but I made sure I kept Rico sipping fast enough to need to refill his glass three times.

"I'll be back, Rico. I forgot to take care of one little thing," I lied.

"Hurry up. Now I'm feeling like putting this bed to good use."

"I'll be right back, silly!" I said. "In fact, I'll turn out the lights to help you stay in the mood while I slip into something more comfortable," I added.

While the room was dark, I sent someone else to please Rico in my place. Little did Rico know I was standing in the corner.

The next thing I heard was Rico moaning lower and deeper than I'd ever recalled. Judging from the sounds he was making, I assumed Wendee was rimming his asshole as planned. As the foreplay continued, Rico had no idea he was feeling up and kissing on a pre-op transvestite, who was more than happy to make love to a straight man. In fact, I had to force Wendee to take at least $50 for his time.

"Oh, mami. You're so good to me. I missed you so much."

"Hit it from the back, papi. I know that's how you like it. Let me turn around and make it easy for you to get at this," I said, throwing a cue to Wendee. I had no doubt Wendee caught my hint when I heard Rico comment.

"Nice and tight, just the way I like it."

"That's my back door, papi. Keep going though," I said breathlessly, making him think I was really into it. All the while I wanted to crack up laughing since I knew he was actually fucking the tranny in the booty hole.

"Harder!" I screamed. "I like it in the ass. Lay that pipe *harder*, Rico!"

"Oh, mami. You like?"

"I love. More, I want more. Trey would never ever hit it like this. Take it like you want it, papi. I'm your woman now, remember? Break my virgin asshole in like a real man."

"Me gusto es mio."

Rico continued doing what he thought was his duty, ramming Wendee in the ass. I screamed, moaned, and even played with myself in the dark to make my pretend lovemaking sounds appear authentic. I was used to faking mind-blowing sex with Trey, but I wanted this episode to really suck Rico into my pit of deception. It was working pretty well until my decoy screwed up. Rico was going to town, talking shit and pounding Wendee a new one, when he reached down to feel what was supposed to be my pussy. Instead he felt a swinging penis. I thought the tranny tied the thing up or whatever they do but I assumed wrong.

"What the fuck! Is that a dick I just—" Rico jumped out of the bed and scurried to find the light switch.

Once the light was on, I smirked at him. "If my pussy was good as you said, you ought to have known the difference," I bragged, amused by the anger that covered his face.

"Why'd you stop? You're a cute, muscular thing. I need to give the girl a refund because I would've showed up for free had I known you had it going on like that," Wendee flirted.

Rico lunged at the tranny looking crazed and behaving like a psychotic madman. He placed one hand around Wendee's throat, gripped her hair with the other and began banging "her" head against the wall. To say he was livid was an under-statement—he exhibited the strength of Hercules, and his re-action to what I'd rigged up began to alarm me.

"Hijoeputa! I do not fuck freaks like you. Latin men are macho men. I should kill you. I should end your life with my bare hands, but I have too much to lose. Where did she meet you? Tell it or I'll alert every policeman in the area about you and trouble will become your first and last name."

"Craigslist. Erotic services. I'm—I'm visiting from San Francisco," Wendee confessed, struggling to breathe.

"Is that right? Oh, I see," Rico's eyes glazed over. He glanced in my direction and then looked back at Wendee. "After I take my hands from around your fucking bony throat, you better find a phone and call all the men you know and make appointments to fuck. If you don't, I'll ruin your life. Don't think I can't find out where you lay your head in your home city, what your real name is, when you shit, pee, burp, fart, or wrap your lips around a dick from here to The Golden Gate Bridge. I'm serious about all of this and I hope you understand this is not a joke—you're in one deep mess."

Then Rico pulled an unexpected number by explaining he was an attorney and had personal affiliation with a slew of policeman who routinely busted prostitutes among other things.

"Leslie is about to receive the lesson of a lifetime. Revenge is what makes Rico's world go round. Let's play you two. Let's play chess. My move next—this game isn't over."

Rico released the tranny from his grip. Wendee fell to the ground and gasped for air. Although visibly shaken, Wendee scrambled to find "her" cell phone and began dialing numbers and staggering appointment times. While that was happening, Rico simultaneously made calls to his policeman friends.

"Bring plenty of condoms," he told each one he called. After that, he threw the tranny out of the hotel room with one strong push in the back. Whatever Rico had planned for me, I knew it was terrible. I took a breath and prepared to take my licks like a grown woman. Since Rico threw Wendee out, I had every reason to suspect I was the one who had gone way too far.

Within ten minutes, men began showing up at the motel room on a mission for sexual attention. As each man showed up with money in an envelope, he was told he'd be busted for soliciting a prostitute. When each one pleaded his case, the plain-clothes female cop guarding the door began extorting money. She took what was meant for Wendee plus whatever was in their wallets.

Rico and the cops ran their little scam for an hour. When it became clear that all of Wendee's customers had come and gone, the female cop was excused with her cut. Then I learned exactly what Rico had in store for me. After she left, Rico grabbed me in front of the room full of cops and kissed me long and slow, dragging out every second of his tongue dancing with mine. Then he sensually led me to remove my clothes. When he pushed me back on the bed and began kissing me all over my neck, and sucking my nipples, I grinned, thinking I was at the top of my game.

"You're the only woman for me. Don't you get that?"

"Yes, Rico. Yes," I murmured as he pressed my breasts together and began to run his dick between them. Every time I thought Rico had given me the ultimate experience, he always seemed to up the ante. Getting titty fucked in front of a room full of men made me forget what I had done to him—at least temporarily.

"Remember her face boys. Remember it well. She's all yours now," Rico said, jumping up. "Until you truly understand you're the only woman for me, you're going to be used like the whore you want to be. Now get your ass over there," he commanded.

The next part of the episode began with one man moving close to me very quickly. In fact, I couldn't even make time to move from the spot where I was. He began squeezing on my rear, occasionally licking my ass crack. I felt his long, dark dick brush against my right hamstring. Simultaneously, a second man sucked my breasts, and a third rolled a condom down on his penis and began exploring my pussy. Just when I felt like things wouldn't be so bad the men began to curse at me brutality, making all sorts of sexual demands. They handled me roughly, and every hole I owned stayed full.

Hours passed, and I had been put into more positions than I could count. I was hot and sweaty and was sure I had screwed at least thirteen cops who were more than happy to take advantage of the situation. Many of them never even undressed completely. I guess it gave them a rush of power to get freaky while remaining partially clothed in their uniforms, although they were smart enough to remove their badges.

I did them all—fat, tall, clean, dirty, black, white, pencil-sized dick, hung like a horse, hairy, bald headed, dark, light, pink—all of them on a cheap motel bed spread. Some took turns continuously passing me around like a rag doll, erupting at random. Others stayed hard and aroused, performing as part of a team, in it for the long haul, on a mission to get a piece of a good slut. They kept groping, touching, and filling my holes up like tomorrow would never come.

"Time just seems to fly, huh Leslie? Are you ready to give true love a try now, or do I need to call in the next crew?"

I managed to lift and shake my head although I was physically worn from being pulled in all directions.

"Three of you stand by the door," Rico instructed. None of them seemed to want to stop lusting over my brown sugar, but a few managed to tear themselves away from my body. "If you really want to stop being a whore, prove it. Get on your knees and beg me to let this all come to an end," he said coldly.

"Please, Rico. No more," I begged, pushing my wet hair away from my eyes and dropping to my knees. I looked up at him. "I'll do whatever it takes to make you happy—just no more of this punishment. Let me go," I pleaded. I managed to squeeze out a few fake tears as he stared at me. Then, unable to hold it in any longer, I broke out in laughter. "I know you were trying to make me feel like a crackhead whore getting fucked in a cheap motel, but as nasty as it sounds, screwing a room full of men has been one of the fantasies I'd buried behind my list of ordinary desires. If you want to send more in go ahead. In case you haven't figured it out by now, I'm a true freak. I can still suck and fuck a whole new crew until they cum, you big dummy. It was nice being worshiped and reminded that I've got something all men want."

Rico looked frustrated that he hadn't broken my spirit—

that after all I'd been through, I was still gloating. Not only had I lived the fantasy, but I felt empowered knowing I'd won a round of boxing with Rico's volatile emotions. I could tell he didn't know what to say.

"It's good sleeping weather, and you're coming home with me to Upper Marlboro. We'll discuss our future because you belong to me."

"Whatever you say, papi," I said, still smirking. Rico grabbed me by the arm, tearing me away from the cops. I rose to my feet, holding my gaze on him.

"If you tell anyone about this, I'll kill you. Now get your clothes and get dressed," he mumbled under his breath so the cops couldn't catch on to his most hostile words. I reached for my shoes but he grabbed my wrist, a clear sign that I should leave them. When Rico and I left the hotel room, his outrageous antics continued.

About two miles down an isolated highway, Rico threw on the brakes, held a switchblade under my neck, and then pulled over.

"You think that was cute what you pulled? No one makes an ass of Rico. You still don't know who you're messing with, I see. Get out, puta. Get out and walk home barefoot while you think about your disrespectful behavior, you whore!" he screamed.

I got out and started walking. Rico drove alongside me on the shoulder of the road, taunting me in every way possible. I had expected him to speed off, leaving a trail of smoke. Instead, he dragged out my agony for at least a quarter of a mile. Out of the blue, his tone changed and suddenly he was gentle and warm.

"Hey, Les. Did I tell you I've got one of your pictures as my computer wallpaper?" I didn't reply. "You know the one with you sucking my balls on that boat ride—that's my favorite. I like the way your jaw line looks so strong and sexy. My mami is such an animal. Don't you agree?"

At that second, a sense of fear surged into my body. What Rico didn't know was that I'd recorded the whole train ride, from Wendee's performance up to the last threat he'd made. The only reason I complied to hoofing it was because all the evidence I needed to finally turn his world upside down was resting in my junky purse. Sure, I had to give something to get something. But as far as I was concerned, a little over four hundred dollars was an extremely wise investment. The digital video camera was the mere size of a pack of smokes, and I was able to blend it in with items sitting on the dresser. It almost slipped my mind, but Innocence was a slick little vixen. Even though the images of Rico and Wendee were shadowy due to the lights being turned off, at least the conversation was recorded, and Rico did eventually shed light upon the situation. When he did, I knew the camera had picked up everything that happened after that, including my act. I just had to find a way to keep him from noticing the contents of my purse.

"Mami, tell Rico you agree that you belong to him."

"I do," I said. "I agree," I answered solemnly.

Rico stopped the car. I hopped in and began to wiggle my toes and rub my feet. Hey, it just be like that sometimes— until the time was right to make a move. Innocence could tolerate thug loving, even if Leslie couldn't. Unbeknownst to Rico, I hadn't learned my lesson one bit.

13

S & M Grooving

Early in the morning, after Rico released me from my "duties," I got cleaned up and went to Arundel Mills to pick out the perfect birthday gift for Trey. It took me three and a half hours to come up with something, but in the end, I found the perfect gift for a man who was always on the go—a user friendly carry-on that was complete with an organizer. As I walked through the mall, I called and called Trey, wishing him a happy birthday. The first call I placed was around nine A.M. If he had in fact slept at home that night, I knew he should answer. When he answered his home line, it was in his typical hurried manner, promising to call me from the car on his way to the office. He didn't keep his word, so I wasn't able to announce my plans of making him a romantic dinner and treating him like the king in my world.

As the day wore on I realized he wasn't going to call me back. By evening, I'd called so much I stopped leaving messages and merely hung up each time I heard his voicemail. I got angrier and angrier, and then I lost my cool. I decided to leave another message, and I stated that he could fuck whom he wanted to fuck and that the wedding was off. Fighting and making up had become a new habit. Although it was getting old fast, Trey should've realized I didn't mean what I said. I really just exploded to make a point—it had everything to do with wanting him to be more attentive.

I turned off my phone and tried to put something into my growling stomach. As usual, I sat at my kitchen table with candles, his favorite Chinese dishes, but no Trey. My appetite quickly vanished, and I was only able to eat about seven bites of food and even that small amount proved tasteless. I made my way to my bed, stripped my clothes off, and cried away the rejection and disappointment that made me question why I even bothered to wear Trey's ring. I was still in tears when I heard a message on my answering machine.

"So you said you want to break up and call off the wedding, and I can fuck who I want to fuck—let's roll with that then."

After the message ended, I began to cry harder. Trey completely missed the point of why I said what I said—it was the same shit, but a different day. My mind flashed back to a couple holding hands at the mall. When they stopped to turn the corner and enter a store, they stood so close their lips almost brushed. As the man smiled at the woman and grabbed her hand, I remembered wanting to feel love like that, but I realized how much the scales were unbalanced in my relationship. Trey never reached deeply into my emotions and pulled anything passionate out of our bond, and that bothered me enough to leave that nasty message on his cell phone.

At 1:10 A.M., Soul Train was blaring from the TV, but everything else was still and quiet. I was bored and hurt, so I logged on to the Internet to keep my mind off my disastrous night. I answered some emails, planning to go back to bed and deal with everything the next morning. The thing was, Innocence wanted to come out and play in order to help Leslie subdue her pain. Her desires were having a contest with Leslie's rational thinking, but by 2:11, she spoke to

Leslie and told her that her destiny was to feel pleasure, not pain. I logged back on, and after about fifteen minutes of scrolling through ads on craigslist, I felt a lot less pain. In fact, I felt quite a sense of relief when I read the one stating 600 REASONS FOR A LADY RIGHT NOW!$$$$$$$—35: I'M A YOUNG, ATTRACTIVE PROFESSIONAL IN NEED OF A PRO OR NON-PRO TO BUST MY BALLS! THIS IS SERIOUS AND NO FULL SERVICE!!!!! JUST TREAT ME VERY BAD! 20 MINUTES OF YOUR TIME IS ALL I ASK.

I responded to the anonymous person with a few simple lines. IF YOU ARE SERIOUS ABOUT CURING THAT KINKY LITTLE FETISH OF YOURS, I CAN ASSURE YOU THAT YOU WILL HAVE A GOOD TIME WITH ME. NO PICTURES AVAILABLE, BUT GUARANTEED TO PLEASE.

I left the PC on and lay down to take a real nap. My eyes were red as fire from crying, and I figured I'd catch a few winks while I gave the man a chance to respond. One hour later, he did. He typed his phone number, and I called it. I got all the pertinent details, gassed up the car, and was off to Tyson's Corner to bust some white guy's balls. I wore thigh-high black stiletto boots, a tight mini skirt, and a black top. I figured my get up would meet the approval of the sick business executive who enjoyed S&M and said he needed to unwind after a stressful day. He wanted to be treated badly, and given my mood, I could easily treat him like shit for a mere twenty minutes. I didn't know what to say or do, so I told myself that I'd think of how frustrated I was with the only man I loved and make up the scenario as I went along.

A man wearing a collar with a dangling choke chain answered the door when I knocked. That told me I'd have to go hard and jump right into the kinky role play.

"Gimme my damn money. I respect my time slave! Gimme my damn money before I turn around and leave. If that happens, you'll miss your chance to be punished well," I shouted as I pushed my way inside of his home.

"Here it is, Mistress. Please don't leave me yet." He scurried to get me the money, which I shoved it in my bra.

"Did I say you could look at me? Don't look at me slave. Get your shit—you now have eighteen minutes and counting. Where's my whip and the blindfold? You aren't prepared to worship me properly?"

I smacked him across the face and punched him in the stomach. The man didn't seem to mind—I'd never seen anyone enjoy something like that. Then he ran to collect his essentials. While he did, I walked around until I found his kitchen. I discovered a row of blue tins pushed against a counter by the stove. I searched each one until I found the sugar then hunted for his dustpan. I returned to the living room and poured the sugar onto the marble foyer as he watched. I dropped the metal dustpan, and then secured the blindfold around his head.

"Clean this mess up with your tongue. Lap it up like a dog," I commanded.

Like an obedient puppy, he dropped on his hands and knees, struggling to push the pile of sugar he couldn't see into the dustpan. After a minute or so, I grabbed the whip he'd brought into the room and smacked his backside with it until his hind parts reddened.

"You're doing a piss poor job. That's not fast enough. What good are you? You can't do anything right, dumb ass!"

I yanked the chain around his neck and pulled him upward. The harder I pulled, the more he begged for me to treat him badly.

"Piss on me, Mistress. Please, please piss on me."

"Are you trying to tell me what to do?" I asked, searching for his bedroom.

"No, Mistress."

"Then behave as if you know your place, you fucking bastard!" After I found the bedroom I pushed him onto the bed. "Come hell or high water, I make the rules around here," I told him.

I picked up the heavy-duty wrist and ankle cuffs that were lying on the bed. After he was attached to the bed face up, I felt as if I was being admired by millions. With every act of humiliation, I punished him. I did it for Trey getting my hopes up high, then crushing my heart's desire to let go of Innocence. I administered more hefty lashes on his legs until I thought of what to do next. I lifted one leg toward his mouth.

First he sucked the dirt from my stiletto like it was something tasty. When he followed my outrageous command, I couldn't believe it! I started to just stand on him, then it hit me that this freak may have a foot fetish, so I took advantage if it. I removed my shoes.

"Suck my toes. If you do a good job and don't waste my time, I just may let my slave have his wish before I leave," I said.

"I'd love to worship your feet, Mistress."

Without hesitation the man licked my foot from the arch to the heel then sucked each toe, one by one. By the time he reached my third toe, I closed my eyes, resting them as my whole body relaxed. I was surprised I felt as if I were being pulled into some erotic current. The sensation of feeling a warm mouth caress my virgin feet almost felt as good as if he were spreading my knees and cheeks then hitting it right with a big dick.

My nipples grew hard and began sticking out into the air as I felt my juices start to flow. After I'd had enough teasing, I pulled my leg down, crawled onto the bed, and then straddled him. I finally opened my eyes, hiked my skirt up then grinded my pussy on top of his face. After I humped his mouth a few seconds my juices began running down his cheeks. He begged to push his tongue inside of me.

"Mistress, can I please lick you."

After all of that toe sucking, I wasn't going to debate or reject the idea.

"Lick it now, slave. Hurry up, and stop when I say stop. If you don't, I won't pee on you before I leave."

As soon as I finished speaking those words I felt a long, warm tongue move upward and caress my pussy lips. I reached inside of my shirt and began twisting my nipples as my eyes shut.

"Lick this. Keep licking this sweet pussy," I demanded. "I'll punish you if you don't do the job right," I added.

The man began to moan with pleasure as he played with my clit and made me gush. Without warning, I placed my hands on the bed and held my ass up in the air slightly. I let a warm stream of pee pour all over his chest and drip down his thighs. I climbed down from the bed and began fingering myself as I watched his penis rise and spurt a stream of cum high into the air.

"Oh, Mistress. You busted my balls so good. Oh Mistress. Oh. Oh, you're soooo mean!" he commented.

I stopped playing with myself and ordered him to turn on his side. "Bad slave. Very bad slave!" I screamed, whipping him at an angle. The more I whipped him, the more cum he shot.

After the man's time was up, I detached only one of the wrist cuffs.

"Mistress, can you please help your slave?"

"Time's up, buddy. In fact, you're ten minutes over the clock. Your free arm can reach the phone. Now share this secret freaky shit you like with your friends and coworkers."

"Please, Mistress. Don't do this to me."

"Only under *one* condition."

"What's that?"

"We do this again next week. I want you to tell me where your wallet is so you can pay me five hundred more to make sure you'll call me to bust those balls again."

"Yes, Mistress. I officially want to be your slave. I would love to see you in nylons, garter belts, and heels while I worship you properly. My wallet's in my top dresser drawer. Take whatever you want," he answered.

I couldn't believe how easy it was to attract the attention of every man but Trey. I didn't intend on coming back, but I did take an extra six hundred for my time. As usual, it really wasn't about the money, it was about the power. After I removed every bill from his wallet, a skinny, white, blonde-haired woman dressed in a business suit walked in the bedroom, toting a maroon briefcase. As I noted her demeanor, she gave me a puzzled look. It led me to believe that she was his wife or girl-friend. I pegged her for a prudish cold one. I spoke up before she had a chance to say anything.

"I don't know where you've been all night but he's all yours now, honey. His cute little ass may be a little sore though, so be gentle on him tonight. Take care," I said. "By the way, nice red power suit. You're working it, girlfriend."

I winked and held my head high as I passed by the stunned woman. I figured since the man's wife or girlfriend came home, she was more than capable of unhooking him from the other wrist cuff—if she chose to free her kinky S&M closet freak. From the expression on her face, I don't believe she knew about his secret life, just as Trey didn't know about mine. I had my own problems to worry about though. Mr. Ball Buster was on his own.

14

My Lover, My Stalker, My Baby's Daddy

Check out the scenario: an old school slow jam was playing on the radio. If memory serves me correctly, it was *You Are My Starship,* by Norman Conners. Trey grabbed me, his hands wandering all over my back. I was caught up in a tender embrace—it was makeup time after our horrible fight. As we slow danced for the first time in months, I smelled the scent of his cologne. My man smelled good.

I should've been basking smack dab in the middle of enjoying a romantic moment, but I was preoccupied by my relentless, unwanted "fan"—Rico. I had recorded his last escapade onto a DVD and was pondering how I could use it to clear a way out of the dense forest. What I'd done in the dark couldn't come to light. I was determined to take the bull by the horns and wrestle it to the arena ground. Innocence was thinking for Leslie, the woman with no game and the plain Jane logic. No matter how crazy things got, Innocence was the captain driving Leslie's ship, and that kept me able to lie and deceive with a straight face. Call me Sybil, but I never really realized one half of my personality was causing trouble for the other, but it was and would prove to deliver too much unforeseen damage and drama. Looking back, I can't even count the times it did during my engagement.

"Sometimes you can love someone so much, the words don't want to come out right," Trey said. "You know I'm not one to say certain things often, but I'll try. Let's figure out what we keep doing wrong. I don't want to go back to being strangers—I need to pride myself in listening to you, Les. I wanna make up. I wanna be a strong man who can be good to you. I wanna make you the happiest woman you can be. I'm sorry for what things have been like over the last few weeks. I'm also sorry for not putting you first. I'm sorry I messed up your birthday surprise for me. It wasn't right for me to spend it with my family, then my boys all night—that was poor judgment on my part. All I can tell you is I know what it feels like to really love someone and my feelings couldn't be any stronger than they are right now. I know it seems as though I'm my family's yes man, but as the only boy, I am the only help they have."

"Don't touch me. Just don't—get off of me, Trey!" I ran away with tears in my eyes as a nauseous feeling hit my stomach. I suddenly felt dirty from being intimate with so many strangers.

"You okay?" Trey asked as I leaned over the toilet bowl.

"Yeah, I lied. Why wouldn't I be?"

"I know I haven't been paying you much attention. You look sick, Les. What's up?"

Unable to speak further, I threw up again. Although I explained it was probably something I ate, Trey insisted on driving me to the hospital. After hours of throwing up, my energy level was shot. My bangs were wet and stuck to my forehead. I felt like I was on my way out. Trey stuck up for me and put his foot down at the hospital. What started out as a three hour wait was reduced to thirty minutes. Trey was taking care of me like a good, strong man would. He was there when I needed him and that counted for so much.

I registered in the hospital, then we waited some more in the back. About ten minutes later, a tall white man came in asking me about my symptoms, what I ate, how I'd been feeling, and if I was under any stress. Before long I was wearing a paper gown, having blood drawn, peeing in small containers, and awaiting test results. Several hours passed and I dozed off somewhere along the way. When I heard footsteps enter the room, my eyes opened. The doctor had returned.

"What is it? What's wrong with my baby?" Trey asked with sincere concern. His eyes were glossy.

"Well, it seems that your baby is having a baby."

"What?" he replied, raising his eyebrows.

"You're going to be parents." The doctor said, smiling.

Trey was elated—I wasn't. I knew the baby wasn't his. He hadn't even thought about it. As little as we made love, he should have known better. Instead, my super duped fiancé was doing some new daddy jig around the room, pumping his fist in the air.

"Aren't you happy?" he asked.

"Why should I be? What a disaster! We didn't plan this."

"I know we didn't plan to have a child so soon but this news can't be anything other than a blessing from God. There are couples who try to get pregnant and can't. Stop being so irritable. We're having a baby!" Trey exclaimed, sounding bubbly and cheerful.

I began setting Trey up without his knowledge. "How's your family going to take this? We're not married yet. Your family won't approve of a bastard child."

"Les, don't say that. Don't ruin this moment."

"It's true. They already hate me, and they'll hate *my* baby. They'll see me as one who forced you into fatherhood under the wrong circumstances. It'll be obvious we had sex before getting married when the baby is born so soon. You know they'll start counting the months." I crossed my arms like I was in the midst of starting a tantrum.

"What are you saying? You're talking crazy. We're talking about a human life here. They'll all love our baby, even if we obviously had a slip up. If you're having a baby, it was meant to be, Les. Just let it be."

After I calmed down the nurse returned with my release papers and some instructions for taking it easy. We walked toward the exit of the hospital. When we reached the car, Trey dropped his head in my lap.

"I know we've been having problems, but it will all work out. We're just both under a lot of pressure, that's all. Come on Les, hang in there with me. I need you . . . and my baby. You know I'll be with you, every step of the way."

I didn't respond. I knew the baby I was carrying was Rico's because he and I hadn't used protection on several occasions since my last cycle. It had been a long day. I just wanted to go home and sleep off a monster headache. I tried to reorganize my thoughts five hundred times, but I kept drawing a blank. In fact, that's all there was to do.

In a few short hours, Trey had changed for the better. He was waiting on me hand and foot, tending to my every need, and was even spoon feeding me soup. All the while, he kept reminding me how I had to make it a point to watch salt and fat intake in my diet. I was finally coming first in his life and liked how that felt. I rested as I paid attention to what Trey was into. I was just beginning to drift off when I heard a door shut. After that, I heard two of the most familiar males I knew engaged in a conversation.

"Did you find out what's ailing the wifey?" Rico said in a sensitive voice.

"Well, Rico . . . you're going to be an uncle."

"What? No shit, man? You're really settling down, Trey. We had some wild times together. So you've officially turned in your player's card to have a family, man. How about that shit! Congratulations to you and the queen, hermano! Can I see the proud momma?"

"Let me make sure she's decent," I heard Trey comment. "Come on in," he said.

"I heard the good news, Leslie. This calls for a celebration," Rico told me as he walked in appearing jovial. "I feel like I should've bought some cigars or champagne through the door—now I regret coming over empty handed."

"I might be able to round up a few cigars," Trey said.

"Rico, it's twelve minutes before one o'clock in the morning. What in the hell are you doing here at this hour?" I asked, ignoring his feigned elation.

"Trey didn't tell you? I'm your new neighbor. I bought the house next door. I saw the light on and came on over."

"Don't pay her any mind, bro. Come over whenever you feel moved to make an appearance. I haven't had a chance to tell her. I'll be back. I'm going to find something to celebrate two great things."

Rico walked toward me with an, I'm-going-to-chill-with-ya'll look on his face. I gulped.

"Get out of my face! Why are you trying to take everything away from me?" I hissed, gritting my teeth.

"So now you're trying to keep the peace at home, Leslie?" he asked, ignoring me.

"What? Why don't you get the hell out of my face! My feet are still sore after the mess you pulled."

"You want me to rub them for you?" he asked, grinning. I spit on him but he just laughed.

"I saw you and my boy acting all lovey dovey with the slow dance," he said sourly, wiping his face.

I looked puzzled wondering how he knew Trey and I had shared special moments. Even though Rico's new house was surrounded by acreage which allowed for some privacy, it was hardly enough. Maybe I could convince Trey to move in my house when we got married, instead of our original plan.

"Some loyalty you have after you've been sucking my balls. If I don't watch you closely, you'll be giving away my kisses to my boy again. We have one little lover's quarrel and you go and turn your back on me and lay up in bed at his place? If I didn't know better, I'd say you are reconsidering a monogamous relationship with Trey, not Rico."

"Stop this madness and show some respect. As you can see, I'm out of commission now. I'm under the covers to prove it. I'm on a tea and crackers diet because I can't hold down food."

"Not exactly. Who said pregnant women don't crave sex? In the second trimester of pregnancy women seem to really get horny. How do you think you got pregnant in the first place? I think we can safely say that I'll be a big help to this family. After all, you and I both know you're carrying my seed. Trey's out. I'm in. Move next door and break the engagement. Now you have every reason to get with me honestly and openly. Until then, I can show up on your future doorstep anytime I want. Now I don't have to take a number and wait around. I've got a baby in your belly to prove you're using Trey, and that you truly prefer the backstabbing rude boy over Mr. Manners. We're two freaky whores who were made for each other. You're the female version of dirty ass Rico. *I* own the pussy, Leslie. When you were screaming my name, I made sure I busted a nut up in what now belongs to me. At least you can be confident the baby will come out halfway good looking. If it's a boy, I'll be the one to teach him how to play baseball. If it's a girl, I'll teach her how to salsa dance someday. I'm a much better dancer than Trey. By my standards, he has two left feet. If only you would give me a chance, I'll prove Rico is all the man you really need, in every way."

"I can't stand another day of this, or of you! You're *sick*," I spat emphatically.

"Maybe so, but I know I'm right. If you're willing to tell the truth, be my guest. I know I will never feel the need to." Rico paused. He reached over and rubbed my belly.

"So, will you name the little seed Rico or Trey?" he asked.

I smacked him across the face.

"I have a funny feeling you haven't quite decided, although it's going to come out looking like me," he replied, massaging his reddening skin. "Here's a perfect example of why whores like you need to tighten up your game by getting on the pill, or being responsible and wrapping it up every time. No harm done though—I love children. If you're wondering how I knew that my wife-to-be was cheating on me with someone else, it's because I know women. When the cat is away, the mouse will play. Rico has been watching your every move through a telescope ever since he moved next door. It's been real entertaining watching you from my bedroom window. Sometimes it turns me on, while other times it makes me mad that you haven't made that change you need to make. For future reference, try being a little more modest. No more walking around nude in Trey's spot, especially if you plan on leaving the curtains open now that you're knocked up by me. I know how much you enjoy being a whore, but it's no longer appropriate to show Trey and these other men out here what's between the legs I own. When the phone rings, you better break your neck getting to it. When Trey goes to sleep, I'll expect my nightly piece of the action."

"I think you should leave, Rico!"

Trey returned to the room with two stogies. One was already hanging out of his mouth, unlit. Rico grinned as he grabbed his and they exited the bedroom to smoke them outside. Recalling how Rico ribbed Trey was like being stuck in traffic and not being able to move. I hated our best man and wanted to expose his evil ways, but there was nothing I could say or do because technically he had Leslie on blackmail lock. Everything I wanted was unfolding with the wrong man. Right then I planned to have an abortion and pretend that a miscarriage was the cause for me not giving birth.

After Rico left, Trey called everyone he knew until three

o'clock in the morning to tell them the big news. My heart sank for him as he ran up his long distance bill. Obviously I'd stepped on a grenade by not having safe sex while cheating with the enemy. Rico was right. He didn't trap me into motherhood. I brought that on myself. Now I would suffer the consequences of getting off unprotected.

It was time for me to put my foot down with my lover, my stalker, and my baby's wicked daddy. I was tired of bracing for more stressful days ahead. I had to make a major move and do something—maybe even an intense smear campaign. Innocence had officially been pushed to the edge of her sanity.

15

The Big Twist

I'd been sick in bed and couldn't seem to encourage my limbs to move or wake up my body, nor did I feel like beginning a new day. I was so sick when I woke up that I couldn't read the alarm clock. I held my head up and looked around my bed. Everything was blurry, even after I put my glasses on my face. I felt nauseous and that gave me a clue that my vision had nothing to do with the matter. It was definitely my pregnancy that was making me feel badly.

There was a lot of work to be done and Trey stepped up to the plate. He started remembering to pay attention to what I said and treated my words as if they were sacred. With me not feeling well, I could only do so much on schedule. My body seemed to have a mind of its own, but there was nothing I could do about it except pass the torch of wedding errands over to my future other half.

It was Trey who met with the minister to discuss the service, sent in my change-of-address information to the post office, picked up the wedding programs, and delivered the final deposits. All of the girlie duties fell in his lap, but he didn't complain even once. Who would've guessed he would hang in there like a super duper trooper and not get wrapped up in woman's work stereotypes?

Since Trey seemed to really open up his heart, we started doing everything together, and my fiancé gave me the best of everything. He started coming straight home from work, and even started cooking dinner and doing the laundry. Freshly cut flowers sat in a vase, and he started to remind me how loved I was as often as he could. Trey's sense of humor came back and he even began telling me jokes. I discovered he was hysterically funny. Fatherhood was changing Trey, but I wasn't assured that his actions were real. I couldn't buy into any of it since I didn't plan on being preggers for long. Plus, it was only days before the wedding. I still hadn't brought up the issue of trying to convince Trey to move in with me. Peace was a nice change of pace. At that time, I didn't feel like rocking the boat anymore.

After I peeled myself out of bed one early afternoon, I checked my to do list since there were a few things I had to handle solo. I had to give a list of "important shots" to our wedding photographer. I'd heard too many horror stories about so-called professional photographers who should've known when to take what, so I wanted to remind the brother that I meant business. If I didn't get what I wanted, I'd put a stop on the final check payment. I also had to book my hair-stylist and makeup artist. Meeting with both of the flaming gay men to experiment with styles and colors included a dry run by doing my hair and making up my face. Like I said, I wanted my day to be as perfect as it could be with no undue surprises. My last issue was—ahem—scheduling a much-needed abortion appointment.

I forced myself to dress and was about to grab my keys when I heard my fax machine sound. It was an undesired love note from Rico. The "fan mail" was unsigned of course, but I knew who would make me regret that my number was un-listed, and it wasn't Tanya the hot fot. I hadn't heard from her in some time. Given her angry state of mind, I expected any-thing . . .

Something told me to check my email, so I did just that. After I logged online, I found out my email box was full with hate mail—sixty messages reminding me that Rico was watching me and following his "future wife." I decided to put dealing with my stalker at the top of my list. It was time to go toe-to-toe with him, or better yet, cut off his whole foot.

I looked up the bar associations code of professional con-duct to get my juices flowing. I typed *lawyer's standard of moral conduct* into the search engine box. The results yielded a link, displaying a headline that read: KANSAS SUPREME COURT RULES FOR DISCIPLINING ATTORNEYS.

A lawyer's conduct should always conform to specific legal standards of the law, both in serving clients professionally and when engaged in business and personal affairs. A lawyer should utilize the law's procedures only for legitimate pur-poses and not to harass or intimidate others. A lawyer should exhibit respect for the legal system and for those who serve it, including judges, other lawyers and public officials. It is a lawyer's duty to challenge the rectitude of official action, but it is also to properly uphold the legal process.

After reading that legal mumbo jumbo I got a hell of an idea—mail the DVD I'd made to the Maryland Bar Associa-tion with a letter explaining that Rico was harassing me and also appear blameless by not signing my name. Since I had some technical skills working for me, I'd been able to edit and splice in the scene where Rico made me beg on my knees for the cops not to have sex with me any longer as well as him enjoying getting vertical with a transsexual.

I found the link for the Maryland Bar Association, clicked on the "contact us" button, and up popped the address and phone number. That piece of information was all I needed to get a stinking pot of shit brewing. To add insult to injury, I looked up the magistrate judges in Maryland then printed off the names of the Southern, Northern, and Eastern Division. Now, Rico would play my way, or all of his colleagues would know what sort of sick man was supposedly upholding the law. I placed a call to him to start reporting my findings, little by little.

"Would you prefer to be reprimanded, suspended, or disbarred? Take your pick, but make it quick," I said casually.

"What are you talking about?"

"The big twist. You know, community service, cleaning parks, jail time, fines, getting in an unemployment line. I'm talking about your future. Aren't you listening, Rico?" He remained silent but I knew he was listening. "You don't have me wrapped around your finger, and you haven't been thinking about *us*. You've been thinking of yourself, and I thought now would be the ideal time to let you know what I've decided. I'm sorry if I'm offending you but this is just the way it is. I could always tack on filing a petition in District Court for a peace order. It would be good for six months. I do my homework. Swing, batter, batter, swing! One point for Leslie."

"It sounds like your hormones are out of whack, so I'll overlook the trash talking you're doing. You're being so vague you're not really saying anything of concern to me," Rico explained.

"Let's clarify things: cooperate or I'm moving forward with my plans to ruin you. You're acting too big for your pants, but what you need to do is delete any pictures from your phone, email, stored, printed, or even filed away in your memory bank. I'm not changing the locks, installing a security system, or making my number public. If you love your career as much as I think you do you'll now play this game my way. If you don't believe I'm prepared to take your life in a new direction, ask me where I am. This is not a threat; it's just a simple request," I said, throwing some of Rico's previous comments back at him.

"If I were to entertain your trash talk, just where would you be?"

"I'm standing over a post office box off of Firehouse Road in Landover, prepared to drop your life inside of it."

"And?"

"And it's all love, papi. Get your ass over here. It's time to watch *my* moves. You were never supposed to be the headline act, only the side dish. How many ways can I tell you to cool your heels and stay the fuck away from me?"

"Nonsense. I was never the appetizer. Rico is always the main course."

"Whatever. The clock is ticking. Fifteen minutes is all you have to get over here and engage in a little mediation session. I'm being generous in case you hit traffic but don't drag your big old feet. Bring every spec of dirt you have on me, even the microscopic pieces, or I will get busy with my master plan."

Click. I flipped the script and waited in the car until I saw his beamer pull up. Once he parked, I stood outside in front of the mailbox so the whole world could watch my back.

"Pictures please," I said, grinning and holding the DVD that was encased in a manila colored padded envelope.

"Package!" Rico yelled, sounding like an immature child.

""Pictures!" I repeated. "You don't even know what I'm holding. It may be something to worry about. Then again, it may be nothing at all," I taunted.

"Package!" he yelled, wrinkling his face. "I want to see what's in there. Give it to me!" he commanded.

"Nothing for nothing equals nothing, Rico. You first," I commanded. "You have ten seconds to hand over what I asked for or else you can kiss your legal career adios, amigo." I began to count as I tapped my foot impatiently. "Ten . . . nine . . . eight . . . seven . . . six . . . five . . . four . . . three . . . two . . . one. It's time to cook a Latin and black goose." I turned to drop the envelope into the postal drop box.

"You led me on so don't hold a grudge. Be sympathetic," Rico said, attempting to snatch the DVD from my fingertips.

I tried to dodge him by swinging my arm high in the air but it did no good. Rico managed to confiscate my booty.

"You're in the heat of a battle. This is war and you're going down, down, down under the ground!" I told him, gritting my teeth and widening my eyes. I bit Rico, kicked him in the balls, then let out a glass-shattering scream as I grabbed the package and ran backward with it under my armpit.

Rico's cell phone dropped from his pocket. I knew at least some of the pictures were stored in it, so I lunged forward to snatch it from his reach. I guessed that I could also copy all of the contacts in his phone book. Two tough looking thugs dressed in wife beaters came running to my aid, but Rico managed to limp away like a dog with his tail between his legs. I finally opened the mailbox door and dropped the envelope in it. I was free to finish running my errands. No more whining, no more complaining, no more pressure-filled episodes of Rico acting needy or insecure. Either way the door swung, I had a back-up plan and sent more than one DVD through the U.S. Postal system. A smart whore like Innocence never put all her eggs in one basket. Someone close to Rico would receive a report of his extracurricular activities very soon.

16

A Big Pack Of Lies

"Tanya, I didn't know who else to call," I said, speaking to her answering machine. "I know you probably hate me right now, but I'm laid up in the hospital, all by myself. I just had an emergency hysterectomy. Can you believe it, no kids? I can't have kids." I started crying. I paused for a moment before adding a few more details to my pack of lies. "I can't tell Trey about the ovarian cancer. It would crush him right before the wedding." I paused again, long enough to interject a few sniffles before going in for the kill. "Look, Tanya, we're girls so I just wanted you to know I would never ever hurt you or the kids. I was just angry, and I never called anyone on you about those kids. I'm scared, Tanya. Real scared. We go way back, girl. You're the first person I told when I got my period back in junior high school, and just because we're not speaking doesn't mean I don't love you. I miss you, girl and I was wrong for laying a finger on Rico. After looking deep into my heart and soul, I think it was just wedding pressure jitters, you know. I'm not perfect, just forgiven. Well, actually, the reason I pulled that ignorant stunt about your kids was because I was jealous. Yes, I said it, *jealous*. I found out my ovaries weren't healthy earlier that week and hid the bad news from everyone. The GYN said they would have to go, and I was angry and in denial. Please call me back if you can ever find it in your heart to forgive me. I'm so alone. I know I deserve this but I could die. I don't want to think of leaving this great big lemon drop without setting the record straight with my ace boon coon. I've got to go now. Love you, sweetie. Take care."

After I hung up, I laid back and waited. There's a sucker born every day, and it was Tanya's birthday. The phone rang about an hour later.

"Leslie?" It was Tanya.

"Oh, you called. I didn't think you would."

"You had a hysterectomy? There was no way to save you're uterus? How unusual, Leslie—you're so young," she commented, sounding concerned.

"I don't want to talk about what happened. It's over now."

"I am pissed as hell over everything you did, but my Christian heart won't allow me not to ask if there's anything I can do."

"I can't bother you after how I behaved. I'll make out."

"Do you need something?"

"Truthfully?"

"Yes, truthfully."

"I do need a hand to hold. I'm really scared, Tanya. I'm still bleeding, and I'm afraid that anything could happen to me. Who knows—tomorrow's not promised to anyone," I said somberly.

"I'm coming to the hospital. Where are you?"

"I can't face you right now. I just wanted to say I'm sorry. I've said too much already." I resumed crying. "Kiss the kids. I'll never have any! I can't be a mother, Tanya. God cursed my body, for good reason I suppose."

"No, no, no! Don't say those things."

"It's true. I'm barren. This will have future implications—

no man wants a woman who can't have his child. Now I'm going to get stood up at the altar. I was lucky to find a man in the D.C. area. You know how hard it is to find a good man since there's at least eight times more of us than there is of them. Now look what happens. There goes my hopes of marrying Trey!" I exclaimed.

"I'm sorry you found out this bad news about your health and everything, but no matter how long we've been friends, I can't forget that you repeatedly slept with my man. Since I don't have anything nice to say, it's best that I stop here," Tanya explained.

"I'm all alone in this world now. Should I take these pills or use this blade? I'm not sure how I'll do it but I'm going to kill myself. My life's a mess and there's nothing worth living for. Don't get me wrong, I accept full responsibility for my actions. I made this hard bed, so now I've got to sleep in it. I better go. I have some decisions to make. Goodbye my friend," I said.

"Wait! Where are you? Suicide is not the answer. I'm angry at you but that doesn't mean that—"

"It has to be. I'm no more good," I said, cutting off Tanya. "You take Trey. You deserve him just like you said. Be happy together and take good care of each other," I said. I sucked in a breath, sounding dramatic, but struggling hard to keep from laughing.

"Where are you?"

"Going to hell."

"Answer me. Talk to me straight," Tanya insisted.

"I'm at my place. I was just released from Washington Hospital for Women. I'm going to slit my wrist. The pain I feel is just too deep. I lost you, now I'm about to lose Trey." Click.

I hung up abruptly with high hopes that Tanya would be roped back into my world. The thing is that after my abortion, I needed some help around the house. I was bleeding, but not for the reasons I said. I had to think up an entirely different version to tell Trey.

"Trey, I hate to bother you at work. I know you're busy."

"What's up, Les?"

"I hate to be the bearer of bad news but I—I . . . sort of had an accident," I announced in a choppy rhythm.

"What!"

"Yep."

"Are you okay? What happened?"

"Sort of. It all depends on your definition of okay. I just got home and I'm trying to calm down and settle my nerves. I just need some peace right now."

"Talk to me, baby. What happened?"

"You know how sometimes in life you think you have it all. Just when you're happy and feeling good about things—bam. Something was happening to me, and it was that one thing I didn't see coming."

"Why won't you just tell me and stop dragging it out!"

"I want to Trey. It's not that I don't want to tell you. It's just that what unfolded is a little bit awkward. No one ever said life was easy, so why should I have expected a fairytale leading up to the wedding?" I rambled. "Do you love me? I mean love me like I'm irreplaceable and our bond is unbreakable?"

"Of course I love you like that, girl. What kind of question is that? I wish you would tell me what is going on. I'm getting tired of talking in circles."

"You may not love me after I tell you the news."

"You can tell me anything. What is it?"

"Two days ago, I fell down the steps, Trey."

"What!"

"I know. I know. I got dizzy and fell down the steps. I really think I blacked out. Everything went dark. The next thing I knew I was dragging over to the phone to call 911. I was rushed to the hospital and everything," I lied.

"Why didn't you call me?"

"I didn't think it was that serious, and I didn't want to bother you. You know I'm not a selfish drama queen."

"Nonsense—you should've called to let me know what was going on. This was a bonafide emergency."

"You're always so busy. I didn't want to ruin your day over something small."

"Our wedding is in just four days. You're almost my wife. What are you saying?" Trey asked, sounding annoyed.

"I'm saying that I didn't think it was a big deal."

"But are you okay?"

"I'm still sore for the DNC procedure. Other than that, a few scrapes and bruises from what I've noticed so far."

"And the baby?" he asked. I remained quiet. He asked me again. "And the baby?"

"I had a miscarriage," I told him softly. "Honey, did you hear me? I said I had a DNC procedure. To put it nicely, that means I had to get some internal things tended to after the doctors discovered the fetus wasn't living."

Trey broke down crying in a way I never imagined. I could feel the hurt pouring from his heart. "Why? Why is this happening to me? No! No!" he shouted between sobs.

"I know this really sucks. I really wanted the baby, too. Well, not at first, but after you showed me that our child is, I mean, was a blessing from God. The bottom line is that I was getting attached to it already," I said, pretending to feel sad. I shifted the conversation with a smooth transition to set Trey up not to come see me. "Tanya put her differences aside to come help me. I'm not up to talking much right now. Go get a beer and catch up with Rico and your crew after work. They're like family to you and getting out may do you some good. Don't try to see me right now because I'm not emotionally equipped to face you. Had I not pushed myself and stayed in bed, this never would've happened. I'll call you later. I'm so sorry. Perhaps we can try to get pregnant again later. I guess this wasn't mean to be—everything happens for a reason. I better go for now." Click.

I hung up the phone letting that cruel pack of lies fall in my man's lap.

I heard Tanya turn into my driveway. While she was parking her car, I poured a bottle of pills all over the kitchen table, then scattered them around. I let Tanya bang on the door while I took the time to set the stage for my acting debut. I also decided that every now and then, I would hold my stomach and wince in pain.

When I unlocked the door, I put on a pathetic face and stood at a slight angle. I was breathing hard from running around so quickly that it added to the credibility of my performance. "I'm sorry it took me so long to get to the door. I have to walk very slowly. Please, Tanya, not a word to Trey. He can't know I had this surgery. Swear you won't tell or I don't want you to see me right now."

"I swear I won't mention a thing," she answered as she walked into the house. "You're winded. Come on now. Let me help you get off your feet," she said, gently grabbing my arm and leading me to the couch.

"I'm going to get you a sheet and pillow so you can lay down while we talk about some things. I'm taking off for a few days and I don't want to hear a word about it. You're wedding is in a few days and we've got to get you well enough to walk down that aisle."

"I can't let you be good to me—not in light of my behavior, Tanya. Just leave. Maybe you being here will be too awkward for both of us. I can't even look you in the eye."

"Let's just forget what happened. In fact, the only way I can deal with it is by not ever talking about it again. Blood is thicker than water, and we're almost blood. A man is not worth losing a friendship. That's what they say, right?"

"Yes. I know you're still pissed though."

"Like I said, we don't need to talk about that right now," Tanya explained.

After she made me more than comfortable, including fetching my slippers like an obedient dog, she ended up begging to be my maid of honor.

Tanya showed up with an overnight bag, and I intended on her staying as long as she could. Just as I'd hoped, the midget shrimp waited on me hand and foot all week, and even stressed herself out with my wedding shit while I got my strength back and slept the day away. I listened to the birds sing and slept while she scrubbed my toilet, cooked me breakfast, and played praise CDs to lift my spirits and ease my pain. Tanya placed her hand on my head and prayed for me to lose the suicide demon, wasting her precious vacation days, and leaving her children with someone she had to pay. Dumb, gullible biyotch!

On day one of her stay, I sent Tanya to the store to get some super-sized maxi pads for my bleeding. While she was out and about, I placed a call to Rico.

"You've been officially relieved of your duties," I said just after he answered. "You are no longer my baby daddy. When you show up for wedding rehearsal, you better act like you have some sense, because I'm in love with Trey, *not* you. Wake up and smell the coffee. I had an abortion. Trey and I have come too far, and you're not going to wreck our future."

Trey's mother showed up with church members, the day after my talk with him. They all came bearing gifts, casseroles, fruit, pies, and holding helium balloons with get well messages written all over them. Mabel began treating me like a human being and apologized profusely for the loss of my first child, three days before my wedding. I scammed everyone with my pack of lies. My alter ego Innocence was unleashing her merciless wrath. Mild-mannered Leslie, who was often mistreated and unsatisfied, was buried deep within. Innocence was having everything handed to her on a silver platter . . . and I was beginning to like doing things her way.

17

The Sister From Hell

"Who are you? Her maid?" I heard someone say.
I'd know that voice anywhere. It belonged to my sister from hell. Although she was part devil, her horns seemed to have fallen off when she was born. She didn't have me fooled though. I always knew what she was and why.

"Maid? No, I'm her sister in the Lord," Tanya replied, standing at the front door. "How cute. I love it. I realize you may have mistaken me for Mariah Carey, but

I'm Angela, Leslie's big sister. Same mother, same father. I got the good genes, and she got whatever was left over. Why am I telling you this? That part's obvious."

"Confidentially, she just had a hysterectomy. She needs to rest," Tanya explained. She didn't bother to tell Angela she'd known me since junior high school.

"Please! She's always been one to exaggerate. She'll be fine. She has nerves of steel and the stamina of a workhorse. She can borrow one of my children—no big deal. Kidding!" Angela said, swinging her hair. "Aren't you going to invite me in?"

I sat on a couch in the background watching Angela.

Tanya replied, "Well, I don't know if . . ."

"Anyway, she can stand to open her doors early for her family," Angela commented, nearly pushing Tanya out of the way. "We lost contact and haven't seen her in years. I did a Google search and up popped her address and phone number. I can imagine she's dying to see me. Our parents will be along a bit later," she explained. I sighed and shook my head as I continued spying. "I'm on my fifth marriage. I have nine years of marriage under my belt—husband number one was an IBM executive, some years ago. If I could survive life with *that* man, anybody else would be like a bed of roses. Weddings are no big deal to me. I just wanted to see who was foolish enough to hook up with Tar Baby. Plus, hopping a plane was no big deal. We have a lot of projects going on at our home in L.A.: a broken water pump that's being fixed, an Italian bedroom, yada, yada, yada." She removed a bottle of Airwick air freshener from a bag and began spraying it around the room. I began to cough from the fumes, so I stood up, trying to find another place to sit.

When Angela spotted me her face lit up with a phony smile. She shoved the spray back in the bag and headed in my direction. "Kissy, kissy," she said, taking her index finger, kissing it, and then placing it on my face. Her sick idea of affection caused my face to wrinkle. "Aren't you going to speak to your big sister?" she asked.

"Hi," I replied dryly.

"You haven't been up for more than ten minutes and forty three seconds. I can tell by the sound of your voice. Ever since you were a little tot it would get that scratchy sound in it. It sort of reminded me of someone running nails across a chalkboard. It fits your appearance though. I see nothing major has changed about Leslie."

From that point on, my *sister* never shut her fat mouth. She hadn't changed either. She was just like the Energizer

Bunny—her trap kept going and going and going, something like diarrhea of the mouth.

"One of mom's friends spotted your marriage announcement in some local D.C. paper then gave her a call. After that, she read it. You made the paper, okay, so now you're a little above average. Mom and I have a running bet. I said your wedding was running two thousand five hundred dollars and fifty-six cents, or lower. Am I right? At this rate, by the time you're sixty you will just scrape the roof of the poverty level," Angela chuckled.

Six pieces of luggage were being hauled in while she talked. A nanny carrying a small dog in a cage came in, followed by who I assumed were her three children. Behind them were her hairdresser and chef, piling in my crib. I was speechless to say the least.

"Is this a makeshift shelter, or is this where you really live?" she asked haughtily. "Do you rent or own?" she asked, looking around.

"Own," I answered with brevity.

"I see you didn't spring for the quality carpet. My toddler won't be crawling on this steel wool pad. She's used to hardwood floors—even linoleum won't do. Where's the love, in the room? Could you treat your guest with a little hospitality and pay the cab drivers?"

I shot her a look. Her presence wasn't going to work. She wasn't invited. *They* weren't invited. "I don't want her here," I whispered to Tanya.

"Don't worry about it. Be the bigger person. I'll pay the driver," Tanya whispered back. She disappeared to find her purse. Moments later she flew out the door to pay two cabs. When the door opened the two older kids nearly knocked Tanya down. They ran outside, but the toddler stayed in the house, trying to keep up with his loquacious mother.

Angela found the bathroom and peeked inside of it.

"Change the toilet seat. That thing has got to go! I don't want to leave here with pimples on my butt," she complained to the nanny. "A home you can see from the street spells c-h-e-a-p. Maybe it's time for a career change. You know, something with a 401K, and actually pays you enough not to live like a pauper." She waved her designer watch in my face, just to tantalize me.

"I have a 401K, Angela."

"And what is it that you do again?"

"I'm a teacher, Angela," I said dryly.

"Oh, right. I guess you do have a point. I'm sure this is the best you can do. I'm a television host on the highest rated morning show in L.A." She nodded her head up and down with affirmation. "You should be incredibly grateful. I didn't imagine that you were doing even this well. Your abode is *cute* . . . for you. I imagine it keeps you good and humble."

Angela sauntered past me into the kitchen. "Do you have soy milk, dear? The baby needs it so she'll have strong bones and teeth when she grows up. We don't want a snaggle-toothed child like you were. Beauty solutions start early. Where's your nearest Fresh Fields? We only eat organic foods. We're a health conscious family. Living in L.A. forces you to keep up with your peers unlike the D.C. hogs who I see roaming around in your zip code. It's all about sensible eating. I don't understand why these porkers can't stay committed to losing weight. Then again, they'll never be on TV for anything prestigious, so they don't have to worry about how huge the camera would make them look."

"I do drink soy milk, but I'm out of it right now, Angela. Had I known you were coming, I would've had a room full of the shit," I snapped, ignoring her bragging tirade about her big time job. My patience was beginning to wear thin, especially since I truly was recovering from losing a great deal of blood.

"While I was on the plane I jotted down a few small things

I'll need for me and my family. It's not much. Bottled water—where's your bottled water? I don't drink a drop from the faucet." Before I could mange to reply she began opening cabinets. "No substitutions. It must be Perrier or nothing at all. Unlike your body, my body knows the difference. Well, a trip to the store will be necessary anyway. I can wait since I'm not hard to please. I try not to be a pest whenever I'm a houseguest."

"Says who?" I mumbled under my breath.

"Here's a list of our visiting requirements, in order of importance." She handed them to me. Angela: A CD player with earphones so I can play my relaxation tapes while I put cucumbers on my eyes in the evenings before retiring. And of course, low lighting. Two satin pillow cases so my hair will stay nice and fresh. The nanny should use my own sheets, pillowcases, and towels. During meal time, the chef should use my own pots. Please remove your own items and get them out of the way.

"For my husband who will be joining us later: A fifth of whisky, a fifth of vodka (Grey Goose or Belvedere will do) and three bottles of Merlot, in the event he is not successful in finding a liquor store. He's out right now looking and refuses to go to a treatment center, and that's just the way it is. Children: Organic chicken strips, soy milk, and Fig Newtons. No candy please. For my dog Miss Lady: Since I'm sure you don't own a set of china, one of your best bowls will be needed for her meals. She eats at the kitchen table to ensure her blood glucose levels are controlled. No table scraps! Lastly, my list ends with a note to myself to ask Leslie where I can hook up my fax machine and PDA.

"Um, Angela. You may want to remember your sister needs rest. She's coming along, but she does need to take it easy," Tanya said diplomatically.

Angela ignored her comment. "Tell me, Leslie, who is this mystery man anyway? Can he afford to take care of the one he *thinks* he loves? I want his name, and I want his personal address. I know you better than anyone, and I need to have a talk with the future head of this household. Oh, never mind. I forgot that I'm going back to my old high school to see if I can have a press conference," she joked. "But really, these hands need help! Where's the nearest upscale day spa?"

I ignored her and walked to the window. That's when I noticed one of her children alternating between kicking my car bumper and trying to pull it off.

"I want a smoothie! I want a smoothie!" yelled the little girl.

The boy crawled underneath the car in the dirt and began pulling on the pipes. I yelled out of the window for them to stop. I was two seconds away from cussing their spoiled asses out, but I was interrupted.

"They're just children. Don't be so mean, Auntie Leslie," Angela told me, sitting down on the couch. Her hairdresser began fixing her hair and set up a curling stove in my living room. Once the man had curled only one piece, vain Angela was already tugging at it and patting her hair.

"I wouldn't have some hair disaster on my big day. I need to test this hairdo out now while I have time to change my mind if it's not to my liking. Come here," she said. I walked toward her. "Bend down. I'm getting my hair done. I can't reach like that." I bent down. Angela began running her hands through my hair. She was obviously checking for tracks or extensions. "Wig, InstaWeave, what? You never had hair. You know it doesn't grow. I could cut my hair off three times, let it grow back, and you still wouldn't have much to pinch!"

"I let it grow out, Angela," I snapped, standing upright.

"Doesn't the way you look just make you want to run and hide? This is the skin you want, soft and smooth. I feel like I can say this because you're my sister. Splotches are not cute. Since you obviously weren't using a personal trainer, I can assume you'll be retouching your wedding photos to do something with those thunder thighs of yours. Maybe he can lighten you up while he's at it. Our maid of honor wants you to look your best. I mean, a photographer can't work miracles, but a little hope is in store for you. At least you appear to be one step above Aunt Jemima."

I felt Innocence preparing to break Leslie out of her polite shell. In fact, she was getting warmed up.

"What do you think this is, the *Live Like a Star* show? Who are you to come in my home and take over? This is not funny. Cool it, you L.A. faker! That is my maid of honor standing over there, and you will not be setting foot anywhere around me on my big day."

Angela rose to her feet and looked into my eyes. The hairdresser tapped her on the small of her back and she sat back down. The hairdresser took a section and resumed curling her locks.

"Where is your compassion? Where is your ability to be a hostess?" she asked. She just kept going and going, just like that Energizer bunny.

It was like a bad reality show. I couldn't stomach my sister's antics any longer. I don't know where the idea came from, but I put my cramps aside, walked down to my basement, grabbed a steel pail, filled it with water, and let Innocence work her magic. I reentered the living room and stood about two inches from her face.

"I *said* shut uuuup! You're such an annoying, self-absorbed bitch!"

"How dare you talk to your big sister this way, Leslie." She patted her hair, feeling the freshly made curls.

I pushed the hairdresser out of the way and dumped a bucket of ice-cold water on her head.

"My hair! My hair! It's ruined," she screamed. Angela was so angry her knees, shoulders, and entire body began to shake. She parted her hair like a curtain and moved her long locks out of her face. "My Manolo Blanicks! Do you know how much these shoes cost? They're ruined!" she said, kicking out one of her feet to survey the damage to her expensive shoes. Angela's toddler was startled and crawled over to her. She began tugging on Angela, begging to be picked up. Angela was too consumed with her ruined hair and shoes to care.

"I listened to your mouth run for the last thirty minutes straight while I'm in pain. I will get some rest, and I will get rid of you. I will seal your children's mouths and hands with duct tape and tie your dog's legs together and feed him table scraps if you don't take you, your little rat on a leash, and your wanna be entourage out of here within five minutes flat! Try me—I am not that little wimp you used to pick on when we were kids. It's a new day and a damn new Leslie! I came out of the same hole you did. It would seem you could treat me right, if only for one damned day. I hated you when we were growing up, and I hate you now! You picked on me then and you're picking on me now! You always treated me like a farmhand. This is no contest!" I screamed at Angela.

"Well, what a malicious pack of lies," she replied, rising to her feet. "And you're scaring my baby," she said.

The little boy was screaming at the top of his lungs. By this time, he was blowing snot bubbles with his nose. The noise was making me even crankier than I was before.

"Lies my ass! Out—every last one of you—out!" I hollered, pointing at the door. "And as far as me dumping cold water on your head, Miss Angela, you should be thanking me—I started to boil it first!"

The bitch ignored me and continued wailing over her wet state. Tanya disappeared with a carton of eggs from my fridge. I guess egg hurling was her specialty. She held the carton steady as I hurled each one at my sister and her entourage. I hit the baby with one egg by accident. The nanny picked him up. He continued blowing those snot bubbles, looking over her shoulder at me. He waved his little arm in my direction like he wanted to hit me. They all scurried around faster, suddenly feeling an urgency to run toward the door and vacate my premises. As a result, Angela left her luggage, fax machine, and everything she'd lugged in behind. I slammed the door, leaving them to sit on the curb and wait on a cab that *she* or *they* would pay for.

Tanya and I fell out laughing like devilish teenagers. Obviously, we stole the horns from my sister from hell and enjoyed tormenting her. Although my sister blew my cover, Tanya never said anything about my telling her that everyone in my family was dead. After all, I had just lost my baby, or so she thought. She knew my emotions were fragile. There was no need to point out that I'd lied my ass off. It should've been obvious why I had stretched the truth a few millimeters.

If people wondered why I couldn't tell the truth they could've easily understood why Leslie became crazy Innocence, the attention whore, in light of my circumstances. My sister had always been the kind of person who could make someone break into jail. Unfortunately, I tore a few pages from Angela's book and proved to follow in her magnificent footsteps . . . in all of my filthy, devious, and psychotic glory.

18

Two Of A Kind

The heat was on, two days before my wedding. In dealing with my sister, I found my strength in wielding my blackmailing power. I excused Tanya by convincing her it would be best if she'd run a long list of miscellaneous errands. Plus, my strength was coming back good enough for me to tend to unfinished business that involved Rico.

After I powered on Rico's phone and examined it, I discovered all zeros were under the number section of Rico's phone book. No photos, no real contacts. The smart ass had removed his SIM Card where all of the info was stored. His ass let me believe I hit gold, but the phone I managed to grab was a mere decoy. As a result, I had to step up the plan to take extra precautions by dropping an identical spiel to what I told Rico in someone else's ear—the police chief.

I stripped someone's ability to be rigid and judgmental by giving them something scandalous to think about. I was in the frame of mind to get obstinate and indulge in tripping—of all people—at the police chief's expense. A free pass to be rotten had been dropped in my hand because I held an edited DVD of his men running a train on me. Of course I knew what to show and what to keep to myself. By my account each of the men were having a good time, at my expense. In fact, that part was true. As far as they knew, they were breaking the law by raping a citizen who didn't want to be treated like a piece of meat. I was taking a chance, but just because I was didn't mean I'd turn out to be the biggest loser.

All of Angela's talk about working in the media gave me a twisted, creative idea. I dressed conservatively, like a reporter on a mission to get a news story. I parked and went inside, insisting that I needed to see the chief about an important matter. He should've known a hot potato was about to drop in his lap . . . but he didn't.

"What's your name? Is Chief Morgan expecting you?" the receptionist asked.

"Of course he is." I flashed the phony press pass I made by cutting out a square and affixing it on a chain.

I walked right past her, and she called after me with that typical D.C. government attitude. I waved, thanked her, and ran down the hall. I knew she was paging security so I hurried my steps. I read the name on the door and busted through it like I owned the place. Saliva dripped from the corner of Chief Morgan's mouth, and a white powder donut sat on his desk on a paper towel. His stomach looked like a huge balloon as it moved up and down when he snored. The chief needed to be on a hunger strike, but he was obviously a steak and potatoes type of man, definitely not among the most fit.

"Chief Morgan!" I called sternly.

The chief's snoring ceased, and he looked all around him stunned—as if he were trying to figure out who had called his name. I awakened him while he was napping, reared back in his chair.

Before he could gather his faculties and respond, I ambushed him. "Sorry to interrupt your midday nap, but I'm itching to know one thing. How can you say you want to clean up your city, when those on the city's payroll are a part of the problem, not the solution? I think hard working taxpayers would like to know about the corruption that is plaguing the city of taxation without representation. You have two choices—underestimate me having the guts to send this to every media outlet by the end of the day, or talk about how you can make this go away by convincing me to forget what really happened. Can you really stand the negative publicity? How much do you really want to keep your job?"

"Do I know you?" he asked, trying to focus his eyes in a rush. "What are you talking about?" he asked, wiping drool from the left corner of his mouth.

"Maybe so, maybe not. Either way, you're in for a surprise or two. Do you have some time for a little drama? I know your constituents are always crying and hollering about something, but this is a legitimate concern. I know you're a wise person." I whipped out a portable DVD player and hooked it up. "Let me enlighten you and show you why I'm here and what my visit is all about," I explained.

Tension rose as we watched the DVD exposing the ugliness of his policeman. I watched the chief sigh and lean forward with shock. He looked as if a one hundred and twenty mile per hour wind had swept him up just as rising flood waters were closing in—clearly devastated as he watched what happened.

"If you tell me something good and cut a deal, you won't have to worry about hearing from me again and again. I would be willing to part with this copy and also the copies of copies, if you put me on the city's payroll somehow. If not, I can get this over to every media outlet so fast it will make your head spin. I've been to the sexual assault center at PG. Hospital and details of what occurred are already on record. If I decide to press charges, everything is in place. Freedom is priceless—more than several of your men could end up behind bars, just like the criminals they arrest. I'll turn your force into rubble.

What kind of scrutiny can you tolerate? I'm barely holding on, and it hurts," I said, a tear escaping from the corner of my eye.

The chief looked confused, as if he didn't quite understand what I was talking about.

"Hey, more power, more problems," I mumbled, wiping my nose with a Kleenex I grabbed from my tote bag. "But there's an answer—do something to make me happy. If you don't want people to know your business, you'll elect to do the right thing. This isn't a game. I'm serious. I hope you take the time to show me you understand this is a very touchy situation. If you don't, things won't go back to the normal routine. I will play hardball if I must expose how I was violated. No bureaucratic red tape, Chief. I don't have the patience for that or a waiting game."

He looked irritated, but then again, so did I.

"Cat got you tongue, Chief?" I teased, changing my disposition. "I would hate to see you have to resign. Would you like to think it over before giving me your reply? Here's my number. When you make up your mind and feel like talking, call me. How about we set a time frame. Let's say—"

Just when I was about to finish laying out my terms of negotiation and place my cell phone number in front of the chief, Rico appeared in a gray, two-piece button down suit and wing tip shoes. He came in like he was on a mission to plan my future. My eyes widened. I quickly snatched the hookups from the wall, pushed the DVD player into my tote bag and turned around.

"Treat me like a lady, Chief. Treat me like a lady," I whispered, looking him in the eye. "He doesn't represent me. In fact, that man over there was mixed up in the whole thing. Remember, if you don't respond, I will go to every major media outlet by the end of the day. You shouldn't waste a moment indulging in doubting limbo. Think about your nest egg before you deny my simple request. And no lawyers. If you contact one of your lawyers, the deal is off the table. Think smart for the sake of everyone involved." I winked.

"Now, Ms. Thompson, I told you not to talk to anyone without counsel. I represent you. As you've noticed, the chief won't talk to you. You shouldn't be here talking to him—let me fight this fire—that's what a qualified legal eagle veteran like me is for. I assure you I'll take care of everything within the proper legal channels. I'm being paid to represent you, remember? You're confusing the situation *and* the chief. We're waiting on his counsel to arrive so our meeting can begin," Rico said.

His accent was absent. I'd never heard his words flow so smoothly and clearly. Rico had a legitimate meeting with the chief and I was stunned.

"Don't be fooled," he continued. "After what she's been through, her mental state is understandable. I can't reveal her medical assessment to you, of course. Confidentiality, you know . . . it's hard to know what she's really thinking," he said in a calm, soothing voice.

I responded by banging my fist on the desk. "I hate you, Rico. You're a mentally imbalanced psychotic scum wad! You can't intimidate me. You can't control me. What are you trying to pull with this bullshit here? You are nowhere near a legitimate servant of the law!" I shouted and ranted, pointing at him.

The chief's head swung in my direction as I exploded. I knew Rico was making me look as if I was the one with some sort of problem, but I couldn't manage to subdue my anger. In fact, since Rico arrived, the chief's neck had been swinging back and forth as if it had a spring in it.

"Someone's not listening," he told me. "Ms. Thompson, please . . . *let me do my job*. I know you thought I was caught up in court, but I suppose you didn't receive the message from my secretary." He smiled. "I strongly urge you to go now. I can take things from here. I know what's best for you and your welfare. There's no need to lose control of yourself," Rico said, sounding professional.

I was so frustrated I backed away from the desk yelling, "Thirty thousand, Chief. Don't be stupid."

Rico laughed. "I'll do the negotiating. *Go home*. I'll be in touch, Ms. Thompson. We'll speak later."

I didn't have the energy to struggle with Rico and wade through his garbage. I couldn't believe he used part of my real name. I managed not to do that before. Now I was naked and playing a mind game with a heavy hitter in authority.

Everywhere I turned, Rico was on my heels like white on rice. Quite frankly, resisting his antics was becoming a daunting task, despite me wanting to regain control over my life and destiny. I knew the chief was considering settling on the dynamic duo's terms—first mine, then Rico's. I could only hope he would be contacting me, not Rico.

When I saw what I assumed to be his counsel entering the room with a briefcase, I figured Rico made a more convincing plea than I had. It didn't seem to matter that he was in no way, shape or form my legal representative. If the part of me that was Leslie had been anywhere in the chief's room that day, I would've explained that I needed help taking the wind out of a crazy stalker's sails. Instead, I made up an elaborate lie, out of sheer desperation. I knew I was in over my head and I didn't know what else to do. Rico's title gave him the power and the edge to play a dirty game much easier. My alter ego's sense of security wasn't shattered, although Rico was determined to see to it that Innocence *and* Leslie would fall apart. Even so, both parts of me remained ambitious and in search of a way to intimidate Rico, despite the fourteen-foot wave heading in my direction. The water was already up to my chin, and I knew I wouldn't rest easy that night. As suspected . . . I didn't.

19

Freaky Friday

In light of the various complications over the last month, I
found a few gray hairs in my head, the day before my wedding. I pulled them out at the root, and dismissed them,
blaming the shortest ones on the wolf that was watching my
every move—Rico. After wedding rehearsal, a number of my
out of town guests joined the wedding party for dinner. It was
a way to kick back before the wedding, although my original
intent was to concentrate on just the essential people involved—Trey's family, us, and the wedding party. I reconsid-
ered since I had so many out of town guests whose presence
could make up for my lack of family presence.

Rehearsal went fine—Tanya was not talking to Rico. Rico
was not talking to Tanya, and Rico barely spoke to me. All of
this sat well with me. Everyone followed directions, and
things were moving along smoothly until I found out that the
best man possessed the qualities of a chameleon. He was giving my alter ego Innocence a run for her money—literally.

Everyone was talking and waiting for dinner to begin. I felt
a tug at my arm. The next thing I knew, the lights went out
and loco Rico was pulling me toward a dark room where the

circuit breaker was housed. He shut the door and pulled me tightly to his chest, sucking on my neck like my skin held sweet nectar inside of it, and then stuck his warm tongue in my ear.

"Will you let me breathe? Damn! Back up off of me," I spat, making a fist.

"I'll be speaking to you later. You know it's my job to call and check on you every day," he said firmly. "What happened to that fun personality, Leslie? You used to enjoy the devoted attention I gave you, so stop bitching. You're not going to take your love away from me—we were making great progress in our relationship. I told you I own the pussy, and I'm not playing. I asked about forever and you turned me down even though I'm smart, hard working, friendly, and good looking. I offered you passion, I offered you purpose and commitment, but you chose to toss me aside like an undesirable sucker. You'll be sorry you changed my plans for you and me, Leslie. We could've been making love tonight, but you want to give me a hard time and choose not to cooperate. The scuffle you know where was a warm up. I'm not letting up on you. I'm going to keep pounding your hard head into the wall. I have experience playing these types of games—you don't," he explained, holding my elbows.

Once he was finished talking, he flung me from his grip, turned the lights back on, and returned to the dinner before anyone noticed we both were missing. They were all engrossed in eating a delicious meal and mingling at the dinner table.

Before long, Rico held onto tradition and made a toast as every best man should. He rose to his feet and grabbed his champagne glass.

"I'll make this quick." He cleared his throat. "To my best friend, mi hermano, my confidant, making this toast on your behalf is indeed an honor and privilege. Words cannot express how much love I have for you. Through thick and thin, you've been there for me and so many others. I appreciate who you are and respect our lifelong friendship. Here's to many years of happiness and marriage. Here's to dreams realized, a family, and enjoying everything that life has in store for you and your new wife to be. I will be lucky if I ever find a woman who loves me as much as Leslie loves you. And Leslie could never find a man who deserves her more. On this day, on this wonderful evening, I propose a toast to my best friend, Trey. Here's to a lifetime of love with your lovely fiancée, Leslie. May you both live in a happy home that cannot be disturbed by anyone or anything. Remember to keep God first and always remember to forgive. Love is not perfect, but it is a priceless gift. Congratulations from me to both of you!"

His lies almost made me gag and vomit. Everyone smiled, raised their glasses toward us, and drank the bubbly down. I heard many remark how much Rico favored Trey, and how handsome he was. Whatever. Loco Rico had the appeal of a stinking, dead animal to me. As far as I was concerned, the dirt he dished made him butt ugly, but then again, only I knew that side of him. The crowd of about seventy people all clapped. Trey rose thanking his best man for the heart warming toast, and also gave thanks and credit to his parents.

"Sometimes, it's the simple things that count the most. To the two people who made all the difference in my life, thank you for teaching me to appreciate what really matters in life. Thank you for your sacrifice, dedication, and raising me in a Christian home," he said. He turned to me, beaming with pride. "I can't wait to marry you, Leslie. My love for you is stronger than ever and it will surely endure forever," he added.

I guess he saved the best for last. Hearing Trey's sentimental comments made my eyes mist as tingles ran through my body. I felt encouraged by the little things—the reassurance of Trey's love. Maybe he desired to put me above everyone else, after all. It seemed as though I had been worried over nothing. I could've sworn I saw scratches on his back the last time he was shirtless, but I figured my imagination was playing tricks on me due to my elevated stress level. My alter ego had made me paranoid, but indeed, I'd found my needle in the haystack. I had a good black man on my hands and that was that.

Outside of a tingling neck, the event ended without consequence. No one had any complaints, even Trey's family. His mother even behaved as if she had finally accepted we were getting hitched, despite her not being crazy about the idea. She kept her jaws locked tight, which was far better than her usual episodes of insults.

Immediately following the rehearsal dinner, I went to pick up a few things from the store, including the thickest foundation that matched my skin tone. A hickey was forming on my neck thanks to Rico sucking the hell out of it like a vampire. Luckily, I was wearing a summer button down blouse that covered the area. By the time I finished picking up odds and ends, night had fully covered the sky. I enjoyed the solitude as I considered that I would soon be moving in with Trey. My next plan of action was to bag and trash my porn tape collection, most of which was still at my place. Don't get me wrong though, I was off to collect a small stash from Trey's, too.

My addiction to watching sex on film was worsening my addiction to act it out. I saw potential sex in every man I crossed paths with, and lately even the female bank teller, and the grocery clerk with large breasts and full lips. As a nearly married woman, I fought for Leslie's logic to return, suppressing thoughts of calling Deja, the first woman I made love to, as well as every other sexually adventurous journey I'd taken.

I parked the car and walked up the sidewalk. When I reached the door I could hear hints of music floating in the air. I turned my key and heard *She Used to Be My Girl* playing in the CD player. In my mind I reasoned that Trey must be trying to get something sentimental out of his system before I took the big plunge.

"Hey, baby. I'm home!" I screamed cheerfully as I reached for the light switch and began singing along with the O'Jays.

"Next time, keep your shiesty itinerary in your head, you dumb bitch!" Rico said. "I've been going through your trash. I know everything about you. One day I went through your garbage and found a post it that said SEE CHIEF. I graduated at the top of my law school class, Leslie. It was easy to put two and two together."

Chills shot through my body as I jumped and dropped the bag of groceries. They fell all over the floor. I was paralyzed by fear when I realized Rico had broken into my house and made himself comfortable. He even had his shoes off, his shirt was open down to the third button, and the psycho was in the middle of inhaling the scent of a pair of my worn panties. He was also wearing one of Trey's silk ties around his neck.

"What the fuck are you doing, Rico? You just can't come barging in here like this," I said once I was finally able to speak.

Rico let my pink panties fall, jumped up and backhanded me so hard I fell to the floor. From the floor, I looked around and noticed he'd ripped my place apart—savings bonds, papers, bills, envelopes, and cards from Trey had been cut in half, and my favorite baby blue cashmere sweater lined the floor. Sentimental stuffed animals had been decapitated, all of my sex toys were broken in pieces, and my favorite picture of Trey was missing from a display shelf. Trey's slacks, belts, and spare razors also littered the floor. Other personal belongings were strewn everywhere, including my caller ID box, which had been ripped from the socket in my bedroom. There was no question the fool had completely lost his mind.

"Which bedroom is it going to be?" he asked as I looked up

at him. I noticed he'd soaked himself in cologne, a scent I'd bought for Trey. "Pick one like you love me, you backstabbing, freak nasty whore," he added, crookedly curling up his lip on the right side.

He looked so ugly and diabolical that I couldn't believe I'd ever tasted his kisses. A man that looked seven feet tall and three hundred pounds appeared. He looked like one of the rapper's bodyguards, he was so massive. The man picked me up as Rico quickly pressed heavy-duty duct tape on my mouth. They both stripped me down to my thong and lay me on the bed face down. To my surprise, my stalker had his kidnapping tools stashed and waiting.

"Don't worry. We don't want none of your stinking, rotten pussy!" Rico snarled.

They secured my wrists to my wrought iron bed with some sort of strong twine. Rico handcuffed my feet together, pulled off his belt then began pelting my body with crashing blows. The tape muffled the howls that erupted from within me as I felt my butt cheeks redden. After about fifty heavy handed lashes, Rico used one of his fingers to plow up my asshole, violating me as much as he could. Next he summoned the large man to help him unfasten my wrists, turn me over, and bind me to the bed face up. When the brawny brother ripped the duct tape from my mouth, I screamed, "That shit hurt! I think my asshole is bleeding. I hate you Rico. I hope you rot in—"

"Hell?" Rico said, cutting me off. He began laughing as he rose up on his toes, and then let his heels press on top of the floor. "Shut this bitch up! Apparently, she doesn't think she's said and done enough," he told the large man.

Rico threw the man a purple ball gag that was equipped with an adjustable leather strap that he fastened snugly around the back of my head. Once that was done, the large man gave Rico some sort of coded handshake and he disappeared. I heard him drive off as my eyes watered from Rico's sinister flogging. Apparently, my stalker was going to finish me off alone. As Rico spoke he raised my legs toward my head and smacked me on the ass. With each blow, he sounded more deranged.

"So you want to send videos to the bar, huh? Bitch, are you crazy? Do you know the trouble you've caused? I got seven calls today about that little video you mailed to the D.A. I went back and got the one out of the mailbox after you left the post office. A small tip to a postal employee goes a long way. Rico thought you had that one copy, but no . . . you had to mail another one. Now those cops are on my ass talking about their pensions and livelihoods being at stake. One guy has fifteen years on the force and could lose everything if the chief breaks the code of the brotherhood and turns this over to internal affairs. Those policemen were on duty when the train thing went down and this is potentially a big scandal. You remember the call I took at the Chinese restaurant and me mentioning my friend was a D.A. here? If I'm implicated, I'll be disbarred. I can lose everything. The chief refused my offer to negotiate a deal for you to shut up, and you made it all worse by back talking me when I showed up in his office. I worked hard to build a good reputation, and you're threatening to ruin my professional standing. You're going to pay for this. You're not getting married. No, no, fuck all this shit. I'm not going down over some puta, and neither are my friends! This is not a game. This is my life!"

Rico quickened the pace of his lashes, and I suddenly wondered how in the hell the S&M guy liked me whipping him.

"Did you mistake me for some stuffy, conservative lawyer who only wears a suit and tie? Wrong—that's not Rico—not even a little bit! Prepare for your world to get shaken up a little, Ms. Leslie. After dinner, I caught Tanya in the parking lot and told her that you used her. After providing proof of your abortion—what the proof is I won't reveal—she looked at things a little differently. She did me the favor of delivering your whore flick for a special viewing at a party hosted by a friend of Trey's. Imagine Trey's surprise when he sees his wife-to-be running through a train like a pro. Of course no one will know I spearheaded this little event. When everyone sees it, you're going to find yourself in a hell of a jam."

He stopped spanking me, and my ass was stinging. My legs fell and landed with one large thump. I tried desperately to get enough air in and out through my nose, but it was rather difficult in light of my restraint. Rico walked to a corner of the room, reminding me what I had done when I set him up with the tranny, Wendee. He watched me for a while and just kept laughing at my vulnerable state. Finally, Rico walked over to the bed and grabbed his penis out of his pants. He began stroking himself, licking his lips, and looking at me. He tapped his penis on my forehead, and then continued masturbating until he released himself on my face and tits. He kept saying something like *tragete la leche*, whatever that means.

He kept asking me if I liked the nice little spanking I got for being a bad little girl. After he finished, he roughly smeared his ejaculation all over my body, some of it just above my privates, then pulled up his pants. I felt as dirty as dirty could be but could do nothing.

I couldn't grunt, let alone talk; my words weren't audible. All I could do was jerk around as Rico untied a felt bag and dumped it on top of my body. Crickets, blood worms, and spiders were moving in all directions across my skin. He knew I hated creepy crawlers because I had mentioned it to him when we were in Annapolis. I spotted a jumping cricket while we were there and had a royal fit, begging him to protect me.

"Well if you'll excuse me, I'm late for a bachelor party that's already started to *jump* off. Everyone's gonna see how you went from having the tightest pussy in D.C. to the loosest, puta! You're a star waiting to be discovered. Can Rico have your autograph? He loves your work. FYI, a little birdie told me to remind you that snitches always do end up in ditches," he said, taking off my engagement ring and laying it up on my chest. "Don't get anymore stupid than you already are. Me cago en tu madre," he added, walking over to the radio in my room.

Rico found a station with classical music and turned it all the way up. Then he walked back over to the bed and executed his last step of madness—securing a chastity belt to my body. I struggled as best I could, but it was in vain. The whole belt required four locks and loco Rico locked every one. Once he was done, Rico left me all alone in bondage—literally.

Hours passed. I wiggled my wrists in every direction possible, but all the twine did was dig into them. They felt raw and battered. I heard a noise under the bed. To my surprise, my sister's dog appeared and licked me in the face. Any other time, I'd be mad as hell. This time I was glad to see her because she was the one that chased the crickets away, most of them scattering when she approached. She sat next to me like I deserved her loyalty, proving that a dog can be a woman's best friend.

I heard my sister's voice calling her dog. I fought to speak but still couldn't.

The dog barked and pressed her nose against the screen in the open window.

"Where are you?" Angela called. The dog barked again. "Did that mean, evil Leslie hurt mommy's baby?" Miss Lady barked once more. "Should I report her for cruelty to animals?" The dog stopped barking as if she understood the question. "I'm going to get you out of there. I'm sorry you got left behind. If I die trying, I'm going to rescue my little wittle poopsie," she said as if she were speaking to an infant.

"Do you think she's home?" I heard someone ask Angela.

"I think so—that's her car in the driveway."

"Well let's find a way in," said a man's voice.

"As I told you both, she made it clear she didn't want to see us. I still can't believe how rude she was to me and my family. I don't care about the other things I left, but Miss Lady can't stay here with that insane girl. At first I was scared to come back for her but then I thought about it. Leslie is very unstable and may kill her or something out of spite. You both spoiled Leslie growing up, that's the problem. She's probably pretending she's not home."

"Nonsense," my mother commented. I finally recognized her voice. "If I were a spare key, where would I be? I raised you girls to think ahead."

I heard my mother searching under flower pots, mats, and whatever she could get her hands on to lift or inspect. Somehow, she managed to find my spare key. Like it or not, I heard the door knob turn. The threesome followed the noise of my sister's barking dog. When they reached my room, they all screamed. What could I do but accept that we were reunited while I was in a very compromising position, to say the least. After ten plus years, this is how it all went down.

20

A Family Affair

"Look at her. Should we call the police? What should we do, Charles?" my mother asked, standing over top of me. She even looked up my nose and poked on my collarbone like a physician.

"For God's sake, Charlotte, stop prodding and probing her like she's an anomaly and let's get her out of this mess so we can get to the bottom of this. Obviously, that's what we should do!" my father responded with impatience in his voice. My father looked away from my direction, obviously embarrassed that I was nearly nude.

"You don't have any respect for yourself do you? How could you dare be naked in front of your own father? I told you they were coming here. What kind of pervert are you?" Angela ranted while petting Miss Lady.

I hurled many expletives Angela's way, but she was unaware because my mouth was still bound by Rico's contraption.

"Get smart again, and I won't take it off!" she snapped. I guess she sensed that I was not paying her compliments. She ripped the device off as hard as she could, obviously hoping to deliver as much pain as possible.

"Ouch! Are you crazy, snatching that ball from out of my mouth like that, bitch?"

"Mother, Father—I told you. Did you hear what that girl said? She called me a bitch!" Angela said, trying to report me like a seven-year-old a tattletale. My parents had disappeared to find something to free my arms and legs. With a glaring look, she turned toward me, crossing her arms around her dog tightly, almost squeezing her to death. "How about a thank you?"

"Fat chance, Angela. You're just as flighty as you can be. And your dog is a much better relative than you'll ever be," I told her. She puffed her jaws with air and stormed out of the room.

"What do I do?" Mom asked, walking around to look at my father.

"Hold your hands steady," my father replied. "With this arthritis, I can't do it. And someone needs to put something over her. I don't enjoy seeing my daughter indecent!"

"Well, if we get her out of this mess, maybe she can put some clothes on," my mother snapped. She cut through the duct tape and freed my legs. I shook them and smiled with relief. "Now what?" she asked, turning to my father again.

"Use this box cutter to cut the rope around her wrist. Be careful, Charlotte. You must be particularly careful."

"Let Angela do it. I'm afraid I might miss."

"Angela, would you?" my father asked.

"Hell no. Let the bitch stay like this for all I care."

"Oh, you girls. I swear. It's just like when you were children all over again," Mom said.

"Yeah, Angela might break a nail. She can't do it anyway. What does she know about using a box cutter up in L.A., with her fu fu, shi shi crowd." I laughed, using reverse psychology.

"I can to do it," she exclaimed, snatching the box cutter from my mother. In ten seconds flat. My wrists were free. I grinned. "I am not touching the chastity belt though. Hell no!"

"Leslie, aren't you glad to see us? Where are our hugs and kisses?" my father commented, ignoring Angela.

I grabbed my robe from the chaise lounge, threw it on, and ran over to my father and gave him a quick peck on the cheek. I left my mother hanging as she turned her cheek, expecting me to greet her.

"Won't you tell us what happened? Should we call the police?" dad asked.

"No more questions, please. I wouldn't want to bore you with all the silly details. This is embarrassing enough."

"Freak. You always were weird," Angela taunted.

I ignored her and ran to my closet to find some fresh clothes. I didn't want to waste time before indulging in an invigorating shower and treating my skin to some sweet smelling Bath and Body Works Pleasures pearberry shower gel, so I cut it short. My mother was following me around like a shadow, but I all but pushed her out of the way and headed for soap and water. I turned on the water, lathered up, and rinsed the bugs and Rico's cum from my skin. I hopped out of the shower, dried off, then threw on my robe and pulled the belt tight.

"Maybe you ought to learn how to please your man so he can stop killing his liver, one bottle of liquor at a time," I told Angela as I bolted past her.

My parents wanted to know why I abandoned the family, but I didn't have time to delve into issues they should've figured out by the time I reached my seventeenth birthday.

"Gotta go . . . gotta go," I mumbled, slinging my purse on my shoulder and grabbing my keys out of a dish on my dresser.

"Should we wait here?" my mother asked.

"Whatever's clever," I said, running down the steps.

"Where are you going?" she called after me.

"Out!"

"When's this wedding you didn't bother to invite us to?" my father shouted.

I paused, looked up at him and said, "Soon. Gotta go . . . gotta go . . . gotta go!"

I felt as if I were the one having the press conference as Angela claimed she was planning. Although my family continued shooting questions toward me, I put my family woes on the back shelf of my mind and squealed tires, eager to break up Rico's shindig. Rico might have scared me a bit, but he didn't make me back down. I put up my dukes and decided to go toe-to-toe, neck and neck, blow for blow, letting him know that if he wouldn't stop, neither would my alter ego, Innocence.

21

Putting Up My Dukes

"Woo wee! That's a freak right there. If I ever found a dime piece like that, I'd take care of business!" Rico shouted.

I was standing in the breezeway near the living room where Trey and his boys were having his bachelor party. When Rico detained me against my will, I don't think he realized how cocky he was. He was so sure I wouldn't get loose in time to stop him from showing the tape that he told me they were partying at Scott's place. I remembered who Scott was and where he lived, so I knew exactly where to go. When I arrived at my destination and rang the bell, one of the men attending the party thought I was a stripper coming to pop my coochie and let me in. Before I stepped through the door I held my left index finger to my mouth, then winked, leading him to believe my strip act was a big surprise. It was a big surprise—just not the one he was expecting! I knew I had to work fast so he couldn't clarify anything.

"They got some freaky, *freaky* freaks in D.C. Try any club, the workplace, bars . . . you didn't know? Where have you been?" another voice said as I eavesdropped.

"Hook a brother up then—please, playboy!" Rico responded.

"Find your own play, bama. Freaks are a dime a dozen in Chocolate City. All you gotta do is put out a few bucks for a drink and pretend you may be that needle in a haystack who's gonna stick around. Ain't no man in the D.C. area gonna settle down and spend no lifetime with these materialistic, shallow bitches."

"Harlem, Atlanta, Detroit, Miami Beach—they're all the same. You can't trust 'em no more than you can chunk 'em, my brother," another said. "The best thing to do is keep them nasty hos on the call and hit it list. The only thing they're good for is getting their brains fucked out. If you start catching feelings for any of these broads out here, you'll be short. My boy at my job is paying some broad a grand every paycheck and she didn't even have to work when they were married. Now that's some expensive pussy for your ass," a third agreed.

"Damn! This bitch is bad though. Listen to the way she's slurping on that thang while those dudes got her role playing in some cop shit. Any freak who takes care of a man in the bedroom like that is worth the extra money and trouble. What I'm looking at doesn't come along every day. Say what you want but that right there is up there with that girl who wrote that book about sleeping with cats in the music industry." Rico snapped his fingers. "Ya'll know who I'm talking about. What's her name again?" he asked.

"Superhead. The one that wrote *Confessions of a Video Vixen*," someone replied.

"Yeah, that's it. Look how much she was supposedly getting paid to take care of brothas. The freak on the tape is about to turn around real soon. This is my favorite flick. The good part is coming. I don't think this ho is acting, either. Wait until you see her pretty face. She's a one of a kind beauty," Rico said.

I searched through my twisted mind to find a way to make

my spiel fly. Before I could think it over, Innocence began to move her lips with confidence. I took a deep breath and busted into the room as the men alternated between bashing women and watching the tape. I stood directly in front of the TV screen to block the picture.

"You're momma wasn't no glassmaker, dear," one of the men shouted.

Without wasting time I quickly found the bottom of the DVD player and ended the show. I ejected the DVD and dropped it in my large purse.

"My number one pet peeve is a hypocrite. Trey, what has come over you? I thought we made it clear that there would be no making love, and obviously watching booty tapes isn't appropriate either."

"How did you find us?" Rico asked, looking as if I could've knocked him over with a feather. "We were just trying to have a little fun—no harm done. We don't even have strippers or anything. It's just the boys, beer, and a few pizzas. Let us watch the tape, master," Rico said, recovering quickly from his apparent shock.

"Don't worry about how I found you. Watch your mouth, Rico," I answered.

I know what he was really wondering was how I managed to escape his bizarre obstacle course and put up my dukes to stand up to his psycho ass. We communicated nonverbally as I squinted my eyes and stared at him like he hadn't shaken my nerves one tiny bit.

"If you're the Christian you say, you shouldn't be lusting over other women—that's ungodly, and I don't appreciate your friends proving to be bad influences. Do you hear me, Trey? Say something."

Trey stood there holding his palms upward as if he were going to provide an explanation. I knew I planned to cut him off as soon as he started speaking in order to shift the blame without suspicion.

"But Leslie—I . . ."

"We're about to start a new chapter of our lives tomorrow, and I refuse to allow you to hold on to a bachelor mentality. The man I'm marrying is one with the cloth and he shouldn't be afraid to admit that he is. I'm not trying to put our business out in the street, but you think it's wrong to even lust after me. Since that's the case, this can't be right either," I reminded Trey. "There's no excuse and don't give me some shit about men being men. I'm not the one to tolerate that sexist mess. Stop acting like women would be in search of you from foreign countries just because you're such a lover boy— there's no mambo party going on in your pants. In fact, you're practically dead from the waist down. I practically have to beg to get some from you. Now put that in your pan and fry it!" I continued shaking my finger like a newly wed wife, standing directly in Trey's space.

His boys snickered as I chided him in front of them. Trey dropped his head as if I were stripping him of his manhood, layer by layer. I knew I was and I enjoyed humiliating him in front of the perfect audience.

One man I didn't know started booing, laughing, and whispering like Trey was a punk. I knew I had embarrassed my fiancée and didn't give a shit. A grown man should've been giving his woman some dick. I'm sure each of them was taking care of business with their freaks of the week.

I pulled Trey to the privacy of an empty corner and convinced him to gather his things then immediately booked a hotel room. I didn't want anyone to know where we were until it was time to show up at church, especially Rico. He kissed my lips and threw up his hands as he exited the scene of my close call.

"Just because he's got to leave doesn't mean we have to. How about leaving us the flick," someone said.

"Get one of your freaks to make your very own," I answered, smirking. I added, "A freak in D.C. is a dime a dozen, right? Furthermore, every one of you old heads needs to grow up and stop picking up young hoppers in clubs. One of these days they're going to mistake you for someone's old ass grandfather who can't give up the game even if there are more of you than there are of them. By the time you settle down you'll need penis pumps."

"Damn! Sister girl don't play. I don't think we'll be seeing too much of Trey anymore!" a man shouted.

"Ya damn skippie!" I answered.

"Who knows," Rico commented. "We may be seeing Leslie and Trey more than we all think."

I ignored Rico's jab and left the party with the evidence that I was the unknown, unofficial porn star who was doing all sorts of things with those officers.

I had two rooms reserved for Trey and I. I started to give him the information and tell him that I'd meet him, but I changed my mind. I couldn't take a chance he'd take any detours. There was no way that Trey could come home with me in case my family decided to remain on the premises. Instead, I had him follow me to check in. After he found a Discovery Channel documentary on sharks, I felt confident he'd stay entertained while I packed my slip, shoes, jewelry, veil and everything else I needed for my big day.

Thankfully, my family was not at my place when I returned. They left a note on the fridge that read: WE WILL BE BACK. THERE'S NO FOOD FOR US TO EAT. WE HAVE YOUR SPARE KEY. Thank goodness it was almost time to put the whole scandalous ordeal behind me because I was beginning to feel the weight of so much pressure. In my left hand, I carried my bat for protection, and put my mace on my key ring, just in case I needed to take a nigga down in the dark.

It almost slipped my mind, but when I was leaving my house I called Tanya and did my best to convince her that Rico was lying to ruin our friendship over what happened before. She didn't answer at home, and her cell phone went straight to voicemail. I found this to be odd, given that I should've heard from my maid of honor the night before my wedding. After all, she did say she didn't want Rico to come between us. No one is all good or all bad. Although I had done my fair share of stabbing her in the back, I did decide that something would be missing if my girl didn't show to participate in my wedding, so I left her a message. I knew there was a reason for everything, and I would soon find out what it was. In less than twenty-four hours, everything would be a wrap. It was a good thing because Leslie didn't know how much more she could take of the mess Innocence got her wrapped up in. And by the way, I won't mention how I escaped from my chastity belt. It wasn't pretty . . . but I did.

22

Crave

Upon returning from my place, I called Trey in his room to let him know I had arrived safely after gathering my things. While at home, I threw a monster vibrator into one of the suitcases. It was a new toy, one Rico hadn't found and destroyed, and I couldn't wait to take it for a spin. I removed it from the hard plastic packaging and snagged some batteries from the hotel's TV remote. I inserted the batteries in my toy and began using it on myself. I must admit I was excited to finally lie down on my back and stroke the vibrator gently up my pussy lips and around my clit.

I longed to share the intense vibration with Trey by stimulating him around his testicles, but I could never even let Trey know I had toys I used to satisfy my sex cravings. He'd never go for it. I wished I could find his million-dollar spot by stroking him with my toy, taking him a half a mile from heaven with me as his penis awakened and rose. I tried to picture him moaning in unison with me as I pumped the vibrator faster and more forcefully moving it in and out of my vagina. I could feel my climax begin to mount as I squeezed my muscles around the large, plastic penis. My moans became repetitive as I forced the vibrator to make love to my body.

"Trey . . . Trey . . . Finally, baby. You feel so good," I screamed, fighting to invite my climax to take me to the sweet place where I anticipated landing. Just when I was preparing for the highlight of my journey, the damn batteries died. I was disgusted that too many guests had scanned TV channels and sucked the life out of my impromptu power source. As good as it felt to wrap myself up in my own fantasy all it did was make me crave a real man who could inspire my body to find much-needed relief. I looked at the toy as I squeezed my legs together and dialed Trey's number on the hotel phone.

"Please come fuck me!" I said bluntly. "I really, really need a little sumthin' sumthin' bad. I need to cum. Bring me some dick, Trey. Come stick me. I'm stressed out about tomorrow, and I need to take the edge off."

"Get some sleep, Leslie."

"Please let me sit on it and ride you. Let me come to your room for just ten minutes. I promise—just ten minutes and I'll leave," I begged.

"We have a long day tomorrow. You just lost a child and you haven't even allowed your body time to heal well. There's plenty of time for sex. I love you," he replied.

"You're right. I love you, too," I responded, masking my disappointment.

I hung up the phone, thinking I wasn't about to let a stupid abortion stop me from getting off as long as I wasn't experiencing any side effects. I cursed the fact that men could sometimes be so damned selfish. Trey's blasé attitude was becoming so predictable I didn't continue trying to figure his lack of libido out. I merely took his response as a green light to please myself.

My next attempt to calm down my hormones was taking a shower. It seemed like a good idea until I started thinking about unscrewing the showerhead to see what a forceful flow of water could do for me. The hotel was no place for shower massage masturbation, but I'd been hearing about it and wanted to give it a try.

I brushed my teeth, and tried to get lost within thoughts most every woman dreams of, but fantasizing about the big day didn't work either. I decided to take my toy on our honeymoon in case Trey planned on doing his usual dead-fish impression, but that was later. At that moment, I wanted to make the annoying feeling of getting so close to what my body wanted go away. Playing with my toy had frustrated me, and all I could think of was getting off.

Still feeling frenzied, I got dressed and went off in search of some ice, but I found myself taking the elevator to get a drink. That way I could go straight to the bar where ice and drink were in one place. Plus, I could fantasize while looking at men sitting at the bar, instead of tossing and turning all night while feeling lonely.

After I sat down I noticed a good-looking bartender. I sat on the stool trying to keep a straight face, squeezing my thighs together, and considering what was in every pair of pants in the bar. The bartender was taking too long to serve me, so I walked behind the counter and proceeded to make my own drink. I craved a glass of liquor to dull the reality of a runaway libido that had me feeling as if I could explode. I was hitting rock bottom.

"Slow down. You can't do that," the bartender said. My hand was firmly wrapped around a bottle of vodka.

"You were taking so long I was beginning to think this was a self-service bar," I replied, returning the bottle to its place.

"What's wrong, Miss?" the bartender asked.

"Life, that's what," I snapped, walking back around toward the other side of the bar.

"If you need a free ear, I'll listen. Let's try this again: what would you like to have?"

"I don't know. How about a strong shot of vodka? Obviously, that's what I had in mind," I told him.

He made the drink and set it in front of me. "Calm down and take a deep breath," he told me. After I did, he added, "What's eating you?"

"I'm getting married."

"Congratulations!" he told me with a smile.

"No, don't congratulate me—please!" I said in between sipping on the vodka. I took one more swallow and added, "Do you tell a man he's a bad lover or do you just fake it for life? I'm tired of Mr. Impotent."

"What?" he asked, looking confused.

"My fiancé is the world's *worst* lover. Trust and believe this much is true," I sighed.

"Maybe he's just a selfish lover. Try telling him what you want. Perhaps communication would help to improve things."

"I have. It doesn't matter. I can't describe how it is to love someone but not be totally into them. I crave affection and crave certain types of gratification, but I know he's not the one who can fully give it to me. Don't men understand that women deserve to be satisfied, too? If sex is bad before marriage, why should I feel it will change just because of two rings? I don't understand why men feel they should have all of the power in a relationship. I guess it's the little emperor syndrome, that's what I call it. Women are supposed to bend over backward to please while accepting whatever from men. Well, we have standards, too," I ranted.

"You can do everything right and some women still won't be satisfied."

"Yes, but as a woman, you can do everything right, and a man still won't completely value what he has. It's hard for some men to behave as if appreciating what you have to give is a wise thing to feel. Women are supposed to be this, and supposed to be that, like it's an obligation. *Hello*, we don't have to do a damned thing. Men don't view what we do as privileges, but they should."

"All men aren't programmed to cheat or behave as little emperors. There are some good ones."

"*Right*. Marriage is so overrated, when you really think it over. Maybe the shacking up game isn't such a bad idea. When you get sick of each other, you can pack all your belongings in a U-Haul and move on, just like that . . . *if* you stick to shacking."

"Would you keep a man around for sex?" a man next to me asked. Apparently, men at the bar became wrapped up in my conversation with the bartender and I hadn't noticed.

"Why? The one I have rations it out and leaves me bored as hell. When I do get it he uses condoms too big for his dick—super-sized Magnums—*whatever*. It's wishful thinking, but who am I to tell him he wasn't blessed with a twelve-incher? If you're guilty of this, stop it," I snapped then turned my head back toward the bartender.

"It sounds like he has a big ego," the bartender said.

"Don't you all? If a condom slips off, there's a reason. Buy your size and stop wasting your money!"

"Since we're speaking honestly about the sexes, how about this: Why do women tend to twist and manipulate information to validate an opinion that already existed? You creatures are masters at doing this."

"If a woman has an affair, there's a reason. Men do things just because they can't control their eyeballs or hands. Take mine for example. I've been playing with myself for the last two hours. Unfortunately, it didn't do a damn thing but make me wet. If I cheat, I have good reason. Shit, I'm sexually frustrated. In towns big and small, all over the globe, there are women in my same position. Maybe it's time for us to change the rules of the game and have some fun."

"Since you put it like that, will you let me have your panties? I'd love to sniff them," the bartender said.

I was shocked because he was a blue-eyed, blonde haired white boy. What was he doing publicly flirting with a black chick? I thought my words would be safe with him but they weren't. Apparently, he was up for openly breaking tradition by offering to mix up the game.

"I'll show you where the bathroom is and you can slip them off," he suggested.

"Why should I give my twenty dollar Victoria Secret panties to you?" I asked, flirting.

He removed his wallet from his pants and handed me a twenty-dollar bill.

"Because I asked for them."

"Give me a free refill and I'll consider it." He did and that encouraged me to play the field.

"So what's your number one fantasy?" he asked.

I took a sip of my drink, and then set the glass down on the bar. "Getting banged over the kitchen sink by someone I'd had brief conversations with on a few occasions. Maybe a man I'd bumped into in the mall, for example," I lied. "Fuck it. The truth is I'd get off fucking someone who doesn't know my first or last name. I'd enjoy every minute of getting slapped, flipped, and rubbed down by a complete stranger with great stamina. I'm sexual, passionate, *and* freaky. There—I said it."

I shut my eyes and grinned as I envisioned Trey's face watching me as I allowed another man's hands, who didn't even know my last name, wander over my body and grip my waist tightly. It felt so real. When the chatter of bar patrons awakened me from my daze, I opened my eyes.

"Who are you here with?" the bartender asked.

"My brother."

"You ever slept with a white man?"

"No, but I'd do a good looking one like you," I told him, I opted not to count getting licked by the S&M guy. "You ever slept with a black woman?" I shot back half flirting.

"No, but I'd get with a beautiful one like you."

A myriad of emotions danced in my head. I'd lusted after Tom Cruise a few times but that's as far as it went. I thought about all of the black men who sleep with white women. Why the hell not? Why can't I or any woman of color reach our hand in the Caucasian candy bowl? Slavery was a long time ago and black women needed to lose the hang-ups and give turning to a white boy a try. If white women were sleeping with our men, I saw no reason not to get with theirs.

"Well, all I've got to say is that it's *all* true," I replied after considering where the conversation could lead.

"What's all true?"

"That old saying I'm sure you've heard. You know how it goes: the blacker the berry, the sweeter the juice."

His cell phone rang. The bartender talked briefly and ended the call.

"The girlfriend's checking in, huh? She must sense another woman is trying to jump on her shit. So white men cheat too, huh?" I joked. "Women have a sixth sense about when their dick is straying and about to introduce itself to a new kitty cat," I added. He laughed.

I was tired of squeezing my thighs together in my short skirt. It was time to move in for the kill. I got up from the seat, intentionally flashing him to show off my sister curves.

"If you want my panties, come to my room and get them yourself. Unless you're intimidated by a beautiful chocolate woman, you'll be there. Why are bartenders always so damned good looking?" I smiled flirtatiously, giving his ego a boost.

"I'm going to get off at 12:00."

"And I need to get off now. So what's it going to be?"

"I'm coming."

"Well in that case, I'm looking forward to doing something I've never done before. I hope you are, too. And if I like you, I'm down for almost anything, including making you cum while those toes curl." I pressed my breasts against the bar, leaned close to him, and whispered my room number in his ear. All of the men watched me leave the bar. My nipples hardened from the mere thought of all of the attention I was getting. Innocence hadn't lost her touch. In fact, it was improving every day.

I showered and waited for the bartender to come and play with me. By 12:05, I felt like a hungry wolf on the move. I needed some quick relief so badly that I was nearly salivating over the thought of having my fun by getting my party started with a white man. One light tap at the door signaled me to get up and unlock it. Once I did, the man didn't waste his words trying to get to know much more about me.

"You've got a wonderful body. And that ass—I've never seen anything like it," he told me.

"So you like this pretty round brown, huh? How about some chocolate dessert?" I teased, undressing down to my birthday suit. "Come lick it from the back and then let me be your whore." When the bartender didn't react after I undressed I said, "Don't you have a sweet tooth for something exotic, white boy?" I teased, holding a box of Trojan condoms in my hand.

He started inserting his finger into my vagina while talking dirty in my ear. I loved it.

"Don't you want to fuck me?" I asked, hoping to keep his boldness flowing. I set the box of condoms down on a nightstand, lay on the bed, then continued grinding my hips in slow circular motions while grabbing his penis.

"No, I just want you to feel good." He turned me down. I couldn't believe it.

"You know what freaks like me want. Get undressed and let's fuck," I insisted.

"You know what I'd really like?"

"What?"

"To watch you masturbate."

"Why are you playing so hard to get? Masturbate! I'm trying to suck and fuck something. You acted like you were down to play at first," I said, getting annoyed.

"I am down. I'm just into voyeurism. It's my thing."

Usually, I have to beat men off with a stick when Innocence is doing her thing. His nonchalant attitude frustrated me and made me want him more. I didn't ask his permission to unbuckle his pants to free his dick—I just started doing my thing. Next, I inserted my vibrator inside of myself with one hand and sucked my fingers with the other. After I did, his hands started roaming over my nude body, and he began to massage my back. It was so intense that I began working my hips into the sheet covering the mattress while grinding, grinding, grinding and continuing to yank on his penis. The more he hardened, the more I stared at it and smacked my hips against the bed like a machine. I imagined his tall erect twelve-incher could lead me to a place where I longed to be—orgasm city. My stereotype regarding little, itty-bitty, white men went flying out of the window. All black men aren't well endowed, and I guessed not all white men are packing pencil peckers. The proof was wrapped around the fingers of my left hand. *A dick is a dick.*

The stranger continued massaging my back, digging his hands into it. I couldn't manage to get off with no penetration or licking, so I resumed smacking my hips against the bed, salivating and imagining that the bartender's large tool was giving me something worth losing my mind over. I picked up the box of condoms, pushed one in his direction, and closed my eyes, expecting him to change his mind about merely watching my body react to being teased.

"I have one small suggestion for you to sleep on tonight—don't get married," he told me. My eyes sprung open and my mouth shut. I felt the tension in my back collect. "How would your man feel if he were here to see what you were up to? If your heart isn't in it, don't do it. Obviously you haven't gotten the idea of cheating out of your system."

I let go of his penis and was about to respond but his phone rang. He merely listened to the caller while never saying more than, "I'll be there in a minute, babe."

I wiped the saliva from the left corner of my mouth, too shocked to say anything. The man hung up his phone and placed it on the night table. I began to feel powerless and frustrated, when he chided me.

"When you play games with love, someone's gonna end up hurt. Marriage is a serious commitment. I know I don't know you, but I feel like I can tell you this. Something tells me you aren't here with your brother. If you don't think you're compatible with your intended, be honest about it. Things will get real ugly if you don't get a grip," he said.

I sat up in bed with my breasts exposed. "Who are you to tell me shit? You pour, mix, and shake drinks for a living—what do you know? You played with this knowing that I'm getting hitched, and now you wanna play the preacher man?" I told him, struggling to redeem my power.

"Look, the easier choice may seem to be an affair because you'll keep your family together. Why go through with this with the possibility of divorcing and changing everyone's lives if it all gets out of hand? I'm trying to save you some heartache."

"Your morals are no different than mine. You're just as shady. It's just like a man to exercise a double standard. Men sow their wild oats right up until it's time for them to take the plunge and it's accepted. If women are supposed to accept the ritual, so should men! Get out and take your ass home to your girlfriend, while you're at it. You don't know me, and you don't know my man. He and I can make it if we try, so mind your damned business and stop acting like you're my shrink. I invited you up here for sex, not a dissertation on the state of morality and marriage in America. People in glass houses should never throw stones. If you thought something was wrong with you and me sharing some intimate time together, you shouldn't have marched your pink ass up here. I'm getting married to my fine black king tomorrow, and that's my business, not yours. Get out, Vanilla Ice! You're not going to curse my blessing!" I yelled, throwing every single condom in his direction.

He quickly stuffed his dick in his pants and buckled his belt. "You're out of control. You're crazy!" he said.

"Go ahead, leave then! Just get out!" I yelled, jumping up in his face. "I can get paid to have sex with men. I don't have to put up with you playing games! Black men are crazy, and so are white men. In fact, you're probably nothing but white trash that changed your mind about fucking a sista!" I taunted as he proceeded to walk out of the room.

Although I was trying to antagonize him, he stayed calm. When the door slammed the bartender faded into a faint, distant memory.

Just like I said, black men are crazy, and so are white men. If I had been smart, I would've been engaged to a Martian, but those sorts of thoughts were all behind me. This was my last opportunity to fool around before getting the man I "really" wanted, even if the man I wanted couldn't put it down under the sheets. I was determined to take this opportunity to get mine. I scrolled through the phone book in my cell phone, found Deja's number and called her, hoping to cheer myself up. I figured I'd see if she was available to give me a much-needed orgasm. If a man couldn't understand, something told me a woman like Deja could.

To my surprise, Deja more than shared my same spirit of adventure. She brought pot, liquor, and leftovers from dinner with her. We did a lot of female bonding, talking about marriage, life, and friendship. After we loosened up, she strapped on a dildo and fucked me as good as a man with the real thing. I loved the way she manhandled me. It was a beautiful thing. In fact, I even told her my real name. I thought she and I were on the same page of the same book until she started talking while she pumped her toy in and out of my vagina. Now I see why men want women to shut up and just fuck! All sorts of things get twisted when words get in the way. She slipped and said too much . . . and so did I!

"I'm so glad you called because I really miss my girlfriend. Her husband tore her out of my life the night you met us, Leslie. Then my husband and I had a terrible fight over something else," she said. "If you'd let me take you on an erotic journey with one of my toys, it would turn me on to do it."

"Oh yeah? Like what?" I asked drawing up on a toke the way she taught me. It was my first time trying any sort of drug—even herb.

"I love putting a big old strap-on harness and fucking a nice wet pussy . . . like his sister's. That's what this fight was over, his little sister who goes to the Black Harvard. If men in this area would do right, we wouldn't be forced to turn to each other, and college girls wouldn't be in bed with other women in their dorms."

Her statement took me by surprise, but I was so horny I put out the joint and bent over to let Deja show me what skills she was working with.

"Damn! Oh shit!" I screamed as Deja gently slid the fake penis in and out of my vagina, hitting it doggy style.

The egg shaped knob of the double-ended dildo allowed Deja to get off at the same time she inserted the long end inside of me. We both began moaning and panting in tandem, compliments of something Deja said was called the vibrating FeelDoe Silicon Harness Dildo. At that point we began making so much noise someone began banging on the wall next door. Deja and I continued doing our thing, just not quite as loud.

"I'm going to leave him. Hell, I don't want dick anymore— I prefer giving it. What does it take for a man to get my attention? A fine woman like you sitting or standing right next to him. Thanks for opening my eyes to what I really want. The good part is I'll be committed to you in every way—from your comfort down to me introducing you to whole grain pasta. No drama, no games. I'll be here for you—you can expect the best from me, sweet baby. Wouldn't you like that? I love turning out mature married chicks. Fuck men, just fuck 'em!"

After she told me that, all bets were off. I was trying to un-complicated my life, not add to the drama.

"Whoa, whoa, Deja. Baby? Pasta offers? Slow your roll. I didn't expect to spend the night getting off and learning how good you've been pussy whipping another woman long term. I hope you don't have a problem with that, but I'm not exactly interested in you showing off your culinary skills in your gourmet kitchen. Although I've discovered I do enjoy how you get down, I'm not a lesbian and never will be, sweetie. My sex life needed a boost, that's all."

"You're just like him! You don't believe anything I say. You just want me for my body!"

She started picking up things and throwing them around the room—glasses, the clock, the remote—whatever she could get her hands on. After she finished she began crying hysterically, and banged her head against the wall about six times. Then she ran out of the room and threatened to jump off the roof of what I think was a twenty story building. Deja stormed into a waiting elevator, in search of a way out, and I was scared her crazy ass was going to take it.

"Calm down, Deja. Please, just calm down," I begged, jumping in behind her. She pressed the button with the high-est number.

"I'm jumping! I'm jumping," she screamed. "I can't do this anymore. You're the last person who will use Deja."

I found a button to stop the elevator and turned on my award-winning actress charm.

"Honey, all of this right here is not necessary. I know

you've been hurt, and I do care about you beyond the physical." I grabbed her head and placed it on my shoulder.

"Do you really care about me?"

"Of course, I care," I lied, patting her back. I rolled my eyes. The last thing I needed was a fresh piece of road kill who some witness may be able to trace back to my company.

As Deja remained in my arms sobbing and begging for a piece of my heart, I felt like screaming from that hotel rooftop. *I was only trying to get off!* Instead, I took her back to my room and rocked her back and forth in my arms like a baby. Revealing how I really felt wouldn't have done an ounce of good. The last thing I needed was a lipstick lesbian version of Rico who swore I was the apple of her eye. Nevertheless, every sign that Deja more than fit the bill of an unstable chick was looking me in the face. If I had a straight jacket, it would've come in very handy. Thanks to the suicidal tantrum she threw, I only got an hour and forty minutes of sleep before my wedding day. Little did I know Deja's pot was laced with something much stronger than I'd ever imagined.

23

Busted

In between yawning and noting my sensitivity to light and sound, I talked to Trey and began to panic about the state of my wedding affairs. As we drove to the church, he assured me that everything was under control, and that Tanya had done her part to tie up the loose ends with the wedding planner while I was recovering from the "miscarriage." I slid on sunglasses to ward off sunlight after using damn near a quarter of a bottle of Visine to cover up my red eyes, courtesy of my late night of smoking pot with the bisexual drama queen. The consequences for getting buck wild with a "fun one" entailed convincing her that I'd call her as soon as I set foot off of the plane from my honeymoon.

In addition to sleep deprivation, I was suffering from a hell of a hangover. Even so, I felt at ease. My life was about to change for the better—Trey wasn't Mr. Everything but he wasn't exactly a slouch, either. After I reassessed everything, in a twisted sort of a way, I understood that I did need him. I suddenly felt the need to have a tight pussy for Trey, so I inserted the Ben-Wa balls that I'd begun using periodically, to tighten my PC muscles. To be honest, I'd been screwing so much, a train could've passed through my hot box!

My big debut had arrived. Inside, I was doing a happy dance because I was out of touch with the world and all of the problems within it. I wasn't thinking about the liquor on my breath, the hickey I forgot to cover up with make up, or my family who managed to track me down and sit at the ceremony. I wondered how they did it until I put two and two together. Nosey Angela most likely lifted an invitation from the stack of extras I had piled on my dining room table. At least my family wasn't bothering me to be in the wedding though. I also wasn't thinking about Rico. He had no choice but to let bygones be bygones. I wasn't thinking about Tanya doubting I had a hysterectomy; she was a true blue Christian and wouldn't hold that sort of grudge. I wasn't thinking about Trey finding out what Innocence had done. I was finally getting my ring, and now Trey would have no excuse not to give me some. I wasn't thinking about a damn thing but marching down the aisle to change my name from Leslie Thompson to Leslie Williams.

The photographer began taking pictures of the blushing bride to create photo albums full of memories. As cameras clicked, I marched down the aisle with a smile plastered on my face. I had to pull an old beauty queen trick I'd heard about and rub Vaseline on my teeth just so I could remember to do it. Everyone remarked how beautiful I looked . . . until the inevitable happened in front of the entire staff of the high school where I worked and the pastor and elders in my church. At some point, the light from the flashes ripped my ability to wear my sober mask to shreds. Feeling lost in space, I officially fell apart, couldn't control my hangover, and began walking in a zigzag pattern. I had no idea how apparent my stagger was, but no one said a word—perhaps their silence said it all. I finally reached Trey and the minister, and the ceremony went by in a blur until he reached those dreaded words.

"If anyone here has a reason why this couple should not be joined in holy matrimony, speak now or forever hold your peace," the minister said in a strong, clear voice.

The room was silent. Just before the reverend was about to proceed with the ceremony, a voice spoke.

"I want to say something here," the voice standing near me said. "As a devoted lawyer, and upstanding member of the community, I can't let this go on in good faith. I'm sorry I have to do this, but I can't let my brother marry that woman. Unfortunately, some information an anonymous source entrusted me with fell into my hands a few moments ago—now I must bring it to Trey's attention. She's a stripper, a whore, obviously a drunk, and the wholesome life you people think she's living is a great big lie. I have evidence that this, this, *woman*, is notorious—I have the guts to expose her filth for the sake of my best friend, Trey."

I watched an image appear on the wall behind us. As the movie played, I watched myself walking to the abortion clinic, having sex with the policemen, and even kissing Maxwell after leaving my little stripping gig. Everyone gasped. There was no way for me to defend myself, so I opted to expose Rico too, however my hangover slowed down my ability to respond quickly.

"Whoa, whoa, whoa. Now who was it on the screen with me? You tell them. You tell them, Rico. Ask Tanya, Trey!"

"You killed my baby," Trey screamed. "You killed my baby! I was supposed to be a father! Plus, you've been sleeping around, you lush!"

Despite my throbbing head, I managed to fall into Rico's trap and speed up my thinking enough to confess my mess in front of a sardine packed church.

"I had an abortion, and I had no choice. You wouldn't pay attention to me."

"I was saving money for after the wedding, working seventy-hour weeks. I wanted us to have a sizeable cushion for our future—to do right by my wife. *That's* why I was so busy. I don't feel one ounce of pity for you—that's what you get for cheating on me—I know all about it." Trey turned to the crowd. "I want to thank everyone for coming out today, and as a token of my appreciation, I have a special gift taped to the bottom of the pew for each guest. Several moans and groans filled the room as guests began looking at 8X10 glossy photos. Suddenly there were four hundred pair of disapproving eyes fixed in my direction.

"That's right, everyone. As you can see, the best man was breaking off my bride-to-be behind my back."

"Rico was the one who said you were cheating on me—that's how all of this started. I thought you didn't care about us anymore when you stopped giving me emotional support and real quality time. Everything seemed to come before Leslie, and I got tired of waiting for you to give me affection. You stopped telling me about your work schedule and even stood me up to be with your boys or your momma. He's behind this. Why do you think the faces of the movie you just saw were blackened out? This is all revenge because he and his police friends are in big trouble for running a train on me. I'm the victim here," I said, trying to defend myself as my secret double life began to flood to the surface.

Trey turned back around.

"If you don't believe me, ask Tanya. I was pregnant by him and that's why I had to get rid of the baby. Rico has been stalking, blackmailing, and terrorizing me. I never wanted to have sex with him. He made me do it one day when you weren't home. How could I manage to tell you that your best friend raped me?" I lied.

"You didn't look like you were being raped in those pictures the P.I. took! Tanya was suspicious and the private investigator she hired after you and Rico first started having an affair never stopped following you, *everywhere*, Leslie. None of that matters though. Tanya and I eloped. We got married two days ago at the Justice of the Peace. I wanted a good Christian woman in my life and now I've got one. I wasn't going to go through with marrying you, Leslie. There was just no way! I went along with the whole charade after I found out what you did with Rico. Since everything was paid for, I wanted to see how far you'd go," Trey explained. "And by the way, I found that condom you were carrying in your purse after you supposedly lost my baby. I marked it and noticed a new one had replaced it. Don't think I didn't notice the gold post office box key on your ring and that I didn't hear you mumbling men's names in your sleep. When I heard you call Rico's name, I knew you were just up to your same old thing that caused my bed slat to break."

The crowd gasped again. Chatter increased in volume. Tears began to flow from my eyes as I felt an incredible sense of humiliation over the fact that I'd been set up and conspired against. I felt abandoned by Trey, and I hated how it felt. I was stood up at the altar, and I just couldn't believe it. Trey stopped wanting to become my husband and no longer believed our marriage could work. I often complained about him, but never in a million years would I have guessed that he would've gotten with Tanya behind my back.

"Now everyone sees this woman for what she really is," Tanya said. "Bible study, singing in the choir, all fake! Her heart was never in it—not for one Sunday. She's an abomination to the Lord," Tanya said, yelling at the crowd. "You deserve more love, Trey. I'm the real woman who'll give it to you right. I got *my* man!" She looked at me, jerking her neck back and forth, and then kissed Trey's lips. I cringed as she tasted the lips I once enjoyed. None of this was supposed to happen. My hurt was multiplying by the second.

"Bitch, you set me up to take my man. He doesn't love you. He loves me!" I yelled at Tanya, lunging at her in my gown, snot dripping down my lip. I smacked her as hard as I could, and then began scratching her face with my long French manicured nails which had been nicely done for the wedding.

Rico began laughing. Trey turned toward him and clocked him in the face. Rico just stood there looking stunned.

"Be out by the time we get back from the honeymoon you paid for. And move all your things out of my house to make room for my wife. I'm going on my honeymoon, with Tanya! We're outta here!" Trey hollered at me.

Feeling speechless from being humiliated, tears began streaming down my face again. I felt degraded and ashamed. The two Ben-Wa balls I'd inserted earlier fell from under my wedding gown and rolled down the aisle. I held my head with my right hand as my thoughts became even more jumbled from my unclear state of mind. I'd never smoked pot before and sharing tokes with Deja was telling on me. Little did I know that all pot is not made equal. Deja's stash was laced with crack cocaine. I found out the big surprise, after listening to a message she left the next day, asking how I enjoyed the special blend. That explained my wacky behavior but I found this out was a little too late.

The crowd gasped once more as Trey flew out of church without saying a single word. I hiked up my dress and held it with both hands as I did a piss poor job of running behind him, trying to keep from zigzagging. I followed him so closely I nearly clipped his heels. Tanya followed me, and I was sure Rico ran behind her. A crowd followed the now four bitter enemies who had once been two close couples. I tripped on the concrete. Trey opened the limo door, and Rico pulled out a small pistol from the cummerbund of his tuxedo. Trey grabbed it from Rico. Tanya wrestled to snatch it from Trey. Rico knocked out one of her teeth by elbowing her in the process, and then aimed the gun at me. When I fell down, the bullet bypassed me and hit Tanya in the chest. I screamed hysterically because my big day was ruined and was shaking the entire time, but Rico wasn't finished yet. When Trey's new wife fell, Rico looked as if he was going to shoot either Trey or me, so Trey wrestled him for the gun, trying to get it away. Rico quickly let go of the gun to make it appear as if Trey fired the deadly shot, when we heard blaring sirens and saw a cop car pull up. Trey stood dumbfounded, holding the gun as Rico threw up his hands to make it appear as if Trey was attempting to shoot him too.

"Don't shoot me, too. Don't do it!" Rico screamed, backing into the crowd. "He killed her!" he screamed, pointing at Trey.

I was in shock and couldn't speak, although I'd seen what really happened. I'd rather not relive the ugly details of how the groom was made into the ideal suspect while Rico walked away from the scene without being charged with anything. I also prefer not to get into the range of emotions I experienced seeing Tanya's dead body hauled away. A strange thing was that right before I left, someone patted me on the ass so quickly, I didn't know who did it and why they'd done it until I recognized the cop's face. Talk about a strange day, yes it was.

Realistically, what man would publicly embarrass his fiancé, as well as himself, in a packed room of people? One who was hurt and embarrassed, that's who. The wedding was paid for, so I guess Trey figured he'd show up and sling dirt because he felt justified to vent. I feel he did so much in front of family and strangers because people will do some crazy things that don't make sense when they're hurt—I should know. Well, who would've thought there would ever be a runaway bride? Who would have guessed a bride would be kidnapped by her parents so she wouldn't marry her intended? And now *my* incredible wedding disaster. I guess you can add it to the growing list of scenarios that seemed too outrageous to be true. Although I was still very torn up, I did remember love didn't come easy to me, even on my big day. Fabulous . . . juuuust fabulous.

24

Knee Deep In the Game

Three months later . . .

I stared through a heavy veil of pouring rain at the large concrete building and the stainless steel wire that encased the structure. I'd finally worked up my nerve to visit Trey in jail. Although I was well aware that he had been wrongfully labeled as a high flight risk with no ties to the community and charged with manslaughter, Leslie nor Innocence chose to rush to deliver an apology. His bail had been set at one million dollars, and that was that. Unbeknownst to Trey, I finally understood why all of the pieces to the puzzle of his case didn't fit. Sometimes it takes me a minute, but. I never forget a man I "experienced." The person who patted me on the ass was one of Rico's associates who was in the group of men who ran the train on me. It's no wonder the dirty cop instantly took Rico's side, not charging him with anything. Plus, Rico is probably connected with dirty judges, too. Trey had a good chance of literally rotting in jail.

Even so, I wasn't interested in running back to his arms. Under my assessment of the situation, if any real comparison could be drawn, Trey was as wrong as I. We were both culpable by violating a divine bond. The only difference is that he had a legal reminder, and I didn't. I wouldn't even admit that though—not to one soul in the world. Everything was all Trey's fault. It was his fault for kicking up the drama a notch, marrying my former best friend, and for hurting me beyond words. In the future, I'd aim higher than a fool, and by my definition of a fool, dear Trey passed, fitting the description with flying colors. Obviously, jealousy and bitterness set in and wouldn't allow me to fully regret that his right to freedom had been revoked.

I was frisked for contraband and drugs by a prison guard. When I was asked to open my purse, it finally hit me that I was preparing to sink knee deep in the game by facing Trey. There were some things I needed to say so I could sleep and think a hell of a lot better—to feel as sense of closure. My motive for showing up was a selfish one, and I didn't give one iota. My main sacrifice to visit him was giving up the sixty-dollar designer bra that I bought with money Rico left for our "honeymoon gift," and a silver toe ring I picked up from a shop when Innocence was on the loose. I guess it wasn't meant to have the bra because it was destroyed due to the presence of wire in it. Cutting through it was a small price to pay, considering Rico could've framed me, instead of the intended groom.

After I showed my ID and signed in, I saw Mabel come in, sit down, and begin reading her Bible. She looked tired, appearing as if she'd been praying and speaking in tongues from morning 'til night. When a man appeared before her, she greeted him by shaking his hand. I assumed that it was Trey's attorney. Without realizing it, I found myself attempting to eavesdrop on their conversation. Their whispers were low and barely audible, but I managed to decipher a few phrases that were linked to Mabel telling Trey's lawyer that she recently had to contact the D.C. Energy Assistance hotline, and that she would finally agree to put her house up to raise money to continue her son's defense. When the lawyer left to talk to someone in the prison, Mabel spotted me in the visiting area. She hopped up from her chair and ran over to shake her ugly, stubby finger in my face.

"I knew I saw your name on the book. The Lord is going to deal with you. I knew you were trouble, you nasty little whore! You're not on the visitor's list. How'd you get in here?"

"I live more than fifty miles away, that's how. You want a piece of me, huh? If you want some, and you can move those fat feet that look like a pack of hot dogs stuffed down in those tight shoes, let's take this outside. I'm waiting. And actually, I'm a *big* whore. Get it right if you're going to start calling me names, trick," I taunted.

"Vengeance is God's, and when His wrath comes down on you, you're gonna wish you were someone else," Mabel snapped.

"I know you're angry, and I know you must be sad too. I may even feel your pain a little bit, but yelling at me is not going to help rebuild your son's life. God is the only judge, so there's your update," I told her.

"I tried to talk some sense into my boy but he just wouldn't listen."

"He wasn't perfect," I told her, defending myself.

"He's a good man, and I will not stand for you trying to destroy his good name. Tanya was his type, not you. This is what happens when men bring trash home."

"I'm not trash. I'm the prize, Ms. Fit and Fabulous!"

"I call it like I see it!"

"You helped to ruin our relationship. Shut up, bitch. Just shut up. I've been waiting to tell you that."

"Who you calling a bitch? You have no respect for your elders."

"You're not my elder. You're Trey's elder. You're the precious baby's momma. The idea of respecting you will never be on my mind, so just accept that I don't like you as much as you don't like me. Move your three chins out of your way and just eat me!"

By the time the guard showed, I was swinging widely and hurling expletives at Mabel. I spat on her and lost sight of the fact that she indeed was an elder.

"If you don't settle down and stop fighting, I will have you arrested," the guard warned, pulling me off of Mabel. Although he was chiding me for my behavior, he was copping feels of my legs and ass . . . *accidentally*.

"Everyone is equal in my world, regardless of age or the need for Fixodent or Depends. She started it. Lock her up so she can join her son. I was just defending myself," I said. As I huffed and puffed, then fixed my clothes, stuffing my breasts back in my shirt after I flashed the guard, he began to play favorites. I was off to see Trey. Even if Mabel couldn't stand me and didn't want me around, my turn came first Oh well, Miss Mabel. Oh well. Before or after fighting, I look good and you just don't.

My throat felt closed when my eyes met Trey's through the glass wall that divided us. I picked up the phone to talk to him and tried to play off my discomfort as I studied his worn, somber looking face. He was wearing an orange jumpsuit and the guard was watching every prisoner's move while they verbally visited with guests.

"How are you?" I asked Trey, speaking into the phone.

"It took you three months to care enough to find out."

"I've been busy," I lied. "I've been wrapped up with my students since school just started and everything."

"So you say. I guess that's why you can't look at me in the eye." He paused. "You know I tried to call you but you didn't accept the collect charges when I did," he said.

I ignored his comment although it was true. "Like I asked the first time, how are you doing?"

"The gun didn't belong to me. I didn't even fire it, and I end up with a million dollar bail. Rico wasn't charged with anything—I just don't get it. I could easily lose my mind, under the circumstances, but I know this is all a test. I know justice will prevail, although I've met many inmates who tell me their horror stories as they comb law books for a loophole or a way out of something they say they didn't do. It's rough in here. I don't even want to discuss the things I've seen. I haven't lost hope that things will turn around for me. The light of God restores and renews me each day. He's helping to maintain."

"Well, at least you're keeping your spirits up."

"Every trial, every burden, every fear, I would have been there, even after twenty-five years of marriage. Why the best man, Leslie? I've always been strong and you did everything you could to take my manhood by making me look like a fool. Was Rico really worth all of this? What is it about you that made you afraid to give your heart to me completely?"

"If I couldn't be with the one I loved, I was going to pretend to love the one I was with—until I realized his ass was crazy. I tried to cut him off but he just wouldn't let things go. I didn't know if your heart still had space for me. I wanted a better life, so I created a fantasy one."

Trey just shook his head as if to pity my tilted rationale. "I can't believe you put our future and health in jeopardy over a lack of communication. Did you use condoms every single time, Leslie? You were out in the street playing Russian roulette with your life and mine. Do yourself a favor and get tested," Trey told me. His eyes were glossy.

"I tried to communicate with you, but you wouldn't listen! And for your information, Rico was the only one. The *only* one, Trey. That's how it was. Rico was just trying to make me look bad. I don't know what he doctored on some tape, but your boy was the only one who touched me."

"*Right*. Men and women out here in these streets aren't all

HIV free, Leslie. Some people will lay down with you not knowing what they could have. Fidelity is a beautiful thing because when you have it you understand that fucking around just isn't worth it. There are some out here who want to behave as though they can't catch AIDS, but anyone can get it. Leslie, I know some things beyond what was revealed at the church. You said it all when you were obviously high, but I know the whole story."

"You're bluffing. You don't know shit, Trey, except what Tanya told you to stab me in the back. Was Rico worth it, you ask? Was Tanya worth it? You preferred to take her down to City Hall and supposedly do all of this to teach me a lesson. Don't preach to me about shit until you acknowledge that you were also creeping behind my back. I know all about HIV, so cool it!"

"You made it clear that you were *settling* for me and that hurt. I wanted all of you or none of you at all. How could I marry a woman who was whoring around? No man wants to take a ho as his bride. We like to look at women like that on tapes, and maybe even hit on them in clubs, but when it's all said and done, no man can truly feel content with a loose booty bitch who opens her legs anytime men want to hit it. You used to remind me of that yourself, remember? According to you it was why your conservative good girl ass was marriage material. Humph, little did I know . . ."

"Thanks for explaining the double standard to me, Trey. I did say something to that effect, but you've taken my fine words out of context. Women just play a game that men created. If you all would pick one woman and stick to her, there would be a hell of a lot less to worry about. And as I keep telling you, Rico was the only one I was creeping with. You just chose to take Tanya's word and run with it as opposed to believing me. She was just frustrated because she couldn't find her own man to get with."

"Leslie, I didn't just take Tanya's word for it. I also hired my own P.I. When we were in the same hotel the night before the wedding, it was me who kept ringing the white guy's phone. I wanted final confirmation about what you were doing behind my back, so I was asking him questions about you. After he left to see his "girlfriend," he came into my room and played back a recording of everything you said. He was wired. After that, I happily made love to Tanya, my wife. Everything she'd been saying about you was correct. I couldn't believe my ears. It's like you have split personalities or something. It was a one in a million chance that you would go to the bar, but that's the number one pickup spot for cheaters so we put the bait there in case you decided to take it. I also had other information about you prostituting yourself. What's wrong with you? Why are you so loose, Leslie?"

"*Me* take the bait? You fucked and married my best friend when you should've had your loving arms around me. It's funny you could do that since you acted like you were a wet mop when it came to making love with me, or paying me any attention. How cynical—you were spying on me, too?"

"Let's just say it was a revised version of the lie detector test my grandmother wanted me to have you take. So I wear the wrong sized condoms, huh?"

"How could you not only fuck my girl, but marry her too?"

"In spite of my best efforts to stay close to you, Tanya was there, I was there . . . you weren't. One thing led to another, and I ended up hiding the marriage certificate in my sock drawer when I told you it was for us. I knew you wouldn't straighten up and fly right. I just knew it. I didn't love Tanya, but it just seemed like a good idea at the time. Don't pin this on me, though. That part never would've happened if you were keeping your legs crossed in the first place." Trey began raising his voice. "Thanks to you, she's dead, and those children have no mother to raise them. I understand perfectly. You had no conscience when you were turning my life into a living hell!" he screamed.

"Who cares about that trifling Mommy Dearest. I'll go spit on her grave." Trey started crying. "You're not over that bitch yet? Apparently, you cared way more about her than you did me, and you deserve to be behind bars. Mr. Morality . . . you're the hypocrite. I can't believe you call yourself a man or a Christian!"

"No matter what you say or think, justice will prevail. My faith in God will see to it that it does," Trey told me.

"You knew what you were doing. I hope you rot in hell for what you did to me. I hate you, Trey. You are the one who caused all of this . . . now deal with the consequences and man up!"

"How could you speak about her that way? She was a good friend to you. There's nothing you could say or do to explain your poor behavior. Cheating with your best friend's boyfriend, and the best man, was just inexcusable. More was at stake than breaking out of a sexual rut. Sex isn't just about what the flesh needs, but also what the soul craves. I tried to ensure our relationship was headed for light, depth, humor, and lifetime love. All of those things could've turned you on before we hit the sheets again had you been paying attention to my intentions. Of course you would miss the intimacy that's attached to the act of making love, as opposed to getting off. You allowed Rico to punk you. Maybe you are a nympho because I don't know anyone, male or female, who wouldn't have been able to see you were nothing more than something forbidden for Rico to conquer—just because you were supposed to be off limits to him and I had you. If this is the last time I see you in life, I'd consider myself lucky, Leslie. I have nothing more to say to you so please leave and don't plan on coming back. I should've known better than to believe I could have a conversation with the sane you!" he screamed again.

"Don't act like you're perfect here, you screaming pussy! I know that you didn't shoot Tanya, and I may be the only one who can corroborate your story at trial. I also know of a few crucial details that you're not even aware of. After the way you talked to my ass, all bets are off. I was going to put up money for your defense and do everything in my power to help free an innocent man. Now, huh, you're on your own, baby cakes—sink or swim."

"Why won't you recognize the reason why my life got fucked up—I wouldn't be stuck in here if I hadn't met you, and I hadn't known you! You're in need of therapy, behavioral counseling, or something," Trey screamed, losing control of his emotions.

"Shame on Leslie? What about Trey the hypocrite, Trey the equal opportunity asshole? You also did some real cruddy things. What about the things you did by playing me and that dead bitch? You're just like Tanya. Now you're just another black man caught up in the prison system. If you knew what I knew, I wouldn't bank on justice prevailing."

"Why don't you deal with your issues before you wreck someone else's life? Better yet, didn't you think I deserved your respect?" he snapped again.

"I was as direct as I could be about what I needed from you without bruising your male ego. As far as the rest of your commentary . . . whatever, Trey," I said, waving my hand. I was about to rise from my seat in the booth, but couldn't help but to try to get in the last word. "You have no idea what difficulties I've been through in life. You just have no idea what it's been like to be Leslie Thompson." I turned my back toward him as I fought to hold back the tears. "You make me out to be some evil monster, but all I wanted was to really be loved and accepted for who I am. I'm not unbreakable . . . I'm just not, Trey. I'm human and I have feelings, just like you do. I never wanted Cartier, Tiffany, Chanel, or Dom Perignon. I could've been happy living in a modest little one-bedroom cottage with the man I thought would wake up and give me what I obviously craved—*attention*. Even so, all I ever got from you was criticism!" I explained, my voice wavering. I extended my arm to hang up the phone as tears began streaming down my face, accepting that I was getting the closure I needed to disconnect every emotion from Trey.

As I wiped the tears clean, I considered that he was getting on my nerves by assuming so much about me and my mindset, until I heard something I never expected. Trey touched the glass with the fingertips of his left hand. I placed the phone back up to my ear to hear his words.

"When I was fifteen, I secretly fathered a child. My parents don't know, but somewhere out there…I have a son. The baby was snatched away from his mother and given up for adoption. I searched high and low for him for years and years to no avail. I never wanted to risk hurting you; I loved you so much, Lesile. You're beautiful and I could hardly manage to resist you. What I felt for you transcended the physical, and I thought you knew that. To me, abstaining was the lesser of two evils. Now you know why I wanted to stop having sex with you, until our wedding day. When I found out you did get pregnant, I figured it was a sign from God that he gave me another child to make up for the sadness I experienced so long ago. You don't have any idea of the life I've led either. Now you know my biggest secret, too. Are you happy now, Leslie . . . are you?"

Trey dropped the phone and broke down in tears. I watched him sob, and the thought of a man revealing his hurt at the most inopportune time made me feel small and defeated. I hung up the phone and left without saying goodbye. As I walked away, all I could do was pretend I didn't hear what he told me. When trial time came, maybe I'd tell the District Attorney the truth . . . but probably *not*. I could always pretend I didn't remember a thing. After all, I was high as a kite when the love train collided and derailed. Unfortunately, our desire to communicate fully was much too late— too much wickedness had already fallen upon us. Despite his surprising confession, I still doubted I could ever forgive him for marrying Tanya behind my back. To me, doing that was completely unforgivable. As a result, I would never fully extend the olive branch and regret what I did to Trey, even if my affair with Rico began over a simple lack of communication

25

Whats Done In the Dark

I would never admit it to Trey, but he was right about a few things. Now the big question was if my lack of self-control led to me being HIV positive, or if it would prove to be a bit of a set up for a strong come back. To answer that question, I took off on a not so fantastic voyage in pursuit of the truth. I went to the health department's STD clinic to get an AIDS test. I didn't desire to make an appointment with my regular medical doctor because I didn't want to generate a paper trail that would follow me on my medical record if anything was in fact wrong with my health. I recalled some prostitutes on craigslist.org mentioning that they got tested at the county health department, so I went to Google and found a number to ask about how things worked. I had never had reason to get tested in the past, but now I truly did.

"Yes, I would like to have some information about getting tested," I said to the woman who answered the phone.

"Get here 8:00 A.M., Monday through Friday, with the exception of Thursday. We're open from 11:30 to 6:00 on Thursdays," the woman told me.

I could tell by the tone of her voice that people pestered

her with those sorts of questions every few minutes. I don't now how she had the patience for it, even if she was being paid.

"What do you test for? Do you get your results the same day?" I asked.

"We test for all of the major sexually transmitted diseases. After you're tested, it takes a week or so to get everything back from the lab."

"So you also test for HIV there?"

"The results take two weeks for that."

"I read something on the Internet about a test where you can find out your results the same day so I'm a bit confused."

"That's the rapid results HIV test. HAP is on the first floor. We're on the second floor. You have to call down there to find out their hours."

"Do you have their number?"

"Yes, it's area code 301 . . . ," she said, rambling off the number.

"Thank you."

"Goodbye," she replied.

As I drove to the clinic to get tested for the ABC's of STD's, I lost myself in wondering if I was going to die. When I was getting mine, I really didn't consider that Rico or even any of the others could have something. I was so afraid of facing my final judgment call that I could feel my heart pound and my throat get dry. Finding out my status was the pits but I had to do it. Everything we do has consequences. When we play any game of chance, sometimes we luck out and get off light, and sometimes we don't. I walked into the room feeling very nervous about all of that. I filled out a form that was obviously created for statistical purposes. There was no way I was going to admit I engaged in any type of high-risk sexual activity with so many random partners, even though I was getting tested anonymously. If I did admit those things, how could I ever look at myself in the mirror again? It was much easier to lie through the pain. Running away from it made me feel a little better, so I let that part of what was done in the dark stay in the dark.

After I filled out the form the receptionist gave me, I waited for my turn to be examined. It alarmed me that people sat in the lobby laughing as if sitting in the STD clinic was some sort of joke. I was amazed that anyone could manage to laugh at a time like that when I was embarrassed just being there, and even more embarrassed when they called me by my first and last name. As I stood to enter the back area, the door opened, and a couple exited with brown bags in hand. I thought their faces looked familiar, so I kept staring at them as we nearly brushed shoulders in the hallway. The woman was carrying a small brown paper bag of what a reasonable person could assume was antibiotics. By the time the man touched the doorway to let the woman through the other side of the door, I finally recalled their identity—it was the man and woman I had picked up at the club in D.C., Deja and her husband! My mouth dropped and I continued looking over my shoulder as the door eased shut. I wanted to run up and smack the both of them, but I had no right to. All I could do was watch them leave the room. I then saw what Trey meant. Some people were burning out here. I swallowed, sighed hard, and caught up with the woman I was supposed to be following.

The next thing I recall was being tormented by a monster migraine headache as I made a fist to have my blood drawn. I kept wondering if I was going to lose the only thing I had left—*my life*. After I walked across the hall, an unemotional doctor told me to undress and put on a paper gown, and then she exited the room. I did what she instructed and was ready by the time she returned. Afterward, she ordered me to move down on the table so she could give me a gynecological exam and take specimens to send to the lab. As I placed my legs in metal stirrups, fear grabbed me and wouldn't let go.

"Open your legs," she told me.

"I did."

"Miss, you must open them more than that," she said sounding annoyed.

I opened them wider and cringed as she struggled to affix the speculum. I was waiting for her to apply KY jelly like my GYN usually did upon examining me but she never did.

"Did you know you have a titled uterus? When's the last time you had sex? Have you had an AIDS test yet? You should have an AIDS test," she said with a distinct accent.

I believe she was Ethiopian, or at least she appeared to be. My head spun as she asked me a series of personal questions I preferred not to answer. As for her cold demeanor, I couldn't blame her. My hole was just one of many to inspect, and after all, I was only paying ten dollars for all of the services that were being rendered on my behalf. Although I understood where she was coming from, I felt intimidated by her sterile approach.

Just as the person who answered the phone when I called for information explained, I had to call back for results the following week. In the meantime, I was given two bottles of medication as a preventive measure: 500 milligrams of something called Metronidazole, and 100 milligrams of Doxycycline Hyclate. Why? I couldn't dare admit to the doctor that I had been sexing all sorts of partners I didn't know so I lied and told her that I was raped a few days prior. I didn't need anyone judging me, and telling a little white lie was the only way I could make it through. But then again, I could argue that Rico led me to be sexually assaulted by a room full of policemen. I never told them to stop what they were doing so that evening fell into a gray area.

Next, I took my last journey to the first floor. HAP was written on the door, so I opened it when I was certain I was in the correct place. I made it in thirty minutes before closing, and the counselor agreed to test me. He explained the procedure and how the rapid results test worked. After he swabbed my mouth below my lower set of teeth, I waited for the big count down. Before leaving the clinic that day, I'd know my status thanks to a modern technique that involved collecting saliva, not blood. In the meantime, I decided to write Trey a letter that would explain the other half of my issues—the half I never revealed to anyone outside of my family. I didn't know if I would mail it after his performance but I knew I at least wanted to put it on paper.

Dear Trey,

I have twenty minutes to wait before I get my HIV test results. While I am waiting, I've decided to tell you my biggest secret, since you shared yours with me. Don't mistake my opening up to you as forgiveness because I never would've married Rico, but you <u>did</u>, I repeat, <u>did</u>, marry Ms. Tanya.

My family was at the wedding. I didn't invite them and you wouldn't have guessed that any of them were related to me, and now I'm going to explain why I lied about them being dead. When I was growing up, I was made to feel that I was an unattractive person. Comments like, "don't play in the sun," and "don't marry no black man, your kids will be cursed to be reminded they are niggers, every day of the week," reminding me that I was the darkest in a family full of light skinned people. In fact, we still had relatives that passed for white, and no one ever would know any different, at least by sight alone. When I asked my mother why her relatives would proclaim to be something they weren't, she would explain the history of our country which ties your amount of hue to the opportunity you seem to deserve. According to her, whites embraced light people more, sometimes without even thinking, because they appeared to be more like them. As a seven-year-old child, I'd shrug my shoulders, considering history books I'd devour about the motherland and all of the wonderful books about black inventors and trailblazers. Initially, I never viewed my deep brown skin as any different from white or lighter skin, but my lack of similarity to those who were in my bloodlines ate away at my self-esteem. Each time I looked in the mirror, my reflection reminded me that I didn't have blue eyes and blonde hair like my mother, aunts, and cousins, nor did I show any signs of an Indian heritage like my father and sister—I was one of the few who stood out like a sore thumb. I felt like a foreigner in my own territory because everyone seemed to question how this happened since both of my parents were born of "mixed" families. Even so, what could I do? This is how my inadequacy complex all began.

My older sister grabbed all my mother's genes, and was often mistaken for Puerto Rican, if she spoke one measly word of Spanish. People would automatically assume she was one of them, if not biracial. She ate up the attention greedily and often reminded me that I was an unworthy after thought. She went from describing me as such to taunting me like she despised me for having fuller lips, a larger nose, and kinky hair. Sometimes I would watch her brush her jet blac,k wavy hair that reached her waist and fantasize about what it must be like to be as beautiful as she was. After she finished, I often walked over to a mirror and began plucking my hair with my fingers. I would turn to her and ask her to help me with my hair and she would laugh, replying that she could do nothing with three-inch naps. My sister would primp in the mirror and would even try to look at her reflection in the microwave or anything with a reflective quality. At every turn, she'd proclaim that she would never cut her hair so she could remind the world that she was no ordinary blackie. Although her insults made tears flow, I continued trying to get her to love me by making her queen for a day, waiting on her hand and foot, and letting her take the credit for completing her chores when I had really done them. In a sense, being nice to her seemed to make her treat me worse.

When my parents went away on a vacation, she once locked me in the basement and told me that my dinner was in the dog's bowl. I shook with fear in the crawl space for the duration of the night. My eyes fell upon snakeskin where one of the critters had left their old ones behind. I finally submitted to my hunger and drank the water from the dog's dish and ate the Alpo that sat clumped on the other side of it. My sister walked around to the outside of the house and pointed at me through a small window. She and a teenage boy ridiculed me for several minutes before disappearing like ghosts. When my parents returned, I explained every detail of what she did that evening, but I was punished for fabricating a tall tale. If I fabricated that tall tale, why couldn't they see the truth of her ugly side through another incident?

On my ninth birthday, only two kids showed up at my birthday party, and she still was jealous that I received any attention and angry that my parents demanded she wear a party hat and sing happy birthday to me with everyone else. When my mother set the cake on the table, my sister punched it with her fist as hard as she could, then gave me a look of death. I ran to my bedroom to escape the humiliation, and I got in trouble for being rude to my guests, while she was permitted to go out with her friends after pitching a fit, behavingas if she were nine, not sixteen. After that incident, I no longer begged for my sister's love. I became withdrawn and stopped vying for the loved little sister spot. It was my parents who continued to force me to interact with her. At this point, she was so mean-spirited that when my father asked her to help me learn how to ride the new bike I was given for my birthday, she intentionally pushed me too hard, and I flew into a tree stump, badly scarring my knees. While I sat on the ground with bloody knees, she laughed and told me no man would ever want me anyway, and having ugly legs would not matter. Enough about that bitch though, I could go on forever about her cruel antics.

As if my "easy going" home life wasn't enough, the kids at school also taunted me for trying to make myself appear lighter with my mother's finishing powder, having short hair, crooked teeth, a string bean- like body, and nerd qualities. After hearing degrading comments yelled from the bus window thrown my way one time too many, I just became desensitized to what others said or did. Feeling spit balls stuck in my hair, kicks at the back of my heels in school, and eating lunch alone became just a day in the life. I never bothered to fight back. My defense was sticking my head in my books and excelling in school. I decided that when I got older I would save my money and move far away from my hometown. Each day I arrived home, I placed aluminum foil over my teeth, in the secrecy of the bathroom. I tossed my head back like my sister did when she wanted to make her hair shake like the white girls did, and I fantasizing about buying braces and boys whistling loudly when I walked by.

My plan to escape the hell at my home address worked. While my parents paid for my sister to attend Fisk University, I wasn't offered one red cent to further my education. Someone suggested I join the military or investigate becoming a maid or caring for wealthy white children. I shook my head respectfully, but inside, I was saying: "Later for that Gone With The Wind mess. I'm about to do bigger and better things." I didn't tell my *parents of my scholarship to a Historically Black College because I knew I would receive zilch in the praise department. I rejoiced with myself and decided to disown my entire family. I prepared myself to lie and tell everyone that inquired that all of my immediate family died in a tragic accident and I didn't care to elaborate. I disappeared into thin air and never saw any of them again, until they looked me up after hearing I was going to get married. If they cared, I'm sure they could have found me somehow—before that time—they failed the test, yet another time.*

While attending college, the zits that plagued my skin dried up, braces did wonders for my jagged teeth, and I'd developed a hell of a figure, which made men scream, hoot, holler, and lust when I walked by. I became very popular on campus and was voted homecoming queen of my class. The verdict was in—everyone liked chocolate, and redbone and yellow girls were no longer hogging all of the male attention.

Every sorority approached me about becoming a sister, every athlete tried to get in my pants, and every semester I made it to the Dean's List. Even with all of this reversal of events, I was lonely as hell. One day I was walking toward the library when this tall, dark, and handsome brother who had a smile like Morris Chestnut, sex appeal like Tyson Beckford, and a body cut like a Greek God, stopped me to ask where a place to grab a bite was located I had met a brother who made me feel something real and I could barely manage to explain that a fast food joint was sitting right behind us. Apparently, he felt something too and invited me to come with him. I had already eaten dinner but my lips prevented me from letting him know that I had been there an hour earlier. The conversation over the worst food of my life proved to be the best one of my life. I felt drawn to the commuter student who attended Morehouse and was also putting himself through school. Well, graduate school.

He was the soul mate kind of real deal, and treated me like a queen from day one. Time proved that his inner self was as beautiful as what made my mouth water—he was the total package. Within one month, we became a couple and never looked back. The day we both graduated from our prospective programs, he professed his love for me and presented a friendship ring to me that he requested I wear until the time came for an engagement ring. A few years later, I got that ring, as promised. As you know, the man I am speaking fondly of is you. With all of my friends complaining they were alone, you would think I would have rejoiced to know that my man was nearly signed, sealed, and delivered. The thing is, Trey, I felt you stopped paying me attention so I turned to another way to get it. I held back my libido and never let go, until we started having relationship problems. When you started turning me down sexually, I was reminded of how good it felt to be chased back in college, based on my looks. This time around, I was out to have some fun while turning some heads again. I had no idea you were making efforts to reinforce our financial future. I don't know if I'm really a nympho; maybe I'm more like attention starved, given that I internalized the hurt of my childhood, or maybe I just love sex and can't get a grip. Quite frankly, I'm not even sure if I truly understand the meaning of love. What I do know is that I acted on my fantasies and screwed all of those people to deaden the pain of rejection, since getting off was the only thing I could seem to control. In fact, I never reconciled with the worst part of my emotional damage. I don't believe I'm about to tell you but the emotions are just pouring out of me right now. It was the time that . . .

"Miss, would you come with me please," the counselor called when I was in the middle of finishing a sentence.

I stuffed the letter I was writing to Trey in my purse and followed him back into the testing area. After I followed him around the corner and sat in the chair, I began to swallow hard and shake. Innocence took off and left Leslie high and dry. Fear rolled up next to me, and I must admit that my bold persona shut down, leaving me vulnerable to the truth.

"You tested anonymously, correct?"

"Yes. I can't look! No, no. I can't. I've been such a whore. What if, what if I'm going to die? I don't want to know," I said, crying after my spontaneous outburst.

"Miss, here it is. Look at your test results, and at least you'll know," he urged.

I cried harder as I began walking around the room in circles, finally resting my head on an army green filing cabinet.

"Miss . . . Miss. It's okay. Look," the man insisted. "I think you'll want to see this."

I swung my head around and looked at the results.

"Now when the line is going across on this top bar, it means that no HIV has been detected in your saliva. You're okay."

"I am?"

"Yes."

I cried and cried as I looked at the testing strip again. I began to shake from becoming so emotional. I finally mustered the strength to speak. "Is this one hundred percent accurate?"

"The rapid results test is 99.8% accurate."

I stared at the testing strip once more. Phase two of my new life had begun, after seeing the results in black and white. I was negative! I thanked Jesus over and over again as my face grew hot.

"Now that you know your status, you have to keep these

test results negative. Use a condom each and every time you have sex," the counselor told me.

"I know. I know. You're right," I agreed, wiping my tears away.

After the counselor and I had a private conversation, I humbly thanked him for his patience. While contemplating what happened, I reached over to hug him.

"Thank you, sir. Thank you so much for being nice to me. I'm going through so much right now," I said, realizing that I'd grabbed him inappropriately.

Afterward, I asked him for free condoms. He left and returned with a small stash to drop in my purse. I dropped them inside of my bag noticing that I heard people leaving for the day. Since I was his last appointment, something came over me—I wanted to hold on to his time and manipulate it.

"I'll never have unprotected sex again. I guess I should know how to put a condom on a man properly though. I know this is awkward but I want to ask while I have the guts," I explained.

"Well, I don't have anything to demonstrate on in here. I'd have to go get something."

I touched his arm. "Yes, you do. *Yourself*," I flirted, smiling.

I began to feel wetness between my legs, and I couldn't ward Innocence off, even during a serious time like this. The man cleared his throat and began to blush. I walked over to him, unfastened and unzipped his pants, then looked him in the eyes.

"Let's celebrate the fact that I won't ever have unprotected sex again," I explained, rolling the condom down on his penis. I lowered my mouth between his slacks and began sucking him. He started to moan, moving my head back and forth toward his erection.

"Miss . . . Miss. Did you hear what I said?" the counselor asked.

"What?"

"I said you're okay."

"Yes, I heard every word," I told him, realizing that I had been fantasizing over the most unlikely "victim." The problem was I was wet as hell and still couldn't control myself. I left the small office, equipped with protection, wishing my libido would give me a break. A new phase of my life had begun, after seeing the results in black and white.

" 'Scuse me, sweetheart. Which way is 495? I'm on my way up the highway and I'm not from around here," the stranger said, pulling over.

"It's easier for me to show you," I explained. "The thing is, I'm waiting on my ride," I said, swaying my hips in that way that made men hoot and holler at me. My newfound knowledge made me more smug, instead of scaring me straight.

"I'll drop you where you need to go, if you answer one question."

"What?" I asked, bending over.

"Do you like orgies, ropes, handcuffs, whips, chains, doggy fucking or sitting on top of a dick? Sex in a car, park, or public bathroom? What's your style, ma?"

I couldn't believe what I was hearing. It was like music to my ears, and I was nearly salivating at the thought of getting off. I put my safety aside and hopped in his car for a quickie.

"To answer your question, I like anything that will make my ride home smoother. I like it all. But for starters, how about anything goes in a car—this car," I said, trying to get a peek at his crotch.

When the man's wheels rolled around to the back of the parking lot, he unfastened his pants and showed me exactly what I wanted to see. I pulled out a condom, and rolled it down on his penis as I had done in my fantasy a few moments prior.

"Here's your appetizer, since you want to know so much about what I do and don't like," I told him. I needed some

dick in my mouth so I sucked on him until my jaws hurt. Although I was giving him a covered blow job, I was giving him
some good head, massaging and sucking on his balls at the
same time. He began to moan so I knew he was enjoying it.
When I raised my head, I slipped and said, "Trey. Oh Trey.
Oooh, baby. Trey. I knew you'd like this if you just let me—"

"Don't be calling no nigga's name at a time like this, bitch,"
the man snapped. I had obviously pissed him off.

"Who are you calling a bitch?"

"You. Give me some respect, you crazy ass—"

"I know you better get off my got damn man!" a woman
screamed, her burgundy braids swinging wildly. She was toting a toddler and put down the carrier to come at me like she
wanted to get something started.

"Um, baby, baby! Um," the man stuttered. "Take it easy!"

"Baby, nothing! You were out here getting your Johnson
sucked by some nasty freak? Now I see why you always want
to wait in the car while the baby gets checkups. I knew you
were up to something . . . out here looking to pick up
hoochies in the parking lot," she ranted.

I raised my head as she opened the car door. She pulled
me out of the car by my hair.

"Why can't you hoes leave married men alone?"

"You ain't all that anyway, so shut up!" I yelled. "Why can't
your man be more careful who he picks up and plays nasty
with in parking lots? Obviously, you're not all that he's living
for because I just left the clinic and he *still* was about to hit
this!"

Her husband flew out of the car and pulled the woman off
of me. Without speaking, I ran toward my vehicle, dodging
expletives, and the sound of the baby screaming for attention.
When I reached my ride, I squealed tires, throwing up my
middle finger as I sped past the woman and her trifling husband. She struggled to throw a used pamper at my car. Small
balls of shit flew in the air as the pamper managed to hit my

trunk. I looked in my rearview mirror and watched it fall. I don't know if it would've mattered if I would've known her little broke down man was married, but I was pissed as hell that I got played.

Rolling down the highway, I wiped saliva from my arm, ashamed of what I'd done, and feeling as though I would've been better off buying batteries for my vibrator until further notice. Whenever I was having sex, I felt in control of my life. I knew I was out of control, but just as Trey claimed, I needed counseling so I could tighten up my life and keep my legs crossed for more than a twenty-four hour period.

I turned my cell phone back on. I noticed I had a total of ten messages. When I began to retrieve them, I could hear bodies smacking and a couple moaning without words being spoken. Bed springs squeaking loudly made my pulse quicken. Was it a wife, girlfriend, or full-time lover of someone's path I crossed? At the time, I just didn't know but something told me Deja's looney self had flipped out. Feeling aggravated, I deleted each one and dismissed it as a childish stunt, until I reached the tenth one. Voices drifted into my ear. When they did, my world went blank. I couldn't help but to want to listen to the bizarre scene, although it would be an understatement to say I was fuming.

"Papi is going to give you a treat today. Do you like this?" the man asked.

"No, I don't like it—I love it," the woman cooed. "Hit that shit, Daddy! Oh yeah, that's the spot. Keep doing it just like that. That's what I'm talkin' about!" she exclaimed sounding like a home girl from the hood.

"What in the heeeell!" I mumbled to myself.

"Did you miss your papi, la joya? Is your mind made up, my jewel?" he asked as the woman kept moaning. She struggled to articulate her words in between heavy breaths. "Act like it and give me my pussy, because you're mine now! Todo de su cuerpo es para mi, you bad girl! Your husband can't compete with Rico. You're out here in the middle of the Chesapeake Bay, so stop holding back," he said. "Fuck me like you mean it. Scream for me, puta. Make Rico's fantasies come true."

At that second, I finally understood how Tanya felt.

As the woman screamed, losing control, I simultaneously screamed, "No! No! No, please. Noooo!" The next thing I remember, I could feel myself breaking out in a cold sweat as I sped along. As my heart pounded, I stuck my foot on the gas as hard as I could, in pursuit of the dirty dog, Rico. Even if I had to wait all evening for him to return from were he'd once taken me, I would. I lost my fiancé because of his stalker ass, and now he was going for my other jugular vein. After all, the voice in the background belonged to someone I knew all too well. This time, my former baby's daddy was using the identical game he used on me to break off my rival and sister . . . *Angela*!

26

The Final SHeBaNG!

I rocked back and forth in the driver's seat, laying on my car horn and cussing out of the window. Innocence's original plans were foiled. I was stuck in rush hour traffic on the Baltimore Washington Parkway and felt the pressure build as I proceeded down the highway at a snail's pace then stopped.

"Get the hell out of my way. Move iiiiiiiit! Move it, you slow driving dick faces!" I yelled like a crazed maniac.

The person in the car in front of me threw up their hands as if to say, "What do you want me to do, can't you see this place is a parking lot? I can't go anywhere either." When I pulled my head back into my car, I turned to the right and noticed a man dressed in a shirt and tie changing his tire on the slim shoulder of the highway. An evil thought crept into my mind as I recalled that pretty boy Rico loved to speed with his convertible top down. My rage-filled screaming bout transformed into a slow diabolical laugh as I finally understood that I'd been going about getting back at Rico in all the wrong ways. I surfed the radio stations until sinister sounding rock and roll music set the mood for evil thoughts to be conjured and collected in my head. While rocking back and forth, I began working out the sordid details of improperly tightened lug nuts breaking and resulting in all four wheels falling off.

The first thing I needed to do was get my hands on a BMW lug wrench, someone else's ride, and a well-informed thug who could help me fuck up some wheels. Hey, that Innocence bitch was always plotting and scheming on how to break the motherfucker up. But this time, I was determined to pull a strategy of a different flavor out of my hat. Nothing was going to stop me this time. Absolutely nothing. Ruining my wedding plans, fucking my sister, and stealing the money that was earned from me laying on my back spelled a final round of I Declare War.

Everyone has at least one person who knows someone with street contacts, so I placed a call to an associate who put me in touch with a friend of a friend with real street smarts and some sort of prison record. Bow Legs came highly recommended to give me some ideas on a "personal matter," so long as I caught up with him while he was good and sober.

My contact urged me not to discuss anything over the phone and agreed to meet me at an isolated address up in the cut of a spot in North East, D.C. I did . . . in Trey's car. I still had his car key on my ring, and I felt like taking advantage of not being spotted in my ride or creating a paper trail by renting one. I explained my loose lug plan to Bow Legs, although I didn't explain why.

"Now shortie, that's some suburban, Marsha Brady thinking shit right there. If you want to risk him trying to figure out that a wobble was coming from loose lug nuts, do thangs your way. But if you really want to be slick, cut each tire down to the cord with a box cutter knife, and stop at a certain place. I'm not saying how I know, but I'm just saying that's how it would go down with peeps in the hood," he told me.

"That's what I want," I said, agreeing. "Can you do this tonight? Time is running out, and I need this done tonight."

"That all depends."

"On what?"

"I've got you, Bow Legs," I said, showing him the money. "How's thirty dollars for gas, plus two hundred to help a sister out?" I showed him the money and handed him a carton of cigarettes for a tip, as my contact suggested, just to be certain he wouldn't say no. "Now I'm not trying to be funny, but I can't hand this over until I come back. Consider the smokes a deposit."

The other tip I was told was not to give Bow Legs the money up front because he'd get his head bad and I wouldn't be able to find him.

He nodded. "We both need to change clothes though. The last thing we want is to draw attention to ourselves. Do you have something black?" he asked, opening the carton of cigarettes.

"Yes. I have an all black outfit I can throw on."

"This is what we're going to do. We'll take separate cars. As soon as I cut the tires, I'm out—you're on your own and Bow Leg's don't know nothing. I never seen you, and you never seen me."

"I got it Bow Legs. I'm not going to say anything," I replied in a whiny voice.

"So how long will it take you to change and come back?"

"Not even forty minutes."

"All right. Now listen, don't take no vacation. Hurry up and ring my phone once when you pull up out front of here," he told me, lighting up a cigarette.

"I will. In fact, I'll be back sooner if I can," I said.

Two hours later, Bow Legs and I were quietly circling the waterfront neighborhood in Annapolis where I had once visited with Rico and his friends. It didn't take me long to spot Rico's car across the street from where his friend's boat was docked before.

Luckily, he didn't drive his crotch rocket. He took the

Beamer out for a spin. I turned off my car lights and nodded to Bow Legs. He turned off his lights, hit all four tires with the box cutter, and then rolled out. I couldn't believe how fast he worked but I took a chance that he wasn't bluffing about knowing what to do.

I waited in the parking lot of a small shopping center off of Arundel on the Bay Road. I fought sleep as I anticipated Rico passing by with Angela at any time. About three o'clock in the morning, I spotted Rico's tail lights moving past my location. While expediting extreme caution, I eased out of the parking lot, getting close enough to confirm his tag number. After I did, I chuckled as I trailed behind and watched him entertain Angela with his same old predictable lover boy routine. As they headed toward Aris T. Allen Boulevard, I shook my head back and forth at the thought that I'd finally stumped the one who thought he knew it all. In fact, when he stopped at the light, Rico grew even more comfortable, cranking the radio while dropping his top. As soon as the light turned green, he was playing in Angela's hair with his right hand, nibbling on her ear instead of keeping his eyes on the road. After playing with Ms. Bimbo Bitch, he turned the curve in the road, and exited off toward Washington D.C., kicking his speed up to a good eighty miles per hour on the dark, sparsely traveled highway.

By the time I popped a Life Saver in my mouth, I watched a deer appear from a wooded area, and dart in Rico's path, from over top of a high hill. Rico smacked on his brakes and laid on his horn. I slowed my car down and stopped as I watched his back left tire blow out, then the right one, and finally the remaining two. About twenty seconds after he hit the animal, I could hear shrill screams and smell burning rubber. Obviously, Rico was fighting to steer the lopsided car but he had no control over the vehicle's direction. The deer rolled up on his windshield, and over his car, then fell off near the driver's side. Rico's convertible spun around in two revolutions, tipped over, and he was ejected in a wooded area near the side of the road. When the vehicle hit the railing, glass shattered and flew in every possible direction. By the time I heard one final crash, I noticed that neither Angela nor Rico's airbag deployed. The hood of the car was crushed, and I heard a steady hissing noise that told me what was left of the car could catch fire or explode any second. My eyes followed the mangled pieces of metal that were strewn all over the highway—even I couldn't believe what had happened so fast.

I smiled when I recalled that Angela was still inside of the vehicle and that Rico had gone flying through the air like a big bird and landed in the woods. When I stopped Trey's car from a distance on the shoulder of the road, I watched a frantic man pull over and hop out. He was so loud and hysterical that I could hear most of what he was saying in between his screams for help into his cell phone.

"I pulled over to help someone at the scene of an accident. There's a woman that's been in a terrible car accident. We're off of route 50 just before the Davidsonville exit. She needs an ambulance now! I don't see the driver. She looks to be unconscious, and I'm not sure if she's even alive—hurry! I don't think I should move her because she could have spinal or neck injuries. Help! What should I do? The car seems like it may explode at any second!"

I snapped my fingers. "Damn! I wonder if I can get a refund for the prepaid phone I bought from 7-11. I was at least prepared to dial 911 for you and dirty Rico, Angela. Like you said, you materialistic, vain bitch, teachers don't make hardly enough money," I mumbled to myself.

I gloated as I started up Trey's ride and rode past the scene of the accident. I headed for home and popped the cork of a bottle of finely aged wine I'd been saving for years. As I sipped on a glass of the best stuff in my house, I washed the stress away with a nice candlelit bath, while listening to one of the relaxation tapes Angela had left. I tilted my head back,

Dear Readers,

I hope that you enjoyed a peak into Leslie's secret world. I know that I've kept you long enough already. Since I have, I'll keep this letter short, sweet, and neat. Let me first say that I love writing about drama in this crazy world. I wrote this story for a great deal of entertainment value, so I won't get into what my research revealed. I promised myself I wouldn't be a preacher this time! I'm sure you were able to pick up on enough commentary toward the end. The only point I'd like to specifically mention is that if you are a sexually active single, I hope this story serves as an example of why it is a *must* do to wrap it up each and every time you engage in sexual activity. Never take your partner for granted, and regard him or her as someone who you may or may not know everything about. If you are living a promiscuous lifestyle, question if it's really worth it. If there is a reason behind your behavior, consider seeking professional counseling. Also, don't forget to pay quality attention to your woman, men. What you may take for granted, someone else may be glad to have. What if that someone turned out to be one of your boys? Oops, I didn't mean to say that.

On another note, some readers have asked me about *Vinegar Blues*, which I refer to in *Schemin'*. I just may revise the story into nonfiction accounts of my life that will serve as my inspirational book.☺ As I previously stated, a portion of the proceeds of my forthcoming inspirational title will be donated for cancer research, so please consider supporting that project or whichever inspiration project I select. I don't think there are many people who haven't been somehow been touched by this terrible disease. If I don't decide to tell all about me, I will continue striving to collect the most heartfelt inspirational stories from people who have walked various paths in life. Hopefully, this project will come to fruition in the future.

Lastly, I welcome your comments and questions. You may send them to *dreamweaverpress@aol.com, andrea@dreamweaverpress. net,* or send them via snail mail. You will find my address on the next page. I appreciate your support and interest in a budding author!

Best wishes always,

Andrea Blackstone

NYMPH

Please help decide how Leslie's world will end. Will it stop here? Email or write to me, and cast your vote today!

GET MONEY CHICKS
BY ANNA J.

A Hustle Gone Dead Wrong

"Bitch, what is you whispering for? I can't hear a thang you sayin'," my girl Karen yelled into the phone over the loud music in the background.

My heart was beating in my throat, and even if I tried I couldn't speak no louder than I was at the moment. I collected my thoughts as best as I could, but all I could hear were sirens, the clink of handcuffs, and bars shutting behind me. I had to get out of there and quick.

"Girl, you gotta go get Shanna and get over here quick. I think I killed him, girl." By now tears were rolling from the corners of my eyes like a run in a pair of stockings. I couldn't breathe, and my vision was blurring as we spoke.

"Over where? Black Ron's house? I thought you was in there pulling a caper?"

"Karen, listen to me. You have to go get Shanna and come over here now! I need y'all. I don't know what to do."

"No, problem. I think I just saw her pull up to the building. We'll be there in like three minutes."

Instead of responding I hung up. Snatching my clothes from behind the chair, I slid into my gear quickly and went downstairs to wait for my friends. In my heart I hoped this nigga was just playing a cruel joke, and was just trying to scare me. I couldn't go to jail for murder. I didn't have time to be fighting no bitches off me 'cause I was fresh meat, and as sexy as I am there's no doubt they'd be trying to get at me.

Not even four minutes passed, and my girls were pulling up to Black Ron's door. I breathed a temporary sigh of relief as I opened the door to let them in, but the moment the door was closed I busted into tears and fell into Shanna's arms. If my morning didn't start out bad, my night was ending in the worst way.

"Mina, pull yourself together and talk to me. Where is Ron, and what happened?" Shanna said, making me stand up on my own two feet and wipe my face. I sniffled a few times in an attempt to catch my breath. We took seats around the living room, and I ran the entire day down to my girls.

"I met Ron at the club last night and we came here to handle our business. He was already drunker then a mu'fucka so I knew getting ends from him was going to be a piece of cake," I said to them as I wiped snot and tears from my face.

I went on to tell them how Black Ron, the largest dealer in all of this side of Yeadon, was popping Xani's like they were lifesavers. He had already been drinking way before I saw him at Heat, a local night spot in Sharon Hill over there on Hook Road where all the ballers hung out. He was up in that piece flashing money like he had just won the damn Power Ball, and I was on his ass before any of those other smut bitches could take advantage of his weak state of mind.

We left there around two in the morning, and I ended up having to help him to his car and drive to his crib so he wouldn't kill me and any other unsuspecting motorist behind the wheel. By the time we got to the crib he was able to walk a little straighter, and he made it upstairs just fine.

My plan was to fuck him to sleep and help myself to a little bit of that money when he was out like a light. I would then ask him for money in the morning because I knew he didn't know how much money he was throwing around the night before. I mean, the late great Notorious B.I.G. said it best, "Never get high on your own supply." A chick like me will catch you slippin' and then the next thing you know, it's curtains.

By the time I got finished taking a shower and came back into the bedroom, this nigga was lying back in the bed with his dick in his hand watching *My Baby Got Back* on the television. Silly me thought he would be out for the night, but I guess I would have to work for my money this evening.

"You feeling better?" I asked him, inching closer to the bed. He turned his attention my way for a split second before looking back at the television.

"Yeah, my head pounding a little, but I'm cool. Thanks for seeing that I got home. Out of all the tricks I fuck with, you are the only one I truly trust."

I didn't say anything, instead I toweled my body dry and began to apply some of the lotion he had on his dresser. I pretended not to pay him any mind, but I saw him go from watching me to watching the porn movie out of the corner of my eye. I made a display of massaging my breasts and spreading my legs, acting the entire time like he wasn't in the room.

"Girl, get over here and ride this dick. What you puttin' all that damn lotion on for anyway? You just gonna be ashy in the morning all over again."

I continued to lotion my body like I didn't hear what he said. He was stroking his dick in a long, slow motion, and I'd be damned if I didn't want some of it. Black Ron was definitely working with some shit. I figured I might as well make it a two for one deal. Get the best nut of my life, and the cash to go with it.

Walking over to the bed, I waited until I got to the side to drop the towel. Through half-closed eyelids, Ron watched me give him head while he finger fucked my pussy and smacked me on my ass.

Now, this nigga had been drinking Henney all night, so I knew this was gonna be forever. My head skills were impeccable, and in no time flat I was swallowing all of his babies. But his dick was still standing at attention.

"Damn, girl. If you used your head for anything else you'd be a genius. Get up and ride Daddy's dick."

Ignoring the comment he made, I did what I was told, riding him like I'd been taking horse riding lessons my entire life. I guess my momma's dreams of me being a ballerina were crushed, because the woman I am now is nothing like the girl I was back in the day.

I was on his dick hard, knowing the payout at the end of the night would be marvelous. He stretched my long legs out in all kinds of directions, and I could have sworn I heard him saying something about loving me before he pulled his dick out and busted yet another nut in my face. I pretended like I enjoyed it while he panted all hard in an effort to catch his breath beside me.

Reaching over to the side of the bed, I grabbed the towel to remove his children from my face. This dude was a beast, and although I could see him falling asleep, I knew it would be on again in the morning. I took that moment to take eight one hundred dollar bills from his pants pocket and put it in my wallet before lying in the bed next to him. He snuggled up close to me, and before I knew it I was 'sleep, too.

In the morning I woke up to him sliding his already hard dick into me from the back, and I had to clear the cold out of my eyes so I could focus. This nut was a little quicker than last night, and I was grateful. I laid back in the bed and watched him stumble around the room, and almost fall into the hallway over one of his Timberland boots. I laughed, but not out loud, because Black Ron is crazy and has been known to knock a chick upside the head for less. When he came back into the room, his eyes looked bloodshot, and he damn near crawled to the bed to get in it.

"You gonna be okay, BR?" I asked, noticing his breathing was getting heavier and he was breaking out in a sweat. I didn't know what was wrong with him, but I wouldn't just leave him like this. I still had to get paid for my services.

"Yeah, I'm cool. Those damn pills got me trippin'," he said in a slurred tone as his eyes closed, and his head fell to the side.

"How many did you take?" I asked, scared as hell. I didn't know what was happening, but I couldn't call the cops because I knew this nigga had drugs or something up in this camp, and I'd be damned if I was going to jail for conspiracy.

"Like four of 'em this morning, but I'm cool. I just need to sleep it off."

I didn't answer; I just moved closer to him and let him put his head on my stomach. Not too long after that he was snoring and I was able to turn him on his back. I watched him for a little while, but before I knew it I was asleep, too.

"And when I woke up he wasn't breathing and was foaming at the mouth. I concluded my story in a loud wail. "Lord, please, if you get me out of this one I promise I'll stop being a hoe!"

"Girl, he prolly just thirsty. Let's go see what's crackin," Karen said, and we all got up and followed her upstairs. When we got into the bedroom, he was the same way I left him: sprawled out on the bed, ass naked, with his dick pointing to the ceiling.

"Damn, that nigga working with that? I had no idea," Karen said as she got closer to the bed. I stayed my ass by the door because I didn't know if he was going to jump up or what.

"Damn girl, I know you said you had a killer pussy, but I didn't know you was for real about that shit," Shanna said.

While Karen and Shanna stood there laughing and high-fiving each other I was a nervous wreck standing in the doorway. I killed a man—I think. And I didn't know what to do. How was I going to get my hot ass out of this mess?

"OK, I gotta plan." Karen's loud-ass mouth brought me out of my trance. At that point I was open to anything, as long as no one pointed the finger at me.

"OK, what is it?" Shanna said while scoping the room out. I'm sure she was looking for something to take, and I could care less. I just wanted to leave.

"Mina, wash him and dry his body off. Fix the sheets around him when you're done. Shanna, go get a trash bag out of the kitchen. It's clean up time."

"I ain't touchin' his dead ass. You do it!" I yelled at her, still stuck in the doorway. I wasn't about to go nowhere near Black Ron. The next time I would see his ass was at his funeral.

"Bitch, that's your pussy juice all over him. You want the feds to come and get your ass?"

I stood there for a second more before I ran to the bathroom to throw up. I couldn't believe the turn my day had taken, and I knew if nothing else I had to walk away clean. Taking the rag from the sink I used the night before, I soaped it up and went to the room to handle my business. It was hard for me to clean up Ron's dead body, but what else could I do?

I didn't want to get caught so I had to handle my business. In the meantime, Karen had found his stash, along with his jewels and a couple of brand new button-down shirts with the tags still on them. We cleaned as best we could and was out of there in no time.

Back at Karen's crib, she counted the money we took from Ron's while Shanna rolled one of five Dutches and I stared out of the window watching the world pass me by. I couldn't believe the life I was living, and I knew after today things had to change.

I got up and changed into a pair of Karen's sweats, taking

the club outfit I wore the night before and throwing it in the garbage. I didn't want anything to remind me of that horrible day. I came back in the living room just in time to get the blunt passed to me. Inhaling deeply, I hoped the effects of the illegal drug would cloud my mind long enough for me to make some sense of what happened. I was scared to death, and even though my girls told me I would be cool, I knew I was waiting for what happened to come around to me.

"So, what do we do now?" I asked Karen and Shanna. The weed started to take effect, and I wanted to enjoy my high as long as possible.

"We wait. I'm sure someone will find his body soon. We just act like we don't know nothing and keep it moving. We got a couple of thousand to spend. So we focus on that."

I knew Karen was right, but I couldn't help but think about it. I was now sure that it was the Xanex pills that killed Black Ron, but I was the last one seen with him, and that was my biggest fear. For right now, I would do my best not to worry, but like they always say . . . what you do in the dark always comes out in the light.

About the Author

Andrea Blackstone was born in Long Island, New York, and moved to Annapolis, Maryland at the age of two. She majored in English and minored in Spanish at Morgan State University. While attending Morgan, she received many recommendations to consider a career in writing and was the recipient of The Zora Neale Hurston Scholarship Award.

After a two-year stint in law school, she later changed her career path. While recovering from an illness, she earned an M.A. from St. John's College in Annapolis, Maryland ahead of schedule and with honors. Afterward, Andrea became frustrated with her inability to find an entry-level job in journalism and considered returning to law school.

Jotting down notes on restaurant napkins and scraps of paper became a habit that she couldn't shake. In 2003, she grew tired of waiting for her first professional break and decided to create Dream Weaver Press. A short time later she self-published *Schemin': Confessions of a Gold Digger*, and the sequel, *Short Changed*. Andrea is also a finalist in *Chicken Soup for the African-American Woman's Soul*, and some of her original work will also be included in an upcoming urban fiction anthology. A lover of all genres and outrageous characters, Andrea aspires to write a wide array of stories. Her work will range from inspirational nonfiction to unconventional plots written under one of many pseudonyms. Andrea recently signed her first book deal with Q-Boro Books and looks forward to having a new work released under a publishing house.

LOOK FOR MORE HOT TITLES FROM

LOOK FOR MORE HOT TITLES FROM

Q-BORO
B O O K S

DARK KARMA - JUNE 2007
$14.95
ISBN 1-933967-12-9

What if the criminal was forced to live the horror that they caused? The drug dealer finds himself in the body of the drug addict and he suffers through the withdrawals, living on the street, the beatings, the rapes and the hunger. The thief steals the rent money and becomes the victim that finds herself living on the street and running for her life and the murderer becomes the victim's father and he deals with the death of a son and a grieving mother.

GET MONEY CHICKS - SEPTEMBER 2007
$14.95
ISBN 1-933967-17-X

For Mina, Shanna, and Karen, using what they had to get what they wanted was always an option. Best friends since day one, they always had a thing for the hottest gear, luxurious lifestyles, and the ballers who made it all possible. All of this changes for Mina when a tragedy makes her open her eyes to the way she's living. Peer pressure and loyalty to her girls collide with her own morality, sending Mina into a no-win situation.

AFTER-HOURS GIRLS - AUGUST 2007
$14.95
ISBN 1-933967-16-1

Take part in this tale of two best friends, Lisa and Tosha, as they stalk the nightclubs and after-hours joints of Detroit searching for excitement, money, and temporary companionship. These two divas stand tall until the unforgivable Motown streets catch up to them. One must fall. You, the reader, decide which.

THE LAST CHANCE - OCTOBER 2007
$14.95
ISBN 1-933967-22-6

Running their L.A. casino has been rewarding for Luke Chance and his three brothers. But recently it seems like everyone is trying to get a piece of the pie. Word of an impending hostile takeover of their casino, which could leave them penniless and possibly dead. That is until their sister Keilah Chance comes home for a short visit. Keilah is not only beautiful, but she also can be ruthless. Will the Chance family be able to protect their family dynasty?

Attention Writers:

Writers looking to get their books published can view our submission guidelines by visiting our website at: *www.QBOROBOOKS.com*

What we're looking for: Contemporary fiction in the tradition of Darrien Lee, Carl Weber, Anna J., Zane, Mary B. Morrison, Noire, Lolita Files, etc; groundbreaking mainstream contemporary fiction.

We prefer email submissions to: candace@qborobooks.com in MS Word, PDF, or rtf format only. However, if you wish to send the submission via snail mail, you can send it to:

Q-BORO BOOKS Acquisitions Department
165-41A Baisley Blvd., Suite 4. Mall #1
Jamaica, New York 11434

*** **By submitting your work to Q-Boro Books, you agree to hold Q-Boro books harmless and not liable for publishing similar works as yours that we may already be considering or may consider in the future.** ***

1. Submissions will not be returned.
2. **Do not contact us for status updates.** If we are interested in receiving your full manuscript, we will contact you via email or telephone.
3. Do not submit if the entire manuscript is not complete.

Due to the heavy volume of submissions, if these requirements are not followed, we will not be able to process your submission.